A [illegible]

BRYONY DOUGLAS

BLACK SWAN
DIGITAL

First published in 2025
Concept created by Black Swan Digital. Developed by Annie Kenyon.

One can find women who have never had one love affair, but it is rare indeed to find any who have had only one.

Francois de La Rochefoucauld

1

Dana Taylor thrived in chaos. She stood at the head of the conference table, the glow of the projector casting shadows across her sharp features, the light bouncing off her perfectly styled hair. The air was thick with tension as the marketing team exchanged nervous glances. The quarterly campaign, months in the making, had imploded overnight. A competitor had blindsided them with a shockingly similar concept.

"So, we pivot," Dana said, her voice calm but electric with conviction. She clicked to the next slide on her laptop. "This is what we do. We're not here to play it safe; we're here to win. Let's reframe our message and own the narrative. By the time their ad airs, we'll have moved the conversation forward."

The room buzzed with murmurs of agreement as Dana outlined a new direction with razor-sharp precision. Her energy was infectious, her confidence unshakable. By the end of the meeting, even the sceptics were nodding, taking furious notes. Dana was the kind of leader who could steer a sinking ship into port with nothing but sheer will and a steady hand.

As the team dispersed, she lingered in the conference room for a moment, gazing at the whiteboard covered in hastily scribbled ideas. She took a deep breath, letting the adrenaline settle. Crisis averted—for now.

"Dana, got a second?" Caroline, her junior account manager, hovered in the doorway, a nervous energy radiating off her.

"Sure," Dana said, gesturing for her to come in. Caroline approached, clutching a folder to her chest like a shield.

"I... I just wanted to say that was incredible," Caroline began. "The way you turned that meeting around. Honestly, I was panicking. But you... you made it look easy."

Dana offered a small smile. "It's never easy, Caroline. But the key is to stay focused. Panic doesn't solve problems."

Caroline nodded. Her admiration evident. "Right. Well, I also wanted to show you these initial concepts for the social media push. I know it's early, but..."

"Let me see," Dana said, taking the folder and flipping through the pages. She scanned the designs quickly, her practiced eye catching both the potential and the flaws. "This is a good start. I like the energy here," she said, pointing to one of the mock-ups. "But this one needs a stronger call to action. And watch the color palette—we want something bold, but not overwhelming. Keep refining, and let's review again tomorrow."

Caroline beamed. "Got it. Thank you, Dana."

As Caroline left, Dana returned to her desk, the folder still in hand. Her office was a testament to her success: sleek, modern furniture, shelves lined with awards, and a view of the city skyline that few in the company enjoyed. But the trappings of achievement did little to quell the quiet dissatisfaction that gnawed at her.

Her assistant, Molly, poked her head in. "Dana, you've got a call with the London team in five minutes. Want me to push it?"

"No, I'll take it," she said, setting the folder down. "Thanks."

The call was yet another test of her diplomatic skills. The London team was frustrated with budget constraints, and tempers were running high. Dana navigated the conversation with her usual finesse, diffusing tension and steering them toward actionable solutions. By the time the call ended, she felt drained but victorious.

Her phone buzzed with a reminder: "Dinner with Ben and Ethan." She opened her texts, staring at the message thread with Ben. "Heading home soon?" she typed, then paused. The cursor blinked accusingly. Instead of sending it, she locked the phone and turned to her laptop. There was always more work to do.

~

By the time Dana walked through the front door of their sleek suburban home, the sun had dipped below the horizon, casting the living room in shades of gold and blue. The house was modern, all clean lines and open spaces, with large windows that framed a perfectly manicured lawn and the distant glow of streetlights. The walls were painted in neutral tones, adorned with a few abstract art pieces Dana had chosen during her brief foray into home design—a hobby she'd abandoned when work consumed her life.

The house smelled of freshly brewed coffee. Ben drank buckets of the stuff. The living room was tidy, almost sterile, with furniture that seemed more suited for a showroom than a family home. Yet, there were small signs of life: Ethan's sneakers kicked off near the door, a blanket draped haphazardly over the arm of a chair, and one of his school projects—a half-finished solar system model—spread across the coffee table.

She could hear the murmur of the TV in the den, Ethan's laughter ringing out like a bell. It was a sound that always made her pause, a reminder of the innocence and joy she worked so hard to nurture.

Ben was at the kitchen island, typing furiously on his laptop.

He glanced up as Dana entered, his face breaking into a warm, if weary, smile. "Hey, you. How was the day?"

"Long. Yours?" Dana asked, setting her bag down and stealing a sip of his coffee. She wrinkled her nose at the lukewarm taste but didn't comment.

"Same," Ben replied, already turning back to his screen. The faint glow from his laptop illuminated his face, making the deepening lines around his eyes more pronounced.

Dana's shoulders sagged imperceptibly, but she forced a smile. She crossed the room and found Ethan sprawled on t, his tablet perched on his knees. He lit up when he saw her. "Mom!"

"Hey, buddy. What are you watching?" she asked, ruffling his hair.

"It's this game stream. The guy's trying to beat this crazy level. Wanna see?"

"Maybe later," she said, kissing the top of his head. "Dinner's soon, okay?"

Ethan nodded, already engrossed again. Dana lingered a moment, watching him. At ten, he was growing up too fast, his world expanding beyond her reach. She noticed the way his hair flopped into his eyes. A haircut long overdue. She made a mental note to schedule an appointment in her already brimming diary.

Dinner was a quiet affair. Ben, true to form, checked his phone periodically, responding to emails between bites of roasted chicken. Ethan chattered about school and his latest obsessions, his enthusiasm filling the void. Dana played the role of attentive mother and wife, nodding and smiling in all the right places, but a knot tightened in her chest with each passing minute. Her irritation with Ben was hard to stifle because if she could put her damn phone and laptop away for a few hours, why couldn't he?

"Did you know, Mom, that Saturn has 82 moons?" Ethan said, his eyes wide with excitement.

"I didn't! That's amazing," Dana replied, genuinely impressed. "Are you including that in your project?"

"Yeah, but I still need to paint them," Ethan said. "Can we do it together?"

"Of course," Dana said, reaching out to squeeze his hand. She glanced at Ben, hoping he'd chime in, but he was engrossed in his phone again, his fork idly poking at his food.

"I'll get the dishes," Ben offered after they'd finished eating. It was a small gesture, but Dana couldn't help noticing how absentmindedly he said it, his phone already in hand as he stood.

As she cleared the table, Ethan tugged at her sleeve. "Mom, can you help me with my science project later? It's due Friday."

"Of course, sweetheart," she said, squeezing his shoulder. She smiled at him, but the weight of unspoken frustrations pressed down on her.

Later, project complete and Ethan had gone to bed, Dana wandered into his room to check on him. His nightlight cast a soft glow across the walls, illuminating the posters of planets and galaxies he loved so much. He was curled up under his blanket, his breathing steady and peaceful. She pulled the covers up around him and kissed his forehead, lingering for a moment before quietly stepping out.

When she returned to the bedroom, Ben was already asleep, his laptop still open on the nightstand. She sat on the edge of the bed, staring at her phone. She opened her text thread with him again and typed a message she would never send: "Do you even see me anymore?"

Instead, she sighed and set the phone down, staring at the ceiling. The room was dark and still, but outside, the wind rustled the trees, a lonely sound that mirrored the ache in her chest. The house, for all its modern elegance, felt cold and distant, a reflection of the life they'd built—successful, but quietly unraveling like the memories of when she and Ben first met.

~

It had been a brisk fall afternoon, the kind of day where the crisp air carried the faint scent of fallen leaves and woodsmoke. Dana had just turned twenty-three and was fresh out of college, juggling her first job as a marketing assistant at a small firm in Boston. Her life had been a whirlwind of deadlines, coffee runs, and late nights trying to prove herself, leaving little room for anything else—especially romance.

Ben, on the other hand, was twenty-seven and already making strides in his career as an architect. He had moved to Boston for a promising position at a prestigious firm, leaving behind the small town he had grown up in. He was driven, confident, and fiercely passionate about his work, but beneath the polished exterior was a man longing for something deeper—a connection he had yet to find.

Their paths crossed at a charity event, one neither of them had particularly wanted to attend. Dana had been coerced by a college friend who'd been stood up, while Ben had reluctantly agreed to go as a favor to a coworker. Dana had been nursing a glass of wine and half-listening to a group of acquaintances, when Ben walked in.

She noticed him immediately. Tall, with dark hair that curled slightly at the ends and a warm, easy smile, he carried himself with an air of quiet confidence. Their eyes met briefly across the room, and Dana quickly looked away, feeling a warmth rise to her cheeks. It wasn't long before Ben made his way over, introducing himself with a handshake and a grin that was both charming and disarming.

"I don't think we've met," he said, his voice smooth but friendly. "I'm Ben."

"Dana," she replied, her voice steady despite the flutter in her chest.

Their conversation started with the usual small talk—how they came to be there, their work, their favorite spots in the city. But as the minutes turned into an hour, something shifted. A calamity occurred that would become part of their history, one that they would recount many ties over the years where Ben became her knight in armor. Afterwards, they found a quiet corner and discovered a shared love of art and design, a fascination with history, and an appreciation for sarcastic humor that had them both laughing until their sides hurt. It was as though the rest of the guests faded away, leaving just the two of them in their own little world.

By the end of the night, Ben had asked for Dana's number, and she had given it to him without hesitation. Their first date was a week later, a casual dinner at a cozy Italian restaurant followed by a walk along the Charles River. They talked for hours, the conversation flowing effortlessly as they learned more about each other. Dana was drawn to Ben's thoughtfulness and intelligence, while Ben admired Dana's wit and ambition.

Their relationship blossomed quickly. Ben's steadiness balanced Dana's impulsiveness, and her optimism brightened his more serious demeanor. They spent weekends exploring the city, trying new restaurants, and losing themselves in bookstores. Ben introduced Dana to the world of architecture, showing her his favorite buildings and sketches, while Dana shared her passion for storytelling and marketing campaigns.

Two years later, on a snowy evening in December, Ben proposed. They had been walking through the Boston Common, the trees twinkling with holiday lights. Ben had stopped near the frozen pond, pulling a small velvet box from his pocket.

Their wedding a year later was a small, intimate affair, held in the garden of a historic inn surrounded by their closest friends and family. Dana had worn a simple, elegant dress, her hair swept up in soft curls, while Ben looked dashing in a tailored navy suit. The day was filled with laughter, love, and promises of a future they both believed would be bright.

Dana often thought back to those early days and compared them to the life they'd somehow slipped into. Both focused on their careers, telling themselves they were playing the long game that would provide security for their family and that going the extra mile at work would pay dividends. It seemed like a sensible plan but at what cost? A few hours together in the evenings where Ethan craved attention from the people he loved the most before he was packed off to bed.

Dana and Ben were always too exhausted to make love, even on the weekends when they had to pack everything family related into forty-eight hours of downtime. Then before they knew it, Monday had arrived and the daily grind began again, and somewhere in between was Ethan.

She compared that to when they met. The simplicity of their love, the joy of discovering each other, and the unshakable belief that together, they could face anything. It was a reminder of what they had been—and perhaps, what they could still be, if only they could find their way back.

2

Dana adjusted the strap of her sleek black dress as she stepped into the expansive downtown Los Angeles hotel ballroom. The energy of the networking event hit her immediately: the hum of conversation, the clinking of glasses, the faint rhythm of a jazz quartet tucked in the corner. The room was a swirl of polished professionals in tailored suits and bold dresses, each radiating ambition. Dana felt a pang of disconnect from the quiet, orderly life she had left behind in the suburbs just hours ago.

She scanned the room with practiced ease, holding a flute of champagne she'd picked up from a passing server. The space was dazzling, illuminated by crystal chandeliers that refracted light across the room. Floor-to-ceiling windows framed the glittering city skyline. It was intoxicating, a world so different from her everyday existence that it almost felt like stepping into a dream. The air was perfumed with a mix of expensive colognes and floral centerpieces, and the low murmur of conversation created an ambiance of understated power.

Clusters of people formed small islands across the ballroom. A group of executives stood near the bar, their laughter carrying over the music, while young professionals hovered near the edges, scanning the room for opportunities. Servers glided through the crowd with trays of hors d'oeuvres: miniature crab cakes, prosciutto-wrapped figs, and bite-sized tartlets that were as artful as the venue itself.

"Dana! You're here," called a familiar voice. Caroline, her junior account manager, approached with a nervous smile. "This is... a lot, isn't it?"

Dana smiled, taking in Caroline's slightly frazzled expression and outfit. Her red dress was striking but understated, and she clutched her clutch bag like it was a lifeline. "It's an opportunity. Just remember, everyone here is just as eager to make an impression as you are. You'll be fine."

Caroline nodded; her confidence visibly bolstered by Dana's calm demeanor. "Thanks. I'll... see you around," she said, disappearing into the crowd.

Dana's focus returned to the room. She moved gracefully, exchanging pleasantries and discussing trends with industry leaders. Her tone was warm, her words polished, but a sense of detachment lingered. No matter how many hands she shook or smiles she offered, she couldn't shake the feeling that she was performing, playing a role that she'd perfected over years of climbing the corporate ladder.

It was during one of these polite exchanges that she noticed him.

Justin Birch stood near the far end of the room, deep in conversation with a group of executives. His dark suit was impeccably tailored, his crisp white shirt open at the collar in a way that felt deliberately casual. His movements were fluid, his posture relaxed yet commanding. A faint shadow of stubble added to his rugged charm, and his eyes—a piercing blue—flitted between his companions with an ease that suggested he was equally at home here as he was in a boardroom.

Even from a distance, Dana could see how the group

gravitated toward him. He laughed at something one of the men said, his smile revealing perfect teeth, and the others followed suit almost instinctively. Justin had a magnetism that made him stand out even in a room full of accomplished people. His energy was undeniable—electric, but with an edge that hinted at something sharper beneath the charm.

Their eyes met briefly, and Dana quickly looked away, feeling a flicker of something she couldn't quite name. She turned back to the person she was speaking to, forcing herself to focus, but moments later, Justin was beside her.

"Dana Taylor, isn't it?" His voice was warm, his smile effortlessly disarming. Up close, he was even more striking, his presence filling the space between them. "I've heard a lot about you."

Dana tilted her head slightly, intrigued but cautious. "You have me at a disadvantage. And you are?"

"Justin Birch," he said, extending a hand. His grip was firm, confident. "We've got a few mutual connections. I've been following your work for a while now. It's impressive."

"Thank you," Dana replied, her tone polite but guarded. Compliments in this setting often came with ulterior motives.

Justin seemed to sense this. "I mean it," he said, his smile softening. "The way you turned that campaign around. That was no small feat. People talk about it for a reason."

Dana couldn't help the small smile that crept onto her face. "Well, it's nice to know someone's paying attention."

"Someone should be," Justin said, his tone shifting slightly, becoming more personal. "People like you deserve to be noticed."

There was something about the way he said it that caught her off guard. His gaze was steady, his words lingering in the air. For a moment, the noise of the room seemed to fade, and Dana felt a faint, inexplicable pull.

Justin reached into his pocket and pulled out a sleek black business card. "If you ever want to talk strategy, or anything else, give me a call."

Dana hesitated for just a second before taking the card. "Thanks, Justin. I'll keep that in mind."

He nodded, his smile returning to its full wattage. "Enjoy the rest of your evening, Dana."

As he walked away, Dana glanced down at the card in her hand. The bold lettering stood out against the matte finish: "Justin Birch, CEO." She tucked it into her clutch, her mind buzzing with questions she couldn't yet articulate.

The rest of the evening passed in a blur of small talk and handshakes, but Justin's words stayed with her, replaying in her mind as she drove home under the glow of the city lights. The distant hum of traffic mixed with the echo of his voice: "You deserve to be noticed."

Dana gripped the steering wheel tightly as her car wound through the quiet streets leading back to her suburban neighborhood. The energy of the event still lingered, an intoxicating mix of adrenaline and unease. She replayed her encounter with Justin, the subtle intensity in his eyes, the confidence in his voice. There was something about him, something that made her feel seen in a way she hadn't felt in years.

But as she turned onto her street, guilt began to creep in. The darkened windows of her home reminded her that she'd missed dinner with Ben and Ethan. She imagined Ethan sitting at the table, his bright chatter filling the silence as Ben half-listened, distracted by his laptop. She could picture the empty seat where she should have been, the warm meals she had promised herself she'd prioritize over work.

Pulling into the driveway, Dana cut the engine and sat in the car for a moment, staring at the faint glow of the porch light. Her reflection in the rearview mirror looked tired, her makeup slightly smudged. She reached into her clutch and pulled out Justin's card again, running her thumb over the embossed lettering.

"You deserve to be noticed," he'd said. The words had felt like a lifeline at the time, but now they hung heavy in her chest, tangled with the ache of neglecting the people waiting inside. She slipped the card back into her bag and stepped out of the car, bracing herself for the quiet that would greet her when she walked through the door.

3

The next morning, Dana's inbox was flooded with the usual clutter: meeting invites, campaign updates, and follow-ups from last night's networking event. Among the emails, one subject line stood out: "Follow-Up from Justin Birch." Her stomach fluttered as she clicked it open.

Subject: Follow-Up from Justin Birch

Dana,

It was great meeting you last night. I'd love the chance to discuss a potential marketing opportunity that I think aligns perfectly with your expertise. Are you available for coffee this week? Let me know what works for you.

Best,

Justin Birch

She stared at the screen for a moment longer than necessary, rereading the email. The tone was professional, but the memory of his lingering gaze and disarming smile at the event made her hesitate. Still, she reasoned, it was just business. Dana's reputation had been built on taking opportunities others might overlook.

After a moment, she typed a response:

Subject: Re: Follow-Up from Justin Birch

Justin,

Thank you for reaching out. Coffee sounds great—how about Thursday morning? Let me know where works best.

Best,

Dana Taylor

By the time Thursday morning arrived, Dana had convinced herself there was nothing unusual about the meeting. She'd told no one—not Ben, not her assistant, not even Caroline. It wasn't secrecy, she reasoned, just a matter of keeping things simple. Explaining the nuances of an informal coffee meeting felt unnecessary.

The cafe Justin had chosen was chic and understated, tucked into a quiet corner of downtown. Dana arrived five minutes early, dressed in a tailored navy blouse and black slacks, her laptop bag slung over one shoulder. The rich aroma of coffee greeted her as she stepped inside, mingling with the hum of soft jazz and muted conversation.

Justin was already there, seated at a corner table with a perfect view of the street outside. He stood as she approached, his smile as warm and confident as she remembered.

"Dana," he said, pulling out a chair for her. "Thanks for making the time."

"Of course," she replied, setting her bag down and taking the seat. "It's not every day someone follows up so quickly after a networking event. You must be busy."

"Never too busy for the right conversation," Justin said, his eyes holding hers for just a beat longer than necessary. "Coffee?"

Dana nodded, and he signaled to the barista, ordering for both of them with an ease that suggested he'd been here many times before. When their drinks arrived, Justin leaned forward slightly, his posture relaxed but engaged.

"Let me cut to the chase," he began. "Your work speaks for itself. That campaign you led. It's exactly the kind of innovative thinking we need for a project I'm working on. I want to bring you in as a consultant."

Dana raised an eyebrow. "Consultant?"

"It's a short-term project," Justin explained, "but it's high impact. A chance to shape something from the ground up. I can't think of anyone better suited for it."

The compliment was direct, but there was a subtle edge to it, a way he spoke that made her feel singular, extraordinary. She sipped her coffee, considering his words carefully.

"It sounds intriguing," she said finally. "But I'd need more details before committing to anything."

"Naturally," Justin said, leaning back slightly. "I'll send over a proposal. But let's not pretend this is just about logistics. People like you don't come around often, Dana. You bring something unique to the table."

There it was again—that subtle shift in tone, the words carrying a weight that felt both flattering and dangerous. Dana brushed off the unease creeping into her thoughts, telling herself it was all part of the pitch.

"I appreciate the confidence," she said, keeping her tone neutral. "But let's keep this professional."

Justin's smile didn't falter. "Of course. Professional is my middle name."

They talked for another thirty minutes, delving into the specifics of the project and exchanging ideas. Justin's charisma was undeniable, his vision sharp, but Dana kept her guard up, aware of how easily he seemed to blur the lines between business and something more personal.

As they finished their coffee, Justin handed her another card —this one handwritten with his personal number. "In case you have questions about the proposal," he said.

Dana slipped it into her bag with a polite nod, her smile carefully measured. "Thanks. I'll take a look and let you know."

As she walked back to her car, Dana had the strangest thought. That she'd just stepped onto a path she didn't fully understand. The line between opportunity and something more complicated felt thinner than she'd anticipated, but she brushed the thought aside. It was just business, she told herself. Nothing more.

Later that evening, Dana sat at the kitchen table with her phone pressed to her ear. The house was quiet; Ethan was upstairs, and Ben was working late. She scrolled aimlessly through her inbox as Ben's voice came through the line, warm but distracted.

"Hey, how was your day?" he asked.

"Busy," Dana said, trying to sound casual. "You know how it is."

"Anything interesting?"

Dana hesitated, her fingers brushing against the edge of Justin's card, which still sat in her bag. "Just the usual," she replied. "Meetings, emails, the usual chaos."

"Well, don't work too hard," Ben said with a chuckle. "We miss you around here when you're buried in work."

"I miss you too," Dana said softly. She glanced at the card one more time before zipping her bag shut. "I'll be home soon."

As the call ended, Dana stared at the darkened screen of her phone, a faint sense of unease settling over her. She told herself again that it was just business, but the omission weighed heavier than she cared to admit.

~

The house was already on edge by the time Dana walked in that evening. Ethan's raised voice echoed from the living room, followed by Ben's measured but frustrated tone. She dropped her bag by the door and sighed, bracing herself for whatever conflict she was about to walk into.

"You're not listening to me!" Ethan's voice cracked with the intensity of his frustration.

"I said no more screen time," Ben replied, his voice tight with exasperation. "It's bedtime, Ethan. I don't want to argue about this again."

Dana stepped into the living room, taking in the scene. Ethan stood at the far end of the couch, clutching his tablet like it was a lifeline. His face was flushed, his eyes brimming with the injustice he clearly felt. Ben stood a few feet away, arms crossed, his posture rigid.

"What's going on here?" Dana asked, her voice calm but firm.

Ethan turned to her, his expression a mix of hope and desperation. "Mom, I just wanted to finish my game! It's not fair, Dad won't let me."

"It's already past his bedtime," Ben interjected, cutting Ethan off. "He's had plenty of time today, but he's still pushing back."

Dana looked between them, her exhaustion weighing heavily. "Ethan, hand me the tablet," she said gently. When he hesitated, she added, "You can finish tomorrow, okay? Right now, it's time for bed."

Reluctantly, Ethan handed her the device, muttering under

his breath as he trudged up the stairs. She watched him go, waiting until his door clicked shut before turning to Ben.

"Was that really necessary?" she asked, setting the tablet on the coffee table.

Ben's eyebrows shot up in disbelief. "What do you mean? He's ten, Dana. If we don't set boundaries now, he'll walk all over us."

"I'm not saying he doesn't need boundaries," Dana replied, keeping her voice measured. "But sometimes, it feels like you're more focused on winning the argument than actually understanding him."

Ben threw up his hands. "Oh, come on. He's not some misunderstood teenager. He's a kid who doesn't like being told no."

Dana pressed her lips together, feeling the familiar frustration bubbling beneath her surface. "It's not just about this," she said quietly. "It's about us, Ben. We're so busy keeping everything together that we're barely connecting anymore."

Ben sighed heavily, sinking onto the couch. "Dana, we're both just busy. That's life. Work, parenting, everything... it's a lot. But it doesn't mean something's wrong."

She sat beside him, though the distance between them felt far greater than the physical space. "It feels like we're going through the motions," she admitted. "And when we do talk, it's always about logistics or Ethan or something that needs fixing. I miss... us."

Ben looked at her, his expression softening. "I know it's hard right now. But it'll get better, okay? We just need to push through."

Dana nodded, though his words felt like a band-aid over a deeper wound. She wanted to believe him, to feel reassured, but the weight of her loneliness only seemed to grow. The argument with Ethan had only highlighted the cracks in their relationship, cracks that she wasn't sure how to mend.

Later, as she climbed into bed, Dana found herself staring at the ceiling. Ben was already asleep beside her, his breathing steady and deep. Her thoughts drifted to Justin's words earlier that week: "People like you don't come around often."

The memory sent a shiver through her, equal parts exhilaration and guilt. Justin had made her feel seen in a way she hadn't felt in years. But that feeling, intoxicating as it was, also terrified her. She turned onto her side, closing her eyes and willing herself to sleep, though her mind refused to quiet.

The dream began innocently enough. Dana was standing in a room that seemed familiar yet unfamiliar, its edges blurred and its light soft. Justin was there, leaning casually against a desk, his gaze fixed on her with that same intensity she remembered from the cafe. He smiled, a slow, deliberate expression that made her heart race.

"You look amazing," he said, his voice low and smooth. He stepped closer, his movements confident, purposeful.

"What are you doing here?" Dana asked, though her voice sounded distant, as though it wasn't really her speaking.

Justin didn't answer. Instead, he reached out, his fingers brushing against her arm. The touch sent a spark through her, and suddenly the room felt smaller, the air heavier. She could feel his warmth, the nearness of him overwhelming.

"You deserve this," he murmured, his hand trailing up to her cheek. "To be seen. To be wanted."

Dana's breath hitched as his lips met hers, the kiss deep and consuming. She felt herself melt into him, her hands clutching his shirt as if to anchor herself. It was electric, a collision of longing and release that left her dizzy.

The dream shifted, the edges of the room dissolving into darkness, but Justin remained, his touch, his presence, all-consuming. For a moment, nothing else existed—not Ben, not Ethan, not the life she'd built so carefully. There was only Justin, and the way he made her feel alive.

When Dana woke, her heart was pounding, her skin flushed. The early morning light filtered through the curtains, and the sound of Ben's steady breathing reminded her where she was. She turned her head to look at him, guilt twisting in her stomach.

It had only been a dream, she told herself. Nothing more. But as she lay there, the vividness of it lingered, refusing to fade.

4

The upscale bar glimmered with an understated elegance, all polished mahogany and ambient golden light. The faint hum of conversation and clinking glasses filled the air, mingling with the soft strains of a jazz quartet tucked into the corner. Dana walked in, her heels clicking against the marble floor, her fitted black dress hugging her figure in a way that felt both empowering and foreign. She hadn't told Ben exactly where she was going tonight. It was a last-minute meeting. Work-related.

Justin was already there, seated at the bar with a tumbler of whiskey in hand. He looked effortlessly composed, his charcoal suit tailored to perfection, the top button of his shirt undone just enough to suggest confidence without arrogance. When he spotted her, his lips curved into a slow, inviting smile.

"Dana," he greeted, standing as she approached. "You look stunning."

She flushed despite herself, brushing off the compliment with a polite smile. "Thanks. Sorry if I kept you waiting."

"Not at all," Justin said, gesturing to the seat beside him. "I was just enjoying the ambiance. But it's much better now that you're here."

Dana slid onto the barstool, her pulse quickening at the way his eyes lingered on her just a fraction too long. The bartender approached, and Justin ordered her a glass of red wine without asking. Somehow, it didn't feel presumptuous. It felt... intimate.

"So, what's the big idea you couldn't wait to share?" Dana asked, keeping her tone light, professional.

Justin leaned in slightly, his gaze locking onto hers. "You're the big idea, Dana. I can't stop thinking about the potential we'd have working together. You're brilliant, creative, and driven. It's rare to find someone like you."

Her breath hitched, and she quickly took a sip of her wine to mask her reaction. "I appreciate the flattery, Justin, but let's not get carried away."

"It's not flattery," he insisted, his tone soft but insistent. "It's the truth. You've built something incredible in your career, but I can't help but feel there's more you're capable of. More you deserve."

Dana's stomach tightened at his words, the weight of them settling somewhere deep within her. She felt exposed, seen in a way that was both thrilling and terrifying.

"You have a way of making everything sound... bigger than it is," she said, attempting to deflect.

"That's because I see things for what they could be," Justin replied. He leaned closer, his voice dropping to a near whisper. "And I see you, Dana. I see what you've been holding back."

Her heart pounded in her chest, her resolve wavering under the intensity of his gaze. The bar seemed to fade away, leaving only the two of them in their small, electrified bubble. When Justin reached out, his fingers brushing lightly against hers on the bar, she didn't pull away.

~

The elevator ride to Justin's penthouse was a blur. Dana stood close to him, the air between them charged with unspoken tension. He had one hand around her waist another slid down her stomach. She told herself she should leave, that this had already gone too far, but her feet stayed rooted to the plush carpet of the elevator. When the doors opened, Justin gestured for her to step out first, his hand resting lightly on the small of her back as he guided her into his home.

The penthouse was as impeccable as Justin himself—sleek, modern, and breathtakingly luxurious. Floor-to-ceiling windows offered a stunning view of the city skyline, its lights twinkling like scattered stars. A low fire crackled in the minimalist hearth, casting a warm glow over the room. The furniture was a blend of muted grays and whites, each piece perfectly curated to exude elegance and restraint. A black leather couch sat in the center; its angular design softened by a cashmere throw draped over one arm. A grand piano stood near the windows, its glossy surface reflecting the ambient light.

"Wow," Dana murmured, stepping further inside. "This is... incredible."

"I'm glad you like it," Justin said, his voice low and smooth. He moved behind her, his presence magnetic. "But it's nothing compared to you."

She turned to face him, her defenses crumbling under the weight of his words and the intensity of his gaze. Before she could overthink it, Justin's hands were on her waist, pulling her closer. His lips found hers, and the kiss was everything her dream had been and more—urgent, consuming, and electric.

Justin guided her toward the couch, his movements deliberate yet gentle. He shrugged off his jacket and tossed it aside, his hands returning immediately to her body. Dana's breath quickened as he traced the curve of her spine, his touch sending shivers through her. She felt her own hands moving, unbuttoning his shirt, her fingers brushing against the warm skin beneath.

"Are you sure?" Justin whispered against her ear, his voice husky.

Dana hesitated for only a fraction of a second before nodding. Words felt unnecessary, the tension between them answering every unspoken question. Justin lifted her effortlessly, laying her back against the cushions. The leather was cool against her skin, a stark contrast to the heat of his body as he pressed against her.

Every touch, every kiss, felt like a revelation, a release of something she hadn't realized she'd been holding back. Justin's movements were confident yet reverent, as if he were memorizing every inch of her. Time seemed to blur, the world outside disappearing until there was only the two of them, entangled in a moment that felt both infinite and fleeting.

~

Dana woke the next morning to the soft light of dawn filtering through sheer curtains. For a moment, she couldn't remember where she was. Then she felt the warmth of Ben's body beside her, his arm draped possessively over her waist, and reality came crashing down.

Her chest tightened as guilt clawed its way to the surface. She slipped out of bed carefully, not wanting to wake him, and gathered her clothes from the evening before in silence. Her cheeks flushed as she remembered waking in Justin's bed, the panic she'd felt when she saw the time was past midnight and the shame of what she'd done began to flood her body. While Justin snored, she'd scrambled for her clothes, unable to find her panties and stockings she dressed hurriedly, ramming on her shoes, grabbing her purse and leaving the apartment in silence.

As she stuffed them into the laundry basket and headed for the shower, her reflection in the mirrored wall of their bathroom caught her eye. Her black, bobbed hair was tousled, her mascara smudged where she'd not removed it properly, and her eyes... they looked different. Brighter. Alive. And guilty.

5

Dana sat at her desk, her fingers hovering over the keyboard, but her mind refused to focus. The glow of her computer screen seemed to mock her as she scrolled through emails without reading one. Her thoughts were consumed by the night before, replaying in vivid, agonizing detail. The warmth of Justin's hands on her skin, the way his voice had sent shivers down her spine—it was as if the memory itself was alive, demanding her attention.

She closed her eyes and leaned back in her chair, willing herself to push it away. It had been a mistake. A terrible, impulsive mistake. She couldn't let it happen again.

Her phone buzzed on the desk, the vibration pulling her back to reality. She glanced at the screen, her stomach flipping when she saw Justin's name. A text message.

Justin: Last night was incredible. Thank you for trusting me. I can't stop thinking about you.

Dana's pulse quickened. She stared at the message, her finger hovering over the screen. Every instinct screamed at her to delete it, to ignore him, to pretend it had never happened. But a small, traitorous part of her hesitated, drawn to the way his words made her feel. Desired.

She locked the phone and shoved it into her desk drawer, as though physically distancing herself from it might help.

"Pull it together," she muttered under her breath.

But the rest of the day was a haze. In meetings, she nodded along, pretending to listen while her mind wandered. At lunch, she picked at her salad, appetite absent. Every glance at her phone felt like a battle, the urge to check it nearly overwhelming. When she finally gave in, the message was still there, unread but undeniably present. She hadn't responded, but the thought of him waiting for her reply made her stomach twist in a way that felt dangerously close to excitement.

By the time the workday ended, Dana had made up her mind. She couldn't let this spiral any further. Justin was a distraction; one she couldn't afford. She had a family, a life she'd worked too hard to build. One mistake didn't have to define her.

When she got home, the house was quiet. Ben and Ethan were out running errands, giving her a rare moment of solitude. She poured herself a glass of wine and sat at the kitchen table, her phone in front of her. The unopened message stared back at her like an accusation.

Taking a deep breath, she opened her contacts and scrolled down to Justin's name. Her finger hovered over the "Delete Contact" button.

"It's for the best," she whispered.

With a decisive tap, his name disappeared from her phone. She deleted the message thread next, her heart pounding as though the act itself was some monumental declaration. When it was done, she set the phone down and exhaled, the weight of the day finally beginning to lift.

She convinced herself it was over. Justin was a mistake; one she wouldn't repeat. She would focus on her family, her work, the life she had built so carefully.

But as she sat there in the quiet kitchen, the memory of his touch lingered, refusing to be erased as easily as a contact in her phone.

~

The next morning, Dana was halfway through answering an email when there was a knock at her office door. Before she could respond, her assistant, Molly, walked in holding a massive bouquet of flowers. The arrangement was striking: a cascade of deep red roses, white lilies, and sprigs of delicate greenery arranged in a glossy black vase.

"Wow," Molly said, her eyes wide as she set the flowers on Dana's desk. "Someone's feeling generous. Any idea who they're from?"

Dana's stomach dropped. She forced a tight smile, her heart pounding as she reached for the small white card tucked into the arrangement. Flipping it open, her fears were confirmed:

Dana, Thank you for an unforgettable night. Justin

Her hands trembled as she quickly slipped the card into her desk drawer, shutting it with more force than she intended. "Probably just a client," she said, her voice strained but light. "You know how some people like to make a statement."

Molly raised an eyebrow but didn't press further. "Well, whoever it is, they have good taste. These are stunning."

"They are," Dana said, forcing a chuckle. "Thanks for bringing them in."

As soon as Molly left, closing the door behind her, Dana slumped back in her chair, staring at the flowers as if they might explode. Her mind raced. What was Justin thinking, sending something so bold to her workplace? Did he not understand how dangerous this was?

She pushed the bouquet to the far corner of her desk, out of her immediate view, and took a deep breath. She needed to act. She couldn't let this go any further. The flowers were just another reminder that Justin wasn't going to fade away quietly. She would have to make it clear that whatever had happened between them was over.

Reaching for her phone, she paused, her finger hovering over the screen. For a fleeting moment, she considered calling him, explaining the boundaries she so desperately needed to enforce. But the thought of hearing his voice, of being drawn back into his orbit, was too much, and she remembered she'd deleted his number.

Instead, she opened her email and typed out a short, curt message:

Subject: About Last Night

Justin,

I appreciate the flowers, but this must stop. Please don't contact me again.

Dana

She hit send before she could second-guess herself, then sat back, exhaling shakily. It was done. She had drawn the line. But even as she stared at the "Message Sent" notification on her screen, a part of her doubted whether Justin would respect it—or whether she wanted him to.

Dana sat at her desk, her fingers hovering over the keyboard, but her mind refused to focus. Her thoughts were consumed by the night before, replaying in vivid, agonizing detail. It was as if the memory itself was alive, demanding her attention.

She closed her eyes and leaned back in her chair, willing herself to push it away. It had been a mistake. A terrible, impulsive mistake. She couldn't let it happen again. She didn't want to hurt Ben or Ethan.

~

The next morning, Dana woke with a heaviness in her chest that hadn't lifted. She needed to do something, anything, to distract herself from the guilt that was eating away at her. As she sipped her coffee, an idea formed. Ethan had been so distant lately, and she hadn't been as present for him as she should have been. Maybe she could make it up to him—even just a little.

By mid-afternoon, following a rather tense call where she resorted to begging Ben to agree to her idea, Dana found herself at the local animal shelter. The rows of cages were filled with hopeful eyes and soft mews. One kitten caught her attention: a tiny tabby with white paws and bright, curious eyes. The shelter worker explained that the kitten was only a few months old and had a sweet, affectionate temperament.

Dana filled out the adoption paperwork on a whim, feeling a small spark of hope for the first time in days. She imagined the look on Ethan's face when he saw the kitten and hoped it would be enough to bridge the emotional gap that had grown between them.

When she arrived home, Ben was at the kitchen counter while Ethan was in the living room, curled up with a book. Signaling that Ben should follow, Dana headed in Ethan's direction. He looked up as they entered the room, his expression neutral.

"Hey, sweetheart," Dana said, setting her bag down. "We have a surprise for you."

Ethan sat up; his curiosity piqued. "What is it?"

Dana opened the small carrier she'd been holding, and the kitten stepped out tentatively, its tiny nose twitching as it explored its new surroundings. Ethan's eyes widened, and a huge grin spread across his face.

"A kitten? Is it for me?" he asked, his voice filled with excitement.

Ben smiled and Dana nodded, her heart swelling at his reaction. "We thought you might like a new friend. But you must help take care of him, okay?"

Ethan dropped to his knees, gently stroking the kitten's soft fur. The kitten purred, nuzzling into his hand, and Ethan let out a delighted laugh. "Thank you, Mom. Thank you, Dad! He's perfect. I'm going to think of the best name for him."

"Be gentle with him buddy. He's only a baby." Ben offered before sloping off to the kitchen and his laptop.

Ignoring her annoyance at Ben's lack of interest, Dana focused on Ethan and smiled, a flicker of relief breaking through her guilt. For a moment, she felt like she was doing something right, even if it was just a small gesture. She watched as Ethan played with his new friend, his laughter filling the room, easing the tension that had lodged in her heart.

But as the evening wore on and Ethan eventually went to bed, taking Snowball with him, the most unsuitable name for a tabby kitten, ever, Dana couldn't shake the nagging feeling that her gift had been more for her than for him. The kitten was a distraction, a way to mask the cracks in her life that were threatening to split wide open. And deep down, she knew no number of gestures could fix what she had secretly, stupidly broken.

6

Dana arrived at her office the next morning with a renewed sense of determination. After the email she'd sent Justin, she hoped that would be the end of it. But when she stepped into her office, she froze. Sitting on her desk was an elegantly wrapped gift box, the kind of packaging that whispered luxury before it was even opened. Beside it was a handwritten note, folded in half with her name scrawled across the front in bold, confident handwriting.

She closed the door behind her and approached the desk cautiously, her heart sinking as she picked up the note.

Dana,

You deserve this.

Justin

Her pulse raced as she peeled back the wrapping paper to reveal an extravagant designer handbag. It was stunning, a piece of art in leather and gold accents, but its presence felt invasive, suffocating. She placed it back in the box and stared at it for a long moment, the weight of her emotions pressing down on her. Fear. Guilt. A tiny, unwelcome flicker of flattery.

Her phone buzzed on the desk. For a moment, she thought it might be another text from Justin, but it was just an email notification. She sat down, opened her laptop, and began typing:

Subject: Please Stop

Justin,

I've been clear that I don't want any further contact. Sending gifts like this is inappropriate and unwelcome. Please respect my boundaries and stop.

Dana

She hit send and closed her laptop with a sense of finality. But within minutes, her phone buzzed again. This time, it was him again.

Unknown number: You don't mean that.

Her hands tightened around the phone as she read the message. The words were simple, but they carried a weight that made her skin crawl. She locked her phone and placed it face down on her desk, fighting the urge to respond.

The rest of the morning passed in a blur of meetings and emails, but Dana couldn't shake the unease that had settled in her chest. She felt like she was being watched, like Justin's presence was lingering even in his absence. Every glance at the handbag on her desk felt like a reminder of how deeply she'd allowed him into her life, a mistake that seemed to grow larger with every passing moment.

Around lunchtime, her phone rang. She glanced at the screen and saw the name of Ethan's school. Her heart sank as she answered.

"Mrs. Taylor, this is Mrs. Bailey from the school. I'm calling about an incident that happened on the playground today," the voice on the other end said.

Dana's grip tightened on the phone. "What happened? Is Ethan okay?"

"He's fine, but there was an altercation with another child," Mrs. Bailey explained. "Ethan got into an argument that escalated into pushing. We've spoken to both children, and Ethan seems very upset. I thought you should know."

Dana closed her eyes, guilt washing over her. "Thank you for letting me know. I'll talk to him about it tonight."

"We'd appreciate that," Mrs. Bailey said. "He's a good boy, but he seemed a little distracted today and unable to focus on his work for long. And I have noticed that he's been quite short tempered lately and a tad disruptive."

Dana couldn't believe this was her son the teacher was talking about. "Ethan, disruptive... are you sure? I can't imagine him behaving like this, it's so unlike him."

Mrs. Bailey made a humming sound, then offered an opinion. "I agree, it is unusual for Ethan, but I have seen behavior like this before in my students and it's a classic example of attention seeking, preventing others from working, interrupting the teacher, not following rules and instructions. It usual indicates the child is struggling with something, possibly within school or more often at home. Is there anything you know of that may be troubling him in this regard?"

Dana was stunned. Mrs. Bailey had succinctly dropped a very unsubtle bomb and the only way to diffuse it was to lie so when she found her voice, Dana did just that. "I'm so sorry Ethan has been behaving this way, and I promise his father and I will speak to him about it tonight. You have my word but for the record, Mrs. Bailey, everything is perfectly fine at home."

There was a moment of silence until Mrs. Bailey conceded graciously. "Well, I'm pleased to hear that but going forward, do let us know if there's anything we can do to support him ."

Dana ended the call and leaned back in her chair, her mind racing. Ethan was distracted. Of course he was. No doubt thinking of his kitten at home. And then another thought; what if he'd seen through the bribe. She'd been so consumed by her own turmoil that she hadn't noticed how it and her frequent absences and long hours might be affecting him. The thought made her chest tighten with shame.

The handbag still sat in its box on the desk, a glaring reminder of the chaos she'd let into her life. Dana resolved then and there to fix things, to protect her family and reclaim the stability of their life together. But as she reached for her phone to text Ben about the incident, she couldn't help but feel the weight of Justin's cryptic message pressing down on her. *You don't mean that.*

That evening, Dana sat in the car outside her house, the engine idling as she tried to collect herself. Her reflection stared back at her in the rearview mirror, eyes shadowed with exhaustion. The day had been a mess of emotions—fear, guilt, frustration. Ethan needed her to be present tonight. Ben needed her to be the partner she hadn't been lately. But the thought of walking inside, of pretending everything was fine, felt almost unbearable.

The guilt was relentless, gnawing at her from every angle.

She'd let Justin's attention distract her, and now it was bleeding into her family's life. Ethan's incident at school was proof of that. She'd thought she could compartmentalize, keep her mistake separate from everything else, but the lines were blurring in ways she couldn't control.

She glanced at her phone on the passenger seat, half expecting another message from Justin to light up the screen. She'd blocked his number after his last text, but that didn't ease the knot of anxiety in her chest. He was persistent, and that persistence felt less flattering and more threatening with every passing moment.

Finally, she turned off the engine and stepped out of the car. Inside, Ethan was sitting at the kitchen table, Snowball curled up on his knee while he scribbled furiously on a piece of paper. He looked up when she walked in, his face brightening for a moment before his expression shifted, more subdued.

"Hey, bud," Dana said, forcing a smile as she set her bag down. "What are you working on?"

"Just drawing," he mumbled, not meeting her eyes.

Dana's heart ached. She walked over and knelt beside him, placing a hand on his back. "Mrs. Bailey called me today. She told me about what happened on the playground. Do you want to talk about it?"

Ethan shrugged. "It's nothing. This kid kept bothering me, and I got mad. That's all."

"That doesn't sound like nothing," Dana said gently. "You know you can talk to me about anything, right?"

He hesitated, then nodded, but his silence lingered, and Dana didn't push. She pressed a kiss to the top of his head, feeling the full weight of her failure to be the mother he needed right now. As she stood, Ben walked in, his gaze flicking between her and Ethan with a question in his eyes.

"We need to talk later," Dana said quietly. Ben nodded, sensing the gravity in her tone.

As the evening wore on, the handbag in its glossy box haunted her thoughts. Justin's presence loomed over everything, a shadow she couldn't shake. She'd made a mistake, but she wasn't the only one paying the price. And that realization made her guilt almost unbearable.

7

The morning sunlight streamed through the kitchen windows as Dana prepared breakfast. The air was heavy with the smell of coffee and the faint hum of the news playing in the background. Ethan sat at the table, poking at his bowl of cereal with a spoon, his usual chatter noticeably absent. Ben leaned against the counter, scrolling through his phone, his expression distant and her hopes that he'd take the lead when they talked to Ethan about his behavior, faded.

The previous evening, once Ethan and Snowball were tucked up in bed, Dana had related her conversation with Mrs. Bailey. Ben had been shocked and as she'd expected, was adamant that nothing was wrong at home, giving credence to her fears that he was oblivious to the cracks in their relationship, and how their lifestyle was affecting their son.

He'd reminded her that most of their colleagues and friends were in the same boat, juggling childcare, pre- and after-school clubs, play dates and their children's extracurricular activities while trying to work a forty-plus hour weak and stay sane. Ben had reinforced this with the fact that Ethan had a good life and lovely home, and parents who cared and wanted the best for him, so he was sorry if there weren't enough hours in the day to spend with Ethan, but that was how it was. His final comment, before he rolled over and switched of the lamp was that they shouldn't pander to his bad behavior or demands and would need to set firm boundaries going forward.

She, however, had been awake for hours going over it all in her head and knew that it was up to her to sort this out. So, smothering her irritation with Ben, Dana took a deep breath and set her mug down. "Ethan, we *all* need to talk about what happened at school yesterday."

Ethan's shoulders stiffened, and he kept his eyes on his cereal. "I already told you. It's nothing."

"Mrs. Bailey didn't think it was nothing," Dana said gently, sitting across from him. "She said you were upset. And that you've been misbehaving in class, too. Is that true? I just want to understand what's going on."

Ethan shrugged, still not meeting her gaze. "Mikey was being a jerk. He kept touching my stuff, my new pencil, so I pushed him. That's it."

Dana exchanged a glance with Ben, who finally set his phone down and joined them at the table. "Ethan, pushing someone isn't the way to handle things," Ben said. "You know that."

"He started it!" Ethan shot back, his voice cracking with frustration.

Dana reached out and placed a hand on Ethan's. "Sweetheart, I know it's hard when someone bothers you, but we need to find better ways to deal with it. Are you feeling okay? Is there something else bothering you? If there is, please say then Dad and I can try to make it right."

Ethan hesitated, his lower lip trembling. For a moment, Dana thought he might open up, but then he shook his head and muttered, "I'm fine. Can I go and say bye to Snowball?"

Dana gave him permission and her heart ached as she watched him slide off the stool then begin his retreat from the room and into himself. She glanced at Ben again, but he only sighed and ran a hand through his hair. "We'll talk more about this tonight," Dana said softly, squeezing Ethan's hand before he pulled away. "Just remember, we're here for you, okay?"

Ethan barely responded, a slight jerk of his chin before he ran into the other room. Dana busied herself with cleaning up, her mind already racing with how she'd address this later. She couldn't shake the nagging guilt that her own distractions had contributed to her son's distress.

~

Later that morning, Dana sat at her desk, catching up on emails when there was a knock at her office door. She looked up to see Molly, her assistant, peeking in nervously.

"Dana, there's someone here to see you," Molly said. "He said he has a meeting, but he... uh... didn't have an appointment on the calendar."

Dana frowned. "Who is it?"

Before Caroline could answer, Justin stepped into the doorway, his signature confident smile plastered across his face. He was dressed impeccably as always, his dark suit tailored to perfection.

"Justin," Dana said, her voice flat as she stood. "What are you doing here?"

"Just in the area for a meeting and thought I'd stop by," Justin said smoothly, ignoring the tension in her tone. "I hope I'm not interrupting."

Dana forced a polite smile, aware of Molly hovering in the background. "Molly, thank you. I'll handle this."

Molly hesitated but eventually nodded and closed the door

behind her. As soon as they were alone, Dana's polite facade dropped.

"You shouldn't be here," she said, keeping her voice low but firm.

Justin took a step closer, his hands casually tucked into his pockets. "I just wanted to see you. Is that so terrible?"

"Yes, it is," Dana snapped. "I've been clear about my boundaries. This is my workplace, Justin. You can't just show up unannounced."

He smiled, unfazed by her anger. "I'm sorry if I overstepped. I just thought we could grab lunch, catch up. You seem stressed. I could help with that."

Dana's jaw tightened. "I'm not going to lunch with you. And this has to stop, Justin. I mean it."

Justin's smile didn't waver. If anything, it deepened, as though he found her resistance amusing. "Come on. One lunch. What harm can it do?," he said softly, his tone almost teasing.

Dana's stomach turned as she stepped back, putting her desk between them. "I mean it. Please leave."

For a moment, Justin held her gaze, the tension in the room palpable. Then he shrugged, as if conceding some unspoken game. "If that's what you want," he said, his voice laced with a confidence that unsettled her. "But I think you'll change your mind."

He turned and walked to the door, pausing to glance back at her. "Take care, Dana."

The door closed behind him, and Dana sank into her chair, her hands trembling. She stared at the door, half-expecting him to come back. The encounter had left her shaken, his calm persistence cutting through her resolve like a knife.

Dana knew she needed to do something, but she felt paralyzed by the weight of it all. Justin wasn't just crossing boundaries—he was obliterating them. And deep down, she feared it was only going to get worse.

An hour later, the pressure at work began to mount. Dana's laptop pinged relentlessly with emails, her inbox filling faster than she could manage. A new campaign deadline had been moved up unexpectedly, and her team was scrambling to put together a presentation for an important client. Caroline popped her head in again, looking frazzled.

"Dana, the client's asking for a complete rework of the visuals," she said. "And the creative team is saying it's impossible to get it done in time."

Dana pinched the bridge of her nose, trying to stave off the headache forming behind her eyes. "Tell them to focus on the key slides. We don't need perfection, just something polished enough to get through the pitch."

Caroline nodded and disappeared, leaving Dana to sift through another wave of emails. As she typed furiously, her mind kept drifting back to Justin. His words, his presence, the way he seemed to linger even after he'd left. She shook her head, trying to push the thoughts away, but they clung to her like cobwebs.

By the time the day ended, Dana felt like she was unraveling. Her professional composure was intact, but beneath the surface, she was a mess of anxiety and self-doubt. Justin's visit had thrown her off balance, and the mounting stress at work wasn't helping.

As she gathered her things to leave, Caroline stopped by her office one last time. "Dana, are you okay? You've seemed... distracted today."

Dana forced a smile. "I'm fine, just a lot on my plate. Thanks for checking in."

Caroline hesitated, then nodded and left but once she was alone, Dana had the urge to call her back. Maybe she needed someone to confide in right now, someone she could trust and if anyone fit the bill, it was her trusted assistant.

Caroline had an uncanny ability to anticipate needs and solve problems before they escalated. Whether it was diffusing office drama or keeping Dana's schedule in check, Caroline handled everything with quiet competence. But no matter how much she relied on her assistant, there were just some things you had to keep private, sort out by yourself and Justin was one of them. Best to keep personal and professional separate, avoid muddying the waters in the office no matter how much you needed some good advice and a friendly ear.

Dana sighed and locked her office door behind her. The weight of the day and her situation pressing down on her shoulders. She couldn't shake the feeling that everything was spiraling out of control—and she didn't know how to stop it.

8

Dana sat at her kitchen table late into the evening, the house quiet except for the faint hum of the refrigerator. She'd put Ethan to bed after watching his favorite show together, her heart aching when she noticed how distant he seemed. His hand stroking Snowball's fur, his eyes watching the screen, his usual chatter and constant questions absent from the room. Ben had already retired to their bedroom, citing a headache and an early meeting in the morning. The loneliness she felt now was all-encompassing, amplified by the unsettling events of the day.

Her phone vibrated on the table, the screen lighting up with a notification. She hesitated before flipping it over. A voicemail. The number wasn't saved.

With trembling fingers, she tapped to listen.

"Dana, it's Justin. I don't like being ignored. I think you know that. Call me back."

The message ended, leaving Dana's chest tight and her breathing uneven. She quickly deleted the voicemail, as though erasing it would make it—and him—disappear. But it didn't. His voice lingered in her mind, that edge of menace buried beneath the smoothness of his tone.

Her stomach churned as she opened her social media accounts, desperate for distraction. But even there, Justin had left his mark. A string of notifications greeted her. Likes and comments on old posts, things she hadn't even remembered sharing. His comments were subtle but unnerving:

"Beautiful memories."

"You've always been remarkable."

"This one made me think of you."

Her hands shook as she scrolled through them, the unease building with every word. She tried to block him, but when she refreshed the page, a new account appeared—one with no photo, no posts, but another comment signed off with his name. He was relentless, and the boundaries she'd tried so hard to enforce were crumbling under the weight of his persistence.

Dana closed the app and set her phone down, her heart pounding. She thought about telling Ben, but the idea filled her with dread. How could she explain this to him without revealing everything? Without admitting how far she'd let things go?

The phone beeped again, and she flinched. This time it was another text from the unknown number:

You can't shut me out forever.

Dana's breath hitched. She quickly deleted the message, but the knot in her chest tightened. She felt trapped, her private life no longer her own. Justin had found a way to infiltrate every corner of her existence, and she didn't know how to make it stop.

The next day, she arrived at work with dark circles under her eyes, her mind clouded with exhaustion and fear. Caroline greeted her with a worried look as soon as she stepped into the office.

"Dana, are you okay? You look... tired," Caroline said carefully.

Dana forced a weak smile. "Just a rough night. Nothing to worry about."

Caroline hesitated. "If you need help with anything today, let me know, okay?"

"Thanks, Caroline. I'll be fine," Dana said, though she didn't believe it.

As she sat at her desk, her phone sounded again. Another text from an unknown number. She didn't open it this time, but the preview was enough to send a chill down her spine:

I'm not going anywhere.

Dana turned off her phone and shoved it into her desk drawer, her hands trembling. She needed to focus, to get through the day without falling apart. But the rising tide of Justin's presence loomed over her, inescapable.

For the first time, she considered going to the police. But what would she say? How could she explain the situation without admitting to her own guilt, her own mistakes? The thought made her stomach twist.

The rest of the day passed in a haze, each notification and email a reminder of the pressure mounting on all sides. By the time she left the office, Dana felt like a shadow of herself, worn thin by fear and anxiety. As she drove home, she had an awful feeling that Justin was watching, waiting for her to slip up.

When she finally stepped into the house, Ethan was waiting for her in the living room, a hopeful smile on his face. "Mom, can we play a boardgame tonight?"

Dana's heart broke at the sight of him. She dropped her bag

and pulled him into a hug, holding on longer than usual. "Of course, sweetheart. Let me just change, and we'll play whatever you want."

For a moment, she felt a flicker of normalcy, a glimpse of the life she was trying so desperately to protect. But as she looked over Ethan's shoulder, her phone buzzed from inside her bag, a blatant reminder that Justin wasn't going to let her go so easily.

That night, after Ethan was asleep and the house had fallen silent, Dana sat in the dimly lit kitchen nursing a glass of wine. Ben was upstairs, oblivious to her turmoil. She had brought this into her family's life, and now it was threatening to unravel everything she had worked so hard to build.

Her phone sounded again, but this time, she didn't even look at it. She stared at the wineglass in her hand, her mind spiraling with worst-case scenarios. What if Justin escalated further? What if Ben found out? The mere thought made her stomach churn.

Work wasn't any easier. The next morning, Caroline approached her with more bad news about the campaign. "The client wants another round of revisions," she said, her voice laced with tension. "They're threatening to pull out if we don't deliver by tomorrow."

Dana rubbed her temples, the headache that had been simmering all week finally coming to a boil. "We'll get it done," she said, her voice lacking conviction. "Schedule a team meeting for this afternoon."

By midday, Dana felt like she was drowning. Justin's texts and social media comments continued to invade her thoughts, distracting her from the mounting demands at work. Her team noticed her distraction, the usual confidence in her leadership replaced by hesitancy and frustration.

"Dana, are you sure you're okay?" Caroline asked again after the meeting.

"I'm fine," Dana snapped, immediately regretting the sharpness in her tone. "I'm sorry, Caroline. It's just... I've got a lot on right now."

Caroline nodded, though her concern lingered. "Let me know if there's anything I can take off your plate."

Dana forced a smile. "Thanks."

By the end of the day, the pressure from work and home felt unbearable. As she drove home in the fading light, her hands gripped the steering wheel tightly, her thoughts racing. She couldn't keep this up. Something had to give. But as she pulled into the driveway and saw Ethan's face in the window, she knew she had to find a way to hold it all together—for him, if nothing else.

9

Dana stepped into the house, balancing her purse and a grocery bag on one arm while calling out for Ethan. The soft jingle of the Snowball's bell greeted her as the tiny tabby darted into the kitchen, skidding slightly on the tiles. She smiled, setting the bag down and crouching to scoop up the kitten.

"Where's your big brother, huh?" she murmured, scratching behind the kitten's ears. Ethan's laughter echoed faintly from the living room, and she relaxed slightly. For the first time in days, the house felt calm, even warm.

She carried the kitten with her as she walked into the living room. Ethan was sprawled on the couch, the TV muted as he fiddled with the Snowball's new toy. He looked up as she entered, grinning. "Hey, Mom! Look, he's learning how to fetch!"

Dana laughed softly. "That's great, sweetheart. Dinner will be ready soon, okay?"

Ethan nodded, already engrossed in his play with Snowball. Dana could hear Ben moving about upstairs and turned back toward the kitchen but froze in her tracks. A chair at the dining table was pulled out—just slightly, but enough to catch her attention. She frowned, certain she'd pushed all the chairs in before leaving that morning.

Shrugging it off, she walked over and slid the chair back into place. But as she turned to the counter, something else caught her eye. A framed photo of her, Ben, and Ethan that usually sat on the mantle was now on the side table near the window. Her heart skipped a beat as she stared at it, her mind racing.

"Did you move the picture?" she called out to Ethan, trying to keep her voice steady.

"What picture?" Ethan asked, glancing up briefly.

"The one of us from last Christmas."

Ethan shook his head. "No. Why?"

Dana forced a smile. "No reason. Must've been me."

But it hadn't been. She knew that. Her hands tightened around the kitten as she carried him back to the kitchen, her mind racing with possibilities. Maybe Ben had moved it before leaving for work. Or maybe Ethan had and was just too distracted to remember. That had to be it.

She tried to push the thought away as she prepared dinner, focusing instead on the mundane rhythm of chopping vegetables and boiling water. But the unease lingered, curling around her thoughts like smoke.

That night, after Ethan had gone to bed, Dana curled up on an armchair with her laptop. Snowball purred softly in her lap, his warmth a small comfort. She scrolled through emails, ignoring the growing pile of unread messages flagged for later. She just needed to keep busy, to distract herself from the gnawing feeling that something wasn't right.

Her phone buzzed on the coffee table, and she glanced at it with a sinking feeling. Another text from an unknown number. She hesitated before picking it up, dread pooling in her stomach as she opened the message.

. . .

Unknown number: Nice place.

Dana held her breath. Her hands began to tremble as she stared at the screen, her mind racing. How did he know? Had he been here? Was he watching her now?

She jumped to her feet, startling Snowball, who leapt to the floor with a soft meow. She checked the locks on the front door, then the back. Everything was secure. She peered out the windows, her heart hammering in her chest, but the street outside was dark and still.

For a moment, she considered calling the police. But what would she say? That she'd had an affair and now the man wouldn't leave her alone? That he might have been in her house? Her stomach twisted with shame and fear.

Instead, she typed out a reply, her fingers shaking with each word.

Dana: Leave me alone. This is harassment.

The message delivered, but there was no response. Dana sat frozen, clutching her phone tightly as she stared at the screen, waiting for it to buzz again. Minutes passed, then an hour, but the silence was almost worse than the message itself.

When she finally went to bed, she locked the bedroom door and left the lamp on, unable to rid herself of the notion that Justin's presence was closer than she'd ever imagined. And as she lay awake, staring at the ceiling, she couldn't help but wonder what she'd done and if she'd ever feel safe in her own home again.

10

Dana could still remember the exact moment she met Lexy. It had been thirteen years ago, during an afternoon at a bustling coffee shop in downtown Boston where Dana worked between classes. She had been juggling an overloaded tray of coffee cups when she stumbled, nearly toppling to the ground. A stranger had reached out and steadied her with a quick grip and a bright laugh.

"Whoa there! You've got enough caffeine to fuel a marathon," the young woman had joked, her voice warm and teasing.

Dana had looked up to see a striking woman with auburn hair pulled into a loose bun, her green eyes sparkling with amusement. She wore a leather jacket over a vintage band t-shirt, and there was an air of effortless confidence about her that immediately intrigued Dana.

"Thanks," Dana had said, flustered but grateful. "I guess I underestimated how heavy these were."

"Happens to the best of us," the woman replied, waving off Dana's embarrassment. "I'm Lexy, by the way. And I think fate just decided we're supposed to talk."

It turned out that Lexy had been waiting for a blind date that never showed. Dana, feeling guilty for her initial awkwardness, had offered to buy her a coffee once her shift ended, and they'd ended up talking for hours. Despite their different personalities and college courses they clicked instantly. Lexy was bold, outspoken, and a little bit wild, while Dana was more reserved and cautious. Yet, beneath their surface differences, they found a shared sense of humor, a love for classic movies, and a mutual drive to prove themselves in a world that often underestimated them.

Lexy had grown up in a small town in upstate New York, the youngest of four siblings and the only girl. Her childhood, as she described it, had been chaotic and loud, filled with arguments over the dinner table and hand-me-down everything. Her father was a mechanic, her mother a nurse, and while her family was loving in their own way, Lexy always felt like she was destined for something more. She dreamed of escaping the confines of her small town and making a name for herself, which she eventually did when she left to go to college and later, pursued a career as a private detective.

But Lexy's life hadn't been without struggles. She had confided in Dana about her tumultuous relationship with her ex-boyfriend, a man who had drained her emotionally and financially. It had taken Lexy years to rebuild her confidence and regain her independence, but she had done it with a determination that Dana deeply admired.

Over the years, their friendship had grown into something more akin to sisterhood. Lexy was the one who had encouraged Dana to take risks, whether it was going after a promotion or stepping outside her comfort zone. She had been there to celebrate Dana's successes and to pick her up after her failures. Likewise, Dana had been Lexy's sounding board, her confidant, and her rock during difficult times.

When Dana married Ben, Lexy had been her maid of honor, delivering a speech that left everyone in tears and laughter. "Dana's the heart," she had said, raising her glass. "And I'm the loudmouth that gets her into trouble. But I think we balance each other out perfectly."

Now, as Dana thought about Lexy's unwavering loyalty and fiery spirit, a pang of guilt gnawed at her. She owed so much to her friend, her lifeline, a constant source of strength and joy and now she needed her more than ever.

The afternoon sunlight filtered through the large windows of the corner café where Dana sat, nursing a cooling cup of tea. Her fingers tapped anxiously against the table as she waited, her thoughts a swirling mix of fear, guilt, and desperation. She'd texted Lexy that morning, asking to meet with an urgency she hadn't been able to explain in the message. Now that she was here, she wasn't even sure where to begin.

The café was a cozy spot Dana and Lexy had frequented for years. Nestled on a quiet street in the center of bustling downtown, its warm wooden tables, mismatched chairs, and the faint scent of freshly brewed coffee created an inviting atmosphere. Strings of fairy lights framed the windows, casting a soft glow that made the space feel intimate even during the busiest hours. For Dana, it was a place of comfort—or at least, it used to be.

The door chimed, and Lexy strode in, her sharp eyes scanning the room until they landed on Dana. Lexy was all business, dressed in tailored slacks and a blazer, her dark hair pulled back into a sleek ponytail. Even in the relaxed setting of the café, she exuded an air of authority. She had always been that way—confident, quick-thinking, and fiercely loyal.

Lexy had always been the pragmatic one, the problem-solver who always seemed to have her life together, even when things were falling apart. After graduation, Lexy pursued a career in private investigation, a field that seemed tailor-made for her sharp mind and unshakable determination. Over the years, Dana had come to rely on Lexy's advice, especially during life's more turbulent moments.

"Hey, you," Lexy said, sliding into the seat across from Dana. Her tone was casual, but her eyes betrayed her concern. "You look like you've seen a ghost. What's going on?" Lexy took a sip of the latte that Dana had ordered in advance.

Dana managed a weak smile but couldn't hold it for long. She glanced around the café, ensuring no one was within earshot, then leaned in closer, half dreading the words she was about to say, totally dreading Lexy's reaction to them.

"I... I don't even know how to say this," Dana began, her voice barely above a whisper. "I've messed up, Lex. Badly."

Lexy frowned, concern flashing in her eyes. "What do you mean? What happened?"

Dana took a deep breath, her hands trembling as she gripped her cup. "Okay. Just hear me out because I think you're going to be mad as hell with me."

Lexy's hand froze, the coffee cup halfway between the table and her mouth. "Go on, although I have to say I'm getting worried."

Dana closed her eyes for a second, as if hiding from what was about to happen, then blurted it out. "There's this guy. Justin. I slept with him. It was brief—just one night. I knew it was wrong, and I ended it immediately. But he... he won't leave me alone."

Lexy's frown deepened, and she leaned back slightly, absorbing the revelation. "Fuck. Dana. How could you be so stupid?" Lexy rubbed her temples and let out a long breath.

"Now he won't he leave you alone, you said? What do you mean?"

"He's been texting me nonstop," Dana said, her voice shaking. "At first, it was just messages, but now it's more. He showed up at my office. And yesterday... yesterday, I think he was in my house."

Lexy's eyes narrowed. "In your house? Are you sure?"

Dana nodded, tears pooling in her eyes. "Things were moved. A chair, a photo frame. And then he texted me saying, 'Nice place.' I don't know how he got in. Everything was locked. I... I feel like I'm losing my mind."

Lexy's expression hardened, a mix of anger and determination. "Okay. First, you're not losing your mind. This guy sounds dangerous, Dana. And if he's escalating like this, we need to take it seriously."

"What can I do?" Dana asked, her voice cracking. "I can't tell Ben. He'd never forgive me. And I can't go to the police. They'll just ask questions I'm not ready to answer."

Lexy reached across the table, placing a firm hand on Dana's. "You don't have to tell Ben right now. But you do need to protect yourself. Start by saving every text, every voicemail, every little thing he sends you. We need evidence in case this gets worse."

Dana nodded, wiping at her eyes. "I've kept some of the messages. But at first, I was deleting them. I didn't want to see them."

"That's okay," Lexy said. "We'll work with what you have. I'll also do some digging on this Justin. If he's done this before—and my gut says he probably has—we need to know about it."

"You think he's done this to someone else?" Dana asked, her stomach twisting.

"Guys like him don't usually just stop at one," Lexy said grimly. "But don't worry. I'm going to find out everything I can. In the meantime, you need to be cautious. Change your locks.

Get a security camera for your house if you can. And if he contacts you again, don't engage. Just document it."

Dana let out a shaky breath, the knot in her chest loosening slightly. "Thank you, Lexy. I don't know what I'd do without you."

Lexy gave her a small, reassuring smile. "We'll get through this, Dana. But you need to be ready for the possibility that it could get worse before it gets better."

Dana could feel tears pricking at her eyes but it was Lexy's next question that caused them to flow.

"Look, I'm not judging... but I have to ask even if it sounds like I'm prying, why? I thought you and Ben were solid, happy. You guys have everything, or that's what I thought and this, this Justin thing is so not like you Dana. It's hard to take in that you'd do something like this, it really is." Dana waited, her eyes never leaving Dana's.

There was only one way to answer and that was with the truth. "I honestly don't know why I did it, Lex, and if I could wind back time I would. It's like I lost my mind for a while, as though someone else took over and I bitterly regret it. All I can say in my defense is that for a while there's been something missing between me and Ben and I don't just mean sex, although I can't remember the last time we... well anyway, there's a disconnect, like we go through the motions of married life, parenthood and work and there's nothing left. I felt like he didn't see me anymore, the Dana he married so when someone else did, I fell for it. The bullshit and flattery and I hate myself so much for being so naïve. There. Does that answer your question?"

Lexy looked so sad and disappointed when she gave a gentle nod, no words required and for that Dana was thankful. Because she knew she deserved both barrels and a dressing down for being spoilt and selfish and stupid.

Later, after Dana settled the bill and left the café, somber farewells and promises to keep in touch made, the weight of her confession lifted slightly, but the fear remained. Lexy's support gave her a glimmer of hope, but she knew the road ahead was going to be anything but easy.

11

The smell of grilled meat and fresh-baked cake filled the air as Dana stood in the kitchen, arranging a platter of appetizers. Laughter echoed from the living room where Ben was surrounded by family friends, his warm smile lighting up the room as Ethan eagerly handed him a homemade birthday card. The house felt alive, buzzing with celebration, a rare moment of happiness that Dana had desperately hoped to create.

"Mom, when do we get to eat cake?" Ethan called from the doorway; his face smeared with traces of frosting he'd clearly swiped from the counter earlier.

Dana chuckled, wiping her hands on a towel. "After dinner, buddy. Go enjoy the party."

Ethan groaned but scampered back to the living room, where one of their family friends, Lisa, was telling a funny story that had the room in stitches. Dana paused for a moment, leaning against the counter and watching the scene unfold. Ben's laughter rang out, his arm slung casually over the back of the couch. He looked relaxed, happy, and for a fleeting moment, Dana felt the guilt and fear that had been gripping her begin to loosen its grip.

She turned back to the kitchen, busying herself with last-minute preparations, when a shadow moved across the window above the sink. Her hands froze, the knife she'd been holding hovering over a slice of bread. It could have been nothing—a trick of the light, a passing car—but her pulse quickened as she strained to see into the darkness beyond the glass.

Nothing. Just the faint outline of the backyard fence and the soft glow of the porch light.

Dana shook her head, forcing herself to breathe. She was letting her paranoia get the better of her. This was Ben's night, and she wasn't going to let her fears ruin it.

"Everything okay in here?" Lisa's voice startled her, and Dana turned to see her friend leaning in the doorway, a glass of wine in hand.

"Yeah, just finishing up," Dana replied, plastering on a smile. "How's the birthday boy?"

"Living it up," Lisa said with a laugh. "You've really outdone yourself, Dana. The house looks great, and the food smells amazing."

"Thanks," Dana said, her smile faltering for a moment. "I just wanted it to be special."

Lisa gave her a knowing look. "It is. Don't overthink it, okay? Go enjoy yourself."

Dana nodded, watching as Lisa disappeared back into the living room. She set the knife down and turned to the window one more time, unable to shake the nagging feeling that someone had been there.

As the evening wore on, they were joined by new neighbors who had moved next door, and the party moved outside to the patio. Strings of fairy lights twinkled above, casting a warm glow over the group as Ben cut into his birthday cake to a chorus of cheers and laughter. Dana stood to the side, her glass of wine untouched, her eyes scanning the faces of their friends and neighbors.

"So, Ben," Lisa began as the group settled into their seats around the patio table, the new neighbors seated opposite. "For the benefit of those who don't know, tell us again how you and Dana met. I love that story."

Ben chuckled, wiping a smudge of frosting from Ethan's cheek before leaning back in his chair. "Ah, the infamous meet-cute," he said, grinning at Dana. "We met at a charity fundraiser. Dana was volunteering as the event coordinator, and I was there on behalf of my firm, trying to make a good impression on some clients."

"And he spilled red wine all over one of the auction items," Dana interjected, rolling her eyes fondly. "It was a vintage tablecloth, and he was mortified."

"I was more mortified by how gracefully you handled it," Ben said, smiling at her. "Instead of chewing me out, you found a way to joke about it and keep the event running smoothly. I was impressed."

"You were impressed?" Dana teased. "You spent the rest of the night following me around, trying to make up for it."

"And it worked," Ben said, raising his glass. "Because here we are, years later, married with this little guy." He reached over to ruffle Ethan's hair, earning a giggle from their son.

Lisa sighed dramatically. "See? That's why I love this story. It's so disgustingly adorable."

"I'm just glad the tablecloth wasn't a total loss," Ben said, earning a round of laughter from the group.

Dana smiled, but her mind was elsewhere. She glanced toward the street, her eyes scanning the darkness just beyond the reach of the porch lights. She wanted to lose herself in the warmth of the evening, the sound of laughter and clinking glasses, Ben's smile.

And then she saw him.

Across the street, just beyond the reach of the streetlights, a figure stood watching. Justin. His silhouette was unmistakable, his stance casual yet deliberate. Dana's heart stopped, as her gaze locked on him. He wasn't moving, just standing there, his presence a silent threat that sent a chill down her spine.

"Dana?" Ben's voice broke through her thoughts, and she turned to find him holding a piece of cake, his brow furrowed with concern. "You okay? You've been quiet."

"I'm fine," she said quickly, forcing a smile. "Just tired, I guess."

Ben studied her for a moment but seemed satisfied with her answer. He kissed her cheek and handed her the plate. "Go sit down. You've done enough tonight."

Dana nodded, clutching the plate as Ben returned to the group. She stole another glance toward the street, but Justin was gone. Her stomach swirled as she scanned the darkness, half-expecting him to reappear at any moment.

The rest of the evening passed in a blur. Dana went through the motions of playing hostess, laughing at jokes she didn't hear and responding to questions she didn't register. All the while, her mind raced with questions she couldn't answer.

How long had Justin been there? How much had he seen? And, most terrifying of all, what was he planning next?

Later, as the last guests said their goodbyes and the house fell quiet, Dana locked every door and window, her hands shaking with adrenaline. She checked on Ethan, who was fast asleep with the Snowball curled up at his feet, then slipped into bed beside Ben who was deep in sleep. Dana turned on her side and watched the rise and fall of his chest, envious of his state of blissful slumber, and ignorance of his wife's actions. If she could make a wish for his birthday it would be that he remained unaware of her betrayal, and that he would never have to know the pain her actions could bear down on their family.

Turning on her back, tears streaming down her cheeks, Dana stared at the ceiling and wondered if she should make a wish for herself until a voice whispered in her ear... *you don't deserve one.*

12

Dana rushed into the office Monday morning to find a storm brewing. The usually calm, corporate hum of the marketing firm was replaced by tense whispers and hurried footsteps. Her assistant, Caroline, met her at the door, looking pale and visibly flustered.

"Dana, we have a problem," Caroline said, thrusting a tablet into her hands.

On the screen was a series of emails that Dana immediately recognized as internal correspondence about their biggest client, Brantwell Industries. Confidential details about the upcoming campaign—strategy, budgets, and even early creative concepts—were all laid out in black and white. Worse yet, the emails had been sent to one of their client's direct competitors.

Dana's stomach dropped. "How did this happen?" she demanded, her voice trembling.

"We don't know," Caroline admitted. "But the leak... it's bad, Dana. Mr. Jacobs is looking for you."

Dana barely had time to process the information before her boss, Tom Jacobs, appeared, his face red with barely contained anger.

"Dana, in my office. Now," he barked, not waiting for her to follow.

She set the tablet down and trailed after him, her heart pounding. The moment she stepped into his office, Tom slammed the door shut and turned to face her.

"Explain to me how this happened," he said, his voice low but menacing. "How does confidential client information end up in the hands of a competitor on your watch?"

"I… I don't know," Dana stammered. "This is the first I'm hearing about it. I'll investigate immediately and—"

"Not good enough," Tom interrupted, slamming his palm against the desk. "Brantwell is furious. They're threatening to pull their account, and if they do, we'll be out millions. I need answers, Dana, and I need them yesterday."

Dana swallowed hard, her mind racing. She had always been meticulous about protecting client information. Something like this shouldn't have been possible. But as she stood there under Tom's withering glare, a sinking feeling crept over her.

Could Justin have done this?

Tom dismissed her with a curt wave, and Dana hurried back to her office. She closed the door behind her and leaned against it, trying to steady her breathing. Her phone buzzed on the desk, and she hesitated before picking it up.

The text was from an unknown number.

Maybe now you'll take me seriously.

Dana's hands trembled as she read the message. Her worst fears were confirmed. Justin had done this. He'd gone beyond invading her personal life—he was now sabotaging her career.

Her stomach roiled with a mix of anger and dread as she typed out a reply.

Dana: What did you do?

The response came almost immediately.

Unknown number: Just a little reminder of what I'm capable of. Meet me, and we can talk about how to fix this.

Dana's vision blurred as panic set in. She couldn't believe this was happening. Justin had crossed a line, and now her job, her reputation, and the company's future were at stake. But meeting him? The very thought made her skin crawl.

She needed to act quickly. Forcing herself to focus, she called Lexy.

"Lex, it's me," Dana said, her voice shaking. "He's done something. He leaked emails from my company. It's bad. Really bad."

Lexy didn't hesitate. "Okay, listen to me. You can't let him manipulate you into meeting him. That's what he wants. Forward me everything he's sent you, and I'll see what I can trace. Also, tell your IT department to secure your accounts immediately. Change every password you have."

"What if he's hacked into our systems?" Dana asked, her voice barely above a whisper.

"Let's not jump to conclusions," Lexy said, her tone calm but firm. "For now, focus on damage control at work. I'll handle

Justin. And Dana. Don't meet him. No matter what he says or threatens, do not meet him alone."

Dana nodded, even though Lexy couldn't see her. "Okay. Thank you."

Hanging up, Dana took a deep breath and steeled herself. She had to pull it together. Justin might have thrown her world into chaos, but she wasn't going to let him destroy everything she'd worked for.

But as she sat at her desk, trying to formulate a plan, the weight of Justin's threat loomed large. She knew this was far from over.

13

The Saturday morning sun was bright, casting long shadows over the local park where Ethan's soccer team gathered for their weekly game. Dana sat on the edge of the bleachers, trying to focus on the chatter of other parents and the cheerful shouts of the children warming up on the field. Normally, this was her favorite time of the week—a rare chance to unplug from the chaos of work and spend time with Ethan. But today, her anxiety was a constant undercurrent, making her fidget with her coffee cup as her eyes scanned the crowd.

Ethan was easy to spot in his bright blue jersey, his hair sticking out from under his cap as he passed the ball to a teammate. Dana smiled briefly, her chest swelling with pride. But the smile faded as her gaze moved beyond the field and landed on a figure she instantly recognized.

Justin.

He was leaning casually against the fence, chatting with a small group of parents. His posture was relaxed, almost as if he belonged there, but Dana's stomach twisted. What was he doing here? How did he even know about Ethan's game?

Her grip tightened on the coffee cup as she watched him

laugh at something one of the parents said. Then he turned toward the coach, extending a hand as if introducing himself. Dana's heart pounded. She rose from the bleachers, barely registering the curious glances from the other parents, and made her way toward him.

As she approached, Justin turned, his face lighting up with a smile that made her blood run cold.

"Dana," he said smoothly, as if they were old friends running into each other by chance. "I didn't expect to see you here."

"What the hell are you doing?" she hissed, keeping her voice low but urgent. "You have no business being here."

Justin's smile didn't falter. "I just wanted to meet Ethan. He's a great kid."

Dana's breath caught, her vision narrowing. "You stay away from him," she said, her voice trembling with barely controlled anger. "Do you hear me? Stay away from my son."

Justin's expression shifted, his eyes darkening with a hint of something more dangerous. "Relax, Dana. I'm just here to watch the game. It's a public park. I haven't done anything wrong."

Her hands balled into fists at her sides. "This ends now. Whatever game you think you're playing. I am not going to let you drag my son into it."

Justin leaned in slightly, lowering his voice. "You made this personal, Dana. Not me. I'm just getting to know the people who matter to you."

Before she could respond, he turned and walked away, casually blending back into the crowd of parents as if nothing had happened. Dana stood frozen, her chest heaving as she tried to process what he'd just said.

The game resumed, but Dana could barely focus. She forced herself to stay until the final whistle blew, clapping weakly as Ethan's team celebrated their win. When Ethan ran up to her, beaming and out of breath, she hugged him tightly, holding on longer than usual.

"Mom, you're squishing me," Ethan said with a laugh, wiggling free.

Dana forced a smile. "Sorry, sweetie. Let's get home, okay?"

That evening, Dana sat on the floor of her bedroom, her back against the bed frame as she stared at her phone. The events of the day replayed in her mind on an endless loop, each moment sharpening her fear and helplessness. She had followed Lexy's advice, stayed firm, and refused to meet Justin on his terms. But now he was pushing boundaries she hadn't even considered.

He had come into Ethan's world. That was a line she couldn't allow him to cross, but how could she stop him? He seemed to know everything about her life—where she worked, where Ethan played, even the people in their circle. The realization made her chest tighten, and tears spilled down her cheeks as she hugged her knees to her chest.

The sound of her phone beeping pulled her out of her thoughts. She picked it up, dreading what she might see, but it was a call from Lexy.

"Hey," Dana said, her voice barely above a whisper.

"I've been digging into Justin," Lexy said without preamble. "We need to talk. I've found some things you need to know."

Dana wiped her face with the back of her hand. "Is it bad?"

Lexy hesitated. "We'll go over it tomorrow. Just lock your doors tonight and try to get some rest. You're not alone in this, okay?"

Dana nodded, even though Lexy couldn't see her. "Thank you."

When the call ended, Dana set her phone down and curled

up on the bed, pulling a blanket around her shoulders. She stared at the shadows on the ceiling, her tears soaking into the pillow as the weight of the situation pressed down on her.

Justin had invaded her life, her work, and now her family. And for the first time, Dana realized she might not be able to protect the people she loved from the consequences of her mistakes.

~

The tension in the house was palpable. Dana stood at the kitchen sink, scrubbing a plate with more force than necessary, her jaw clenched. The sound of Ethan's laughter from the living room grated on her nerves, not because it annoyed her, but because it reminded her of how fragile their happiness was. Every moment of joy felt like a cruel illusion, overshadowed by Justin's looming presence.

"Mom, where's my soccer cleats?" Ethan called from the hallway.

"I don't know, Ethan," Dana snapped, her voice sharper than she intended. "Did you check the shoe rack?"

Ethan appeared in the doorway, his face falling at her tone. "I... I thought you might have moved them."

"I don't have time to keep track of everything," she said, turning back to the sink. "You're old enough to look for your own things."

Ethan's shoulders slumped, and he walked away without another word. Dana closed her eyes, guilt washing over her. She knew she was being unfair, but the stress had reached boiling point. Her chest felt tight, her thoughts spiraling out of control.

From the living room, Ben's voice carried into the kitchen. "Ethan, come here. Let's see if we can find those cleats together."

Dana glanced over her shoulder to see Ben kneeling beside

Ethan at the shoe rack, pulling out pairs and holding them up for inspection. Ethan's face lit up when Ben finally unearthed the missing cleats, and the two of them shared a high five. The sight should have brought her comfort, but instead, it made the knot in her stomach tighten.

She couldn't keep this up. Justin's harassment was seeping into every corner of her life, turning her into someone she didn't recognize. She'd snapped at her son over something trivial, and for what? Because she was too afraid to tell Ben the truth?

The truth. The word lingered in her mind, heavy and oppressive. She had to tell Ben. It was the only way to regain some semblance of control. But as she wiped her hands on a towel and stepped into the living room, her resolve faltered.

Ben and Ethan were on the floor, playing with a set of building blocks. They were constructing a tower, each piece placed with careful precision as they laughed and joked together. Ethan's eyes sparkled with delight; his earlier disappointment forgotten. And Ben... Ben looked so content, so at ease.

Dana stood in the doorway; the words she'd rehearsed a thousand times catching in her throat. How could she destroy this moment? How could she burden Ben with the knowledge of what she'd done.

"Hey, everything okay?" Ben asked, looking up and noticing her standing there.

Dana forced a smile, nodding. "Yeah, just... thinking about dinner. Do you guys want spaghetti tonight?"

"Sounds great," Ben said, turning back to the tower. "What do you think, champ?"

"Spaghetti!" Ethan cheered, adding another block to the tower.

Dana retreated to the kitchen, her heart heavy with guilt and indecision. She wanted to tell Ben. She needed to tell him. But every time she came close, the fear of losing everything—her family, her stability, her son's happiness—held her back.

As she stirred the pot of sauce on the stove, her phone buzzed on the counter. She didn't have to look at the screen to know who it was. Justin's texts had become a constant presence, a reminder that no matter how much she tried to ignore him, he wasn't going away.

She picked up the phone and opened the message, her hands trembling.

Unknown number: How long are you going to keep lying to him? He deserves to know the truth.

Dana's chest tightened as she stared at the words. Justin was relentless, chipping away at her resolve with every message, every veiled threat. She wanted to scream, to throw the phone across the room, but she knew it wouldn't change anything.

Taking a deep breath, she locked the phone and set it down. She would tell Ben. Maybe not tonight, but soon. She couldn't keep living like this, caught between fear and guilt, letting Justin control her life. But as she glanced into the living room and saw Ethan's joyful face, she couldn't bring herself to break the illusion just yet.

14

Dana sat at a corner table in the bustling coffee shop, her hands wrapped around a mug of lukewarm tea. The place was packed, the hum of conversation and clinking cups filling the air, but Dana felt completely isolated. She kept glancing at the door, her heart sinking a little more each time someone entered, and it wasn't Lexy.

She checked her phone again. No messages, no missed calls. Lexy had always been reliable, and the silence now felt ominous. Dana had texted her twice and left a voicemail, but there was no response. It wasn't like Lexy to ghost her, especially not when they had agreed to meet to discuss Justin.

Dana's anxiety grew with every passing minute. She stirred her tea absently, her mind racing with possibilities. Maybe Lexy had gotten tied up with work. Or maybe she had found something important about Justin and was following a lead. But the thought that gnawed at the edge of her mind was far darker: what if something had happened to her?

An hour passed, and Dana couldn't sit still any longer. She grabbed her bag, left a few dollars on the table, and headed out into the crisp evening air. Her mind was made up. If Lexy wasn't answering her phone, Dana would go to her apartment. She needed answers, because instinct told her that something was very wrong.

The drive to Lexy's apartment was a blur. Dana's knuckles were white on the steering wheel as she navigated the city streets, her mind a whirlwind of worst-case scenarios. When she pulled up in front of the building, the sight of Lexy's car in the parking lot sent a small wave of relief through her. At least she was home.

Dana hurried up the stairs to the second floor, her heart pounding in her chest. She knocked on the door and waited, her ear pressed to the wood. No sound. She knocked again, louder this time.

"Lexy? It's Dana. Are you in there?"

Still nothing.

Her hand hovered over the doorknob. It was locked, of course, but she jiggled it anyway, as if hoping it might miraculously open. Panic began to set in. She fumbled for her phone and dialed Lexy's number again, pressing the device to her ear as she strained to hear any sound from inside the apartment.

The call went straight to voicemail.

Dana bit her lip, glancing around the hallway. She considered her options. Should she call the police? She didn't even know if Lexy was in any real danger, but her instincts told her something was off. Maybe she could check with the building manager, see if they had a spare key.

As she turned to head back down the hallway, a noise stopped her. It was faint, almost imperceptible, but it came from inside Lexy's apartment. Dana pressed her ear to the door, her breath catching as she listened. The sound was so soft she could barely make it out—a shuffle, a creak of floorboards, maybe.

"Lexy?" she called again, her voice trembling. "If you're in there, please answer me."

Silence.

The hair on the back of Dana's neck stood up. She took a step back from the door, her heart pounding. Something was wrong. She turned and hurried back down the stairs, her phone already in her hand as she dialed the building manager's number, which Lexy had given her once in case of emergencies.

After a few rings, an older man's voice answered. "Hello?"

"Hi, this is Dana, a friend of Lexy's," she said, trying to keep her voice steady. "I... I'm at her apartment, and I'm worried about her. She's not answering her phone or the door, and I think something might be wrong. Do you have a spare key? Could you let me in to check?"

The man hesitated. "I... I'm not really supposed to do that without the tenant's permission."

"Please," Dana said, her voice breaking. "I'm really scared for her. Just come up and let me look. If everything's fine, I'll leave, I promise."

There was a long pause, and then the man sighed. "All right. I'll be up in a minute."

Dana paced the hallway while she waited, her nerves stretched to the breaking point. When the building manager finally arrived, holding a ring of keys, she almost cried with relief.

"Let's get this over with," he muttered, pushing the key into the lock. The door clicked open, and he stepped aside, letting Dana enter first.

The apartment was eerily quiet. Dana's eyes darted around the space, taking in the neat living room, the untouched coffee cup on the table, the jacket draped over the back of a chair. Nothing looked out of place, but the silence felt oppressive.

"Lexy?" Dana called, her voice echoing slightly in the stillness.

There was no answer.

She moved deeper into the apartment, her heart pounding in her chest. The building manager lingered by the door, looking uncomfortable. When Dana reached the bedroom, she froze. The bed was unmade, the sheets tangled as if someone had left in a hurry. On the nightstand, her phone buzzed but Lexy was nowhere to be seen.

She turned slowly, feeling the weight of the empty apartment settle around her like a shroud. Something wasn't right, and she had no idea what she would do next.

Her own phone buzzed in her hand, startling her. She looked down at the screen and felt her blood run cold. A message from an unknown number.

Unknown number: You really shouldn't have asked Lexy to dig into my past.

Dana's breath caught as she stared at the screen, her hands trembling. Her mind raced with possibilities, none of them good. She turned back to the building manager, her voice shaking. "We need to call the police."

The man nodded, pulling out his own phone. Dana stepped out of the apartment; her knees weak as she leaned against the wall. Justin's reach was deeper than she had imagined, and now Lexy's disappearance was undeniable proof that he wasn't just playing games anymore.

15

Dana sat across from Ben at the dinner table, the clink of silverware against plates filling the silence between them. Ethan was spending the evening at a friend's house, and the quiet felt heavier than usual. Ben was focused on his food, his attention divided as he scrolled through his phone every few minutes. Dana watched him, her stomach twisting with unease.

"How's the pasta?" she asked, her voice breaking the stillness.

Ben glanced up, nodding. "It's good. Thanks for making it."

Dana tried to smile but failed. She pushed a piece of garlic bread around her plate, her appetite completely gone. Her mind was racing, the weight of what she needed to say pressing down on her like a boulder. She had rehearsed this moment in her head countless times, but now that it was here, the words refused to come.

"Ben," she started, her voice trembling slightly. "Can we talk about something?"

Ben set his fork down, his brow furrowing. "Sure. What's going on?"

Dana took a deep breath, her hands trembling as she

gripped the edge of the table. "There's something I need to tell you. Something I should have told you a long time ago."

Ben leaned back in his chair, his expression shifting to one of concern. "Okay..."

"I made a mistake," Dana said, her voice cracking. "A huge mistake. And I've been carrying it around, trying to fix it on my own, but I can't anymore."

Ben's eyes narrowed slightly, a flicker of apprehension crossing his face. "What kind of mistake?"

Dana forced herself to meet his gaze, tears brimming in her eyes. "I had an affair."

The words hung in the air, heavy, life changing. Ben's face froze, his expression a mix of shock and disbelief. He opened his mouth to speak, then closed it again, as though he couldn't find the words.

"It was just one night," Dana continued, her voice barely above a whisper. "I ended it immediately, and I've regretted it every second since. But the man I was with... Justin... he won't let it go. He's been harassing me, Ben. Showing up at work, at Ethan's soccer games. And now Lexy is missing, and I think it's because of him."

Ben finally found his voice, but it was low and trembling with anger. "You... you had an affair?" he said, his words slow and deliberate. "Are you fucking kidding me? And now this guy is... stalking you? Harassing you?"

Dana nodded, tears streaming down her face. "I didn't know how to tell you. I was so scared of losing you, of breaking up our family. But I can't keep this from you anymore. Justin has crossed every line, and I don't know what to do."

Ben stood abruptly, his chair scraping loudly against the floor. He ran a hand through his hair, pacing the length of the room as he tried to process what he'd just heard. "You... you cheated on me," he said, his voice rising. "You betrayed me, and now you've dragged this psycho into our lives?"

"I'm sorry," Dana said, her voice breaking. "I know I've hurt you. I've hurt us. But I'm trying to fix it, Ben. I'm trying to protect you and Ethan."

Ben stopped pacing, turning to face her. His eyes were filled with a mix of anger, pain, and something else. Betrayal. "Protect us? By hiding this from me? By letting this guy get close to our son. For fuck's sake Dana."

"I didn't know he would go this far," Dana said, her voice trembling. "I thought I could handle it, but I was wrong. I need your help, Ben. Please."

Ben shook his head, his hands on his hips as he stared at the floor. For a long moment, the only sound in the room was the faint hum of the refrigerator. Finally, he looked up, his jaw set with determination.

"First, we're going to deal with this Justin guy," he said. "Whatever it takes. And after that..." He paused, his voice softening slightly. "After that, we'll figure out what happens with us."

Dana's heart ached at his words, but she nodded. She couldn't expect him to forgive her right away—maybe not ever. But for now, they were on the same side, and that was what mattered.

"We should contact a lawyer," Dana said. "Someone who can help us figure out how to protect ourselves and... and Ethan."

Ben nodded. His expression grim. "I'll make some calls tomorrow. But Dana... if he's gone this far, we might need to involve the police."

Dana hesitated, her stomach twisting. "I know. I'm just scared they won't believe me. Or that Justin will find a way to twist everything around."

Ben stepped closer, his voice firm. "Then we'll make sure they believe you. We'll show them the texts, the emails, whatever evidence you have. This guy doesn't get to keep doing this."

Dana nodded again, her tears falling freely now. Ben's anger and hurt were still palpable, but for the first time in weeks, she felt a flicker of hope. She wasn't alone anymore.

As Ben walked toward the kitchen to pour himself a drink, Dana sat back on the couch, her head spinning. Confessing the affair had been the hardest thing she'd ever done, but it was also a step forward. She had spent too long letting Justin control her through fear and shame. Now, it was time to take that control back—for herself, for Ben, and for Ethan.

~

The plates sat untouched on the table; the dinner long forgotten. Ben stood by the window, his back to Dana, staring out at the darkened yard. His hands were shoved deep into his pockets, his posture tense. Dana sat at the table, her arms wrapped around herself, as if trying to hold herself together.

"I need to know everything," Ben said finally, his voice low but sharp. "All of it. Don't leave anything out."

Dana's breath hitched. "Ben, I..."

He turned, his face etched with pain. "Don't." His voice cracked. "Don't try to soften it. Just tell me."

Dana nodded, her hands trembling as she clasped them together. "It happened after that work event last month. The networking one downtown. You remember?"

Ben gave a short, bitter laugh. "Yeah, the one you said went late. The one I told you not to stress about because I had everything covered at home."

"I didn't plan for it to happen," Dana said, her voice

breaking. "He was charming, and I was... I don't know. I was feeling lost. Invisible. He made me feel... noticed."

Ben's jaw tightened, his fists clenching at his sides. "Noticed?" he repeated, his tone dripping with disdain. "So, what? You just... what, Dana? Went back to his place? Did you even think about me? About Ethan?"

Tears streamed down Dana's face as she shook her head. "It wasn't like that. It was one night, and I regretted it the second it happened. I told him it was a mistake, that it would never happen again. But he... he didn't take it well."

"Didn't take it well?" Ben's voice rose, his anger barely contained. "Dana, this man is stalking you. Harassing you. He's gotten close to our son! How could you let it get this far?"

"I thought I could handle it," Dana said, her voice trembling. "I didn't want to bring it into our home. I didn't want to hurt you or Ethan. I thought if I ignored him, he'd stop. But he's escalated, Ben. He's dangerous. And now Lexy... Lexy is missing because of me."

Ben stared at her, his eyes searching hers for answers, perhaps for something that would make sense of the chaos she'd brought into their lives. All Dana saw was her guilt and fear reflected in his, and it only deepened the ache in her chest.

"How could you do this to us?" he asked, his voice breaking. "To me? To Ethan? I thought we were happy. I thought we were solid."

"I thought so too," Dana whispered, her voice barely audible. "But somewhere along the way, I got lost. And I made a terrible mistake. But I love you, Ben. I love our family. And I will do whatever it takes to fix this. Please believe me."

Ben turned away, his shoulders heaving as he struggled to compose himself. He looked like the ground had been ripped out from under him, leaving him adrift in a sea of betrayal and pain. Finally, he spoke, his voice quiet but firm.

"I think I need to speak to a lawyer," he said, his words like a knife to Dana's heart.

She froze, her breath catching. "Ben... are you... are you saying you want a divorce?"

He turned to her, his face unreadable. "I don't know what I want right now. But I need to protect Ethan. I need to protect myself. And we need to figure out how to deal with this Justin guy before he does any more damage."

Dana nodded, her tears falling freely now. She couldn't blame him for feeling this way. She'd betrayed his trust in the worst possible way, and now they were both paying the price.

"I'll show you everything," she said. "The texts, the emails. Whatever you need. Just tell me what to do."

Ben nodded stiffly, his gaze lingering on her for a moment before he turned away again. "I'll call someone in the morning. For now, I... I just need some space."

Dana watched him leave the room, her heart breaking all over again. She sat alone at the table, the silence pressing down on her like a weight she could barely bear. She had hoped that confessing the truth would bring them closer, but instead, it felt like the beginning of the end. And as much as she wanted to hold on to the life they'd built, an in-built warning system told her that it was already slipping through her fingers.

16

The next morning, Dana and Ben walked into the law office, side by side but hardly united. Their tension palpable. Dana felt the weight of Ben's silence, his eyes fixed ahead as they followed the receptionist into a sleek conference room. The polished wood table and leather chairs did nothing to ease the knot in her stomach. She had barely slept, her thoughts consumed by Justin, by Lexy's disappearance, and by the gaping chasm that had formed between her and Ben.

"Mr. and Mrs. Taylor?" A woman entered the room, her sharp navy suit and no-nonsense demeanor radiating authority. She extended her hand. "I'm Eleanor Graves. Please, have a seat."

They sat across from her, Dana clutching her bag tightly in her lap while Ben leaned forward, his hands clasped together on the table. Eleanor opened a notebook, her pen poised.

"I understand you're dealing with a harassment situation," Eleanor began, her voice calm but direct. "Can you start by telling me exactly what's been happening?"

Dana hesitated, glancing at Ben, who gave her a curt nod.

She took a deep breath and began. "Justin Birch. He... he's someone I met briefly through work. We had a... personal encounter. I ended it immediately, but since then, he's been harassing me. He's shown up at my office, at my son's soccer games. He's sent texts and emails, and he's even... he's even implied he was in our home."

Eleanor's pen moved swiftly across the page as Dana spoke. "And you've kept records of these communications?"

"Yes," Dana said, her voice trembling. "I've saved all the texts and emails I could. I also received a message from him yesterday after a friend of mine went missing. He implied... he implied it was connected to her helping me investigate his background."

Eleanor's pen stopped. She looked up sharply. "Your friend is missing?"

Dana nodded. "Lexy. She was helping me investigate Justin. She didn't show up for a meeting, and when I went to her apartment, she wasn't there. Justin texted me afterward, saying I shouldn't have asked her to dig into his past."

Eleanor's expression hardened. "Have you reported your friend's disappearance to the police?"

"Yes," Dana said. "But they said there's no evidence of foul play yet. They're treating it as a missing persons case for now."

Eleanor nodded, her pen resuming its steady movement. "All right. Let's focus on what we can control. First, I need everything you have on Justin so I can prepare. Given the harassment and the implied threats, we may have enough to file for a restraining order at some point but for now, I think we should let the police do their work."

"Can you not file now?" Ben asked, his voice tight.

"I don't advise it," Eleanor said. "Let's see where the investigation takes us before you spend thousands of dollars in court but, it does no harm to prepare so we can act swiftly if need be. It's an important first step. Beyond that, we can explore other legal options, depending on how this develops."

Ben nodded; his jaw clenched. "What about our son? Can we make sure he's protected?"

"I'd advise notifying his school and any extracurricular organizations, like his soccer league, about the situation. They need to be aware in case Justin attempts to approach him there."

Dana's chest tightened at the thought of having to explain this to Ethan's teachers and coaches, but she nodded. "I'll do whatever it takes to keep him safe."

Eleanor looked at Dana with a mixture of compassion and professionalism. "Dana, I know this is difficult, but it's important that you're honest with law enforcement and anyone else involved. The more they understand the severity of the situation, the better they can help you."

"I understand," Dana said quietly.

Eleanor turned to Ben. "Mr. Taylor, I'll need your support as well. This is a family issue now, and presenting a united front will be crucial."

Ben nodded, though his expression remained strained. "You have it," he said firmly.

Eleanor stood, extending her hand. "Gather all the communications from Justin—texts, emails, anything you have. I'll need copies. And if you hear from him again, document everything. Keep me posted of the police investigation and if anything happens."

Dana and Ben shook her hand, and as they left the office, the tension between them was as thick as ever. They walked to the car in silence, the weight of everything they had discussed pressing down on them.

As Ben started the engine, Dana turned to him. "Thank you for coming with me. For... for standing by me."

Ben's grip tightened on the steering wheel. "I'm doing this

for Ethan," he said, his voice flat. "We'll deal with Justin. But after that..." He didn't finish the sentence, and Dana didn't press him. She stared out the window, her heart heavy. Whatever happened next, she knew the road ahead would be anything but easy.

17

The following morning started like any other. Dana shuffled into the kitchen, still groggy from another night of restless sleep. Ben was already there, sipping coffee as he flipped through his phone, his expression neutral but distant. Ethan's laughter echoed faintly from the living room, where he was watching cartoons.

Dana busied herself at the counter, slicing fruit for Ethan's breakfast and trying to ignore the oppressive tension that had settled over the house. The next few hours loomed large because once Ethan was in school they were going to call the police. It was something she dreaded and for that reason, after the appointment with the lawyer and having had her fill of humiliation for one day, had persuaded Ben to stall the inevitable for at least twenty-four hours.

She glanced out the window, the early sunlight streaming in and casting long shadows across the backyard. For a moment, she allowed herself to breathe, to hope that maybe today would be better.

"Mom, have you seen Snowball?" Ethan's voice startled her,

and she turned to see him standing in the doorway, his brow furrowed. "I can't find him."

"He's probably hiding," Dana said, forcing a smile. "You know how he loves to sneak under the furniture."

Ethan nodded, but his frown didn't lift. "Can you help me look?"

"Of course," Dana said, setting the knife down. She followed Ethan into the living room, where he was already on his hands and knees, peering under the furniture. Ben appeared in the doorway, his coffee mug in hand, watching them with a faintly puzzled expression.

They searched the entire house, checking every corner, every hiding spot Snowball usually favored. But the kitten was nowhere to be found. Dana's unease grew with each passing minute, her mind racing with possibilities.

"Maybe he got outside," Ben suggested, his tone uncertain.

Ethan's eyes widened. "Can we check the yard?"

Dana nodded, her heart pounding as they stepped out onto the patio. The yard was quiet, the morning air crisp and still. They split up, calling Snowball's name as they searched the bushes and flowerbeds. It was Dana who found him.

The sight made her stomach lurch. Snowball's tiny body lay motionless in the grass near the fence, his tabby fur matted and stained with something dark. Dana's hand flew to her mouth, a strangled cry escaping her lips.

Ben was at her side in an instant, his face paling as he followed her gaze. "Ethan, stay back," he called over his shoulder, his voice sharp.

"What? Did you find him?" Ethan's voice was filled with hope as he started toward them.

"No!" Dana said quickly, turning to block his view. "Go inside, sweetheart. We'll keep looking out here."

Ethan hesitated, confusion flickering across his face. Ben

stepped in, his tone firm but gentle. "Listen to your mom, buddy. Go wait inside. We'll let you know when we find him."

Reluctantly, Ethan obeyed, his small figure disappearing into the house. As soon as the door closed, Dana fell to her knees, her hands trembling as tears streamed down her face.

"Ben," she whispered, her voice breaking. "Who would do this?"

Ben crouched beside her; his jaw clenched tightly. "We both know who," he said, his voice low and filled with barely restrained fury.

Dana's phone buzzed in her pocket, the sound making her flinch. She pulled it out with shaking hands, her breath catching as she read the message on the screen.

Justin: Take care of those you love.

A sob escaped her lips as she handed the phone to Ben. His face darkened as he read the text, his hands curling into fists.

"That bastard," Ben muttered, his voice trembling with rage. "He's crossed a line, Dana. We're not waiting anymore. We should have done it the second we left the lawyers yesterday. We're calling the police. Now."

Dana nodded, too overwhelmed to speak. She rose unsteadily to her feet, leaning on Ben for support as they walked back into the house. Ethan met them at the door, his eyes wide with worry.

"Did you find him?" he asked, his voice small.

Dana's heart broke all over again. She knelt, pulling him into a tight hug. "We... we think he might have gotten sick, sweetheart," she said, her voice trembling. "I'm so sorry."

Ethan began to cry, his small body shaking against hers. Ben placed a hand on his son's shoulder, his expression grim as he looked down at them.

"Go upstairs and wash up," Ben said softly. "We'll talk more later, okay?"

Ethan nodded reluctantly, wiping his eyes as he headed for the stairs. When he was out of earshot, Ben turned to Dana, his face set with determination.

"We're ending this," he said. "Whatever it takes, Dana. Justin doesn't get to terrorize our family anymore."

Dana nodded, her tears falling silently as she reached for her phone to make the call. The image of Snowball's lifeless body burned into her mind, a cruel reminder of just how far Justin was willing to go.

As Dana spoke to the police dispatcher, relaying the details of Justin's harassment and the gruesome discovery in their yard, Ben paced the living room like a caged animal. His anger simmered just below the surface, threatening to boil over. Every creak of the floorboards, every faint sound from outside made him flinch, his eyes darting toward the windows.

"This guy is unhinged. He's not going to stop until…" He trailed off, his voice tight with emotion.

Dana hung up the phone, her hands still trembling. "They're sending someone over," she said, her voice shaky. "But what if it's not enough? What if…"

Ben stopped pacing, turning to face her. "It has to be enough," he said firmly. "We'll give them everything we have—the texts, the emails, all of it. And if they can't do something, we'll find another way. I'm not letting him destroy our family."

Dana looked at him, her heart aching at the mix of anger and determination in his eyes. She wanted to believe him, to trust that they could stop Justin before he did any more damage. But the fear that had taken root in her chest was consuming her, and she didn't know how much longer she could hold on.

The sound of a car pulling into the driveway made them both jump. Ben moved quickly to the window, peering through the curtain. "It's the police," he said, his voice a mix of relief and tension.

Dana nodded, wiping her eyes as she prepared herself to relive the nightmare once again. She only hoped that this time, someone would finally be able to help.

18

Ben's grip on the steering wheel was so tight that his knuckles turned white as he drove to Justin's office. Every thought in his mind was fueled by anger—the dead kitten, the smug text, the relentless terror Justin had unleashed on their family. He wasn't sure what he planned to do when he got there, but the seething rage in his chest demanded an outlet.

The glass-and-steel office building loomed ahead, its modern facade gleaming in the late morning sun. Ben pulled into a parking space, his hands shaking as he turned off the engine. For a moment, he sat there, breathing heavily, trying to calm himself. But the image of Snowball's lifeless body flashed in his mind, and the fury surged anew.

He stormed into the building, barely registering the receptionist's cheerful greeting as he demanded to see Justin Birch.

"Do you have an appointment, sir?" the young woman asked, her smile faltering at his demeanor.

"Just tell him Ben Taylor is here," Ben snapped, his voice sharp.

The receptionist hesitated, her fingers hovering over the phone. "Let me see if he's available."

Ben paced the lobby, his fists clenching and unclenching as he waited. After a few moments, the receptionist gestured toward a sleek glass door. "Mr. Birch will see you now. Third door on the right."

Ben didn't thank her. He pushed through the door and strode down the hallway, his footsteps echoing against the polished floors. When he reached Justin's office, he didn't bother knocking. He shoved the door open, his eyes locking onto Justin, who was seated behind an immaculate desk, his suit perfectly tailored and his expression infuriatingly calm.

"Ben," Justin said, leaning back in his chair with a smirk. "What a surprise."

Ben slammed the door behind him, his voice trembling with rage. "You think this is a game? You think you can terrorize my family and get away with it, you fucking freak?"

Justin's smirk deepened. His tone maddeningly casual. "I don't know what you're talking about. But I assume Dana's been telling stories again. She does have a flair for the dramatic, doesn't she?"

Ben took a step forward, his hands clenched into fists. "Don't you dare talk about her. You killed my son's kitten. You sent that text. You're a sick, twisted bastard..."

"Careful," Justin interrupted, his voice still calm but with an edge of warning. "Accusations like that could be considered slander. Do you have any proof?"

Ben's chest heaved as he struggled to keep himself in check. "You're a coward. You hide behind your money and your charm, but I see you for what you are. You're pathetic."

Justin's eyes narrowed slightly, though his smirk remained. "You're awfully bold for someone whose wife came to me willingly. You might want to ask her how much she really regrets it. She seemed pretty... enthusiastic at the time."

Ben's vision blurred with rage. He lunged forward, slamming his hands down on Justin's desk, sending papers scattering. "If you come near my family again, I swear to God..."

Justin didn't flinch. He leaned forward slightly, his smile chilling. "What, Ben? You'll hit me? Go ahead. It'll just make you look worse. And trust me, I'll make sure Dana and everyone else sees what a loser you are."

Ben's hands trembled, his nails digging into the wood of the desk. He wanted nothing more than to wipe that smug expression off Justin's face, but he knew Justin was right. Any outburst would only give him more power.

With a growl of frustration, Ben straightened and stepped back. "You're not going to win," he said, his voice low and steady. "You're not going to break my family."

Justin leaned back in his chair again, his expression unreadable. "We'll see about that."

Ben turned and stormed onto the corridor, calling loud enough so everyone it the adjoining offices and the receptionist would hear. "Go to hell, you sad twisted pervert."

As he walked back through the lobby and out to his car, his hands still shaking, he realized Justin's calm demeanor had left him more unsettled than ever. The man was dangerous, not just because of what he'd done, but because of how much control he seemed to have over the situation. He hadn't flinched and appeared to be enjoying himself.

Sitting in his car, Ben took a deep breath, trying to steady his nerves and temper. He had gone there to confront Justin; to take back some of the power Justin had stolen from them. But now, he felt more vulnerable than ever. Justin's words echoed in his mind, planting seeds of doubt and anger that threatened to consume him.

But Ben shook his head. He wouldn't let Justin win. He would protect Dana, protect Ethan, protect their family. Whatever it took.

19

Dana had been dreading this moment for days. The signs were all there—the nausea, the exhaustion, the subtle changes in her body that she could no longer dismiss as stress or lack of sleep. She had tried to ignore it, to convince herself it was nothing, but the doubt lingered, gnawing at her every waking thought.

Sitting in her car in the pharmacy parking lot, she stared at the small brown bag containing the test, her hands gripping the steering wheel so tightly her knuckles turned white. She had debated for hours whether to buy it, hoping she could avoid the truth for just a little longer. But the uncertainty was unbearable, and now she had no choice.

Back home, the house was quiet. Ethan was at with a friend for the afternoon, and Ben had left for an errand. Dana stood in the bathroom; the test clutched in her trembling hand. Her reflection in the mirror looked like a stranger—pale, wide-eyed, and fragile. She took a deep breath and followed the instructions, her heart pounding as she set the test on the counter and waited.

The three minutes felt like an eternity. Dana paced the small bathroom, her stomach twisting into knots. When the timer on her phone buzzed, she froze, her chest tight with dread. Slowly, she turned and picked up the test, her eyes locking onto the result.

Two pink lines.

Positive.

A wave of nausea rolled over her, and she barely made it to the toilet before she began to retch. Her body shook as she emptied her stomach, tears streaming down her face. The truth she had feared was now undeniable. She leaned against the cool bathroom tiles, her breath coming in shallow gasps.

This baby wasn't Ben's. It couldn't be. He had a vasectomy three years ago, a decision they had both made together after deciding their family was complete. There was no doubt in her mind who the father was. Justin. The name echoed in her mind like a cruel taunt, sending another shiver of nausea through her.

She wiped her mouth with a tissue, her hands trembling as she sat back against the wall. The enormity of the situation threatened to crush her. How could this be happening? How could her life have spiraled so far out of control?

Dana's thoughts turned to Ben. How could she tell him? He was already struggling to come to terms with everything she had confessed. This... this would destroy him. Destroy them. She imagined the look on his face, the betrayal in his eyes, and the thought made her chest tighten painfully.

And Ethan. Her sweet, innocent boy, who had already endured the loss of his pet because of her mistakes. How could she bring a child into this chaos, a child who would be a constant reminder of the worst decision she had ever made?

Dana climbed unsteadily to her feet, her gaze falling on the positive test sitting on the counter. She wanted to throw it away, to pretend this wasn't real, but the truth was growing inside her, impossible to ignore. She gripped the edge of the sink, her knuckles white as she tried to steady herself. Her reflection in the mirror was a portrait of despair, her tear-streaked face a silent witness to her stupidity.

She couldn't hide from this, not forever. But the thought of telling Ben, of shattering what little remained of their marriage, was more than she could bear. For now, all she could do was breathe and try to figure out what to do next.

~

Dana wasn't ready to admit the truth to Ben. Not yet. She hadn't even fully come to terms with it herself. The positive test was tucked away in a drawer in the bathroom, out of sight but impossible to forget. Every time she thought about it, her chest tightened, and her mind turned to Lexy. If there was anyone she needed right now, it was her friend—the one person who had always been honest, unflinching, and supportive. But Lexy had vanished, and Dana's fear for her friend's safety gnawed at her constantly.

Dana sat at the kitchen table, her laptop in front of her as she scoured social media and any news sites she could think of, hoping for some clue about Lexy's whereabouts. Her calls had gone unanswered, her texts unread. Even Lexy's usual online activity—posting sarcastic comments or sharing pictures of her favorite coffee spots—had stopped. It was as if she had disappeared off the face of the earth.

Frustrated, Dana slammed the laptop shut and grabbed her keys. She couldn't sit in the house any longer. She needed to do something—anything—to find Lexy. The police had assured her they were looking into it, and into her harassment claim, but Dana's gut told her they weren't taking either seriously enough. To them, she was a cheating wife who was getting her just deserts and Lexy was just another adult who might have chosen to go off the grid for a while. But Dana knew better. Lexy wouldn't just vanish. Not without telling her.

Her first stop was Lexy's apartment. She had already been there once, but this time she was determined to dig deeper. When she arrived, the building felt creepy, quiet. The faint hum of a vacuum cleaner echoed from somewhere down the hall, but otherwise, it was still.

Dana knocked on Lexy's door, her heart pounding. "Lexy? It's me, Dana. Are you in there?"

No response. She pressed her ear to the door, straining to hear any sound from inside, but there was only silence. Swallowing her fear, she tried the doorknob, but it was locked, just as it had been before. She considered calling the building manager again but hesitated. The last time, he had seemed reluctant to get involved, and she didn't want to waste time convincing him.

Instead, she walked down the hall and knocked on a neighbor's door. After a few moments, an older woman answered, her face lined with curiosity and concern.

"Hi," Dana said, forcing a polite smile. "I'm a friend of Lexy's. I haven't been able to get in touch with her, and I'm worried. Have you seen her recently?"

The woman frowned, shaking her head. "No, not for a few days. She's usually in and out, but now that you mention it, I haven't heard her coming or going."

"Did anything seem unusual the last time you saw her?" Dana pressed.

The woman's brow furrowed. "I did hear raised voices one night. Couldn't make out what was being said, but it sounded like an argument. That was a few days ago."

Dana's stomach dropped. "Did you hear a man's voice?"

The neighbor nodded. "Yes, but I'm afraid I didn't see anything. I didn't want to pry."

"Thank you," Dana said, her voice tight. She forced another smile before turning away, her mind racing. An argument. A man. Her thoughts immediately turned to Justin. Was it possible he had confronted Lexy? Had he hurt her?

Desperation clawed at her as she left the building and got back into her car. She pulled out her phone and stared at the screen. She had no idea where to go next, but she couldn't stop now. The thought of Lexy being in danger, of Justin having something to do with her disappearance, was too much to bear.

Dana decided to retrace Lexy's steps, starting with the last place she knew Lexy had planned to go. She remembered Lexy mentioning she was meeting a contact who had information about Justin. Dana drove to the coffee shop Lexy had frequented, her hands gripping the steering wheel tightly as she navigated the familiar streets.

The shop was busy when Dana arrived, the smell of freshly brewed coffee wafting through the air. She approached the barista, a young woman with dyed blue hair and a friendly smile.

"Hi," Dana said, her voice shaky. "I'm looking for my friend, Lexy. She comes here all the time. Have you seen her recently?"

The barista tilted her head, thinking. "Lexy? Yeah, she was here a few days ago. Met with some guy, I think. They sat in the corner booth over there." She gestured toward the back of the shop.

"Do you remember what he looked like?" Dana asked, her heart racing.

The barista shrugged. "Tall, dark hair, kind of intense looking. They didn't stay long. He left first, and she left a little while after."

Dana's breath caught. It had to be Justin. She thanked the barista and walked over to the booth, her mind spinning. Sitting there, she tried to imagine the conversation Lexy might have had. What had Justin said to her? Had he threatened her?

Her phone buzzed, pulling her out of her thoughts. She glanced at the screen, her heart sinking when she saw the message.

Unknown Number: Need some help looking for your friend?.

Dana's blood ran cold. She looked around the coffee shop, her eyes darting to every face, every shadow. Was he watching her? How did he always seem to know what she was doing?

Fear gripped her, but she clenched her jaw and forced herself to stay calm. She wouldn't stop. She couldn't. Lexy needed her, and no matter how terrified she was, Dana was determined to find her friend. Justin had taken too much from her already. She refused to let him take Lexy too.

20

Dana sat at the edge of the chair, her hands nervously twisting the hem of her sweater as she waited for Ben to come in from the garage. She had spent the entire afternoon circling around what she needed to say, practicing the words in her head but never quite finding the courage to say them aloud. The weight of Lexy's disappearance and the secret she was carrying were eroding her. She couldn't keep it all inside anymore—not if she wanted to survive this.

Ben entered the room, wiping his hands on a rag. He glanced at her, his brow furrowing slightly. "You okay?" he asked, tossing the rag onto a nearby chair.

Dana forced a weak smile. "We need to talk."

He sat down in the armchair across from her, his expression cautious. "What is it?"

Dana took a deep breath, her hands trembling in her lap. "It's about Lexy. I... I'm scared, Ben. I really think something bad has happened to her."

Ben's eyes softened, and he leaned forward, resting his elbows on his knees. "We'll find her. The police are looking, and you've done everything you can. She's smart, Dana. She'll be okay."

"But what if she's not?" Dana's voice cracked, and she blinked back tears. "I... I went to her apartment again, and I talked to her neighbor. They heard an argument—a man's voice. And the barista at the coffee shop said she met with someone who sounded like Justin."

Ben's jaw tightened at the mention of Justin. "That bastard," he muttered. "If he's involved in this, we'll make sure he pays for it."

Dana closed her eyes, holding in tears, her throat tight. "I just... I feel like I'm running out of time. I can't stop thinking about her. She's always been there for me, Ben. She's the one who stood by me when everything started falling apart. Didn't judge me. And now she's gone, and it's my fault."

Ben reached over and took her hand, his grip firm and steady. "This isn't your fault, Dana. Justin is the one doing this. You didn't make him the monster he is."

She looked at him, her tears spilling over. "There's something else I need to tell you. Something I've been keeping from you."

Ben's eyes narrowed slightly, but he didn't let go of her hand. "What is it?"

Dana hesitated, the words catching in her throat. Finally, she forced them out. "I... I'm pregnant."

The silence that followed was deafening. Ben stared at her. His expression unreadable. His hand slipped from hers, and he leaned back in the chair, his mouth opening and closing as if searching for words.

"Pregnant," he repeated finally, his voice flat.

Dana nodded, her stomach twisting. "I didn't know how to tell you. I... I only just found out."

Ben's eyes locked onto hers, a storm of emotions swirling in their depths. "It's not mine," he said, the words more a statement than a question.

Dana's chest tightened, and she looked down at her lap, unable to meet his gaze. "No. It's not."

He stood abruptly, pacing the room as his hands raked through his hair. "Jesus, Dana. I don't even know what to say."

"I'm sorry," she whispered, her voice breaking. "I'm so sorry. I never wanted this to happen. I never wanted to hurt you."

Ben stopped, turning to face her. "How far along are you?"

"I don't know. Maybe four weeks? Five?" she said, her voice trembling.

He shook his head, his face a mixture of disbelief and pain. "And you're sure it's..." He trailed off, unable to finish the sentence.

"It has to be Justin's," Dana said, tears streaming down her face. "There's no other possibility."

Ben let out a harsh laugh, full of bitterness. "This just keeps getting better and better."

"Ben, please," Dana pleaded, standing and reaching for him. "I need you. I can't do this alone."

He stepped back, avoiding her touch. "I don't even know if I can look at you right now, Dana. You've lied to me, you've dragged this psychopath into our lives, and now this?" He gestured toward her stomach, his voice rising. "How am I supposed to deal with this?"

Dana sank back, her sobs quiet and raw. "I don't know. I don't know how to fix this. But I'm scared, Ben. I'm scared for Lexy, for Ethan, for this baby. I need you to help me figure this out."

Ben stared at her for a long moment, his jaw tight. Finally, he exhaled sharply, running a hand over his face. "We'll deal with Justin. We'll find Lexy. The baby is your problem. After that..." He shook his head. "I don't know, Dana. I just don't know."

He turned and walked out of the room, leaving Dana alone

with her thoughts, her tears, and the crushing weight of everything she had unleashed.

21

Dana sat at the kitchen table, staring at the clock on the wall as it ticked away the minutes. She hadn't touched the cup of tea in front of her; the steam had long since dissipated. Her decision had been made, but the weight of it pressed down on her chest like a stone. There was no other choice. She couldn't bring a child into a life where Justin's shadow loomed over everything.

Ben stood by the sink, his arms crossed and his expression cold. He hadn't said much since she told him about her decision, but the silence between them was deafening. Finally, he spoke, his voice flat and devoid of emotion.

"I mean it Dana. You'll have to deal with the baby thing on your own," he said. "This isn't my mistake to fix."

Dana flinched at his words, but she didn't argue. She had hoped, foolishly, that he might support her, that he might at least offer some small measure of comfort. But she could see now that it was too much to ask. Ben was still reeling from everything she had put him through, and this was one step too far.

"I... I understand," she said quietly, her voice barely above a whisper.

He didn't respond. Instead, he turned and walked out of the kitchen, leaving her alone with her thoughts and the cold, empty silence of the house.

The clinic was small and unassuming, tucked away on a quiet street far from the bustling city center. Dana parked her car in the lot and sat for a moment, her hands clenched in her lap. The sky was overcast, the gray clouds matching the heaviness she felt in her chest.

She glanced at her phone, half-hoping for a message from Ben, even though she knew there wouldn't be one. The screen remained blank. With a deep breath, she stepped out of the car and walked toward the entrance, her footsteps echoing in the stillness.

Inside, the waiting room was calm and sterile, the walls painted a soothing shade of blue. A receptionist greeted her with a kind smile and handed her a clipboard with forms to fill out. Dana's hands trembled as she filled in her information, the reality of what she was about to do sinking in with every stroke of the pen.

When she handed the clipboard back, the receptionist gestured for her to take a seat. Dana chose a chair near the corner, away from the few other women waiting. She folded her hands in her lap once more, staring down at them as the minutes dragged by.

A nurse eventually called her name, and Dana followed her down a quiet hallway to a small room. The nurse's voice was gentle as she explained the procedure and asked if Dana had any questions. Dana shook her head, her throat too tight to speak.

She lay back on the table, staring up at the ceiling as the

nurse prepared everything. The room was quiet except for the metallic clunk of equipment. Dana's mind raced, a torrent of emotions swirling through her: guilt, fear, sadness, and an aching loneliness that felt unbearable. But as she thought about Justin—his smug smile, his relentless torment, the way he had invaded every corner of her life—she also felt a strange sense of relief. This was one thing he wouldn't take from her. One connection she wouldn't have to share with him.

The procedure was over quicker than she had expected. The nurse helped her to a recovery room, where she sat in a recliner with a blanket draped over her lap. The physical discomfort was minimal, but the emotional weight was crushing. She felt hollow, as though a part of her had been carved away, leaving only an aching void in its place.

But beneath the sorrow was a faint glimmer of relief. She wouldn't have to bring Justin's child into the world. She wouldn't have to see his face in her child's features, wouldn't have to explain to Ethan who the baby's father was, wouldn't have to endure the constant reminder of her worst mistake. For the first time in weeks, she felt like she had regained a small measure of control over her life.

When the nurse returned, she handed Dana a packet of instructions and medication, her voice kind but professional. "Take all the time you need before leaving," she said. "If you have any concerns, don't hesitate to call us."

Dana nodded; her voice still caught in her throat. She sat for a while longer, staring blankly at the wall, before finally gathering her things and making her way back to her car. The drive home was a blur, the world outside passing in a haze of gray.

When she pulled into the driveway, the house loomed before her, its windows dark and unwelcoming. She sat in the car for a long moment as tears spilled down her cheeks. She wiped them away quickly and took a deep, shaky breath before stepping out and heading inside.

The house was quiet, as it always seemed to be now. Ben was nowhere to be seen, and Ethan was at his friend's house. Dana sank onto the couch, her body heavy with exhaustion. She stared at the blank television screen, her mind numb.

As the minutes passed, accusatory thoughts began to creep back in, intertwining with the relief of her decision. She had made so many mistakes—mistakes that had brought Justin into their lives, that had shattered her family, that had led her to this moment. But at least this one, unbearable mistake wouldn't grow into something that would haunt her forever.

She had made her choice, and there was no going back. But as she sat there, alone in the silence, she couldn't help but wonder if the relief she felt now would ever outweigh the guilt.

22

The email hit Dana's inbox at exactly 8:00 a.m., its subject line stark and jarring: "**Your Reputation.**"

She hesitated before opening it, her stomach already twisting with dread. When she clicked, her heart dropped. There, in vivid, undeniable color, were photos of her and Justin —not just at the bar or entering his penthouse, but far more intimate ones. Photos of her in his bed, partially clothed and completely exposed, captured from angles that made her blood run cold.

Her breath caught in her throat as she scrolled through the images, horror mounting with every click. She had no idea these photos existed. She didn't remember Justin ever taking them, not even with her consent. Then it hit her like a freight train: there must have been a camera in his apartment. He had recorded her without her knowledge, violating her in ways she hadn't even thought possible.

Attached to the email was a brief message:

. . .

Justin: It's only fair that your colleagues know what you've been up to. Unless, of course, you decide to finally talk to me. Time is ticking, Dana.

Dana's hands trembled as she read and reread the words. She felt trapped, suffocated by the images on the screen. Justin had crossed another line, threatening not just her personal life but her professional one as well. Her career was one of the few things she had left—her last semblance of control in a life that felt like it was crumbling around her.

She slammed the laptop shut and pressed her hands to her temples, trying to think. What was she supposed to do? If Justin followed through, if he sent these photos to her colleagues, it would destroy her reputation. Her years of hard work, the respect she had earned—all of it would be gone. And the photos themselves... the idea that anyone else might see them made her feel physically ill.

A door slammed, followed by footsteps, causing her to jump, half-expecting it to be Justin. But it was Ben, his tone curt as he entered the room.

"What now?" he asked, noticing the panic on her face.

Dana hesitated, then opened the laptop again, turning the screen toward him. "He sent me this," she said, her voice shaky. "He's threatening to send it to my colleagues."

Ben's jaw tightened as he scanned the email, his knuckles turning white as he gripped the edge of the table. "This guy is a psychopath," he muttered. "He's not going to stop, Dana. You know that, right?"

Dana nodded; her throat too tight to respond. Tears pricked at her eyes, but she blinked them away, refusing to break down. "I don't know what to do," she admitted. "If he finds out about the termination... I'm scared he'll escalate."

Ben ran a hand through his hair, his expression a mix of anger and frustration. "I need to tell you what happened when I went to his office."

Dana's eyes widened. "What do you mean? What happened?"

Ben sighed heavily, pulling out a chair and sitting down across from her. "I confronted him. I thought if I showed him I wasn't afraid, he'd back off. But he didn't. He was smug, Dana. Smug and calm, like he's always ten steps ahead. He even had the nerve to… to suggest you enjoyed it."

Dana's stomach turned. She clenched her fists, anger rising alongside her fear. "I hate him," she whispered. "I hate him for everything he's done to us."

Ben leaned forward, his voice low and firm. "We're going to figure this out, Dana. We're going to stop him."

Dana nodded, the weight of his words settling over her. Together, they would find a way to end this nightmare—no matter what it took.

Dana and Ben sat in their dimly lit living room; the laptop open on the coffee table as they waited for the Zoom call to connect. The tech expert Lexy had recommended weeks ago—a wiry man named Jake with sharp eyes and an air of quiet competence —appeared on the screen, his face illuminated by the glow of multiple monitors in his cluttered workspace.

"Thanks for agreeing to help us," Dana said, her voice tight with tension.

"No problem," Jake replied, his fingers flying across a keyboard just out of view. "Lexy spoke highly of you before she…" He trailed off awkwardly, his eyes darting away from the camera. "Anyway, let's get started. You said this guy has been cyberstalking you? Sending emails, texts, and... other things?"

Dana exchanged a glance with Ben before nodding. "Yes. He's sent photos and videos of me that... I didn't know existed. He's threatened to leak them to my colleagues."

Jake's face hardened. "If he's recording you without your consent, that's a serious crime. I'll do everything I can to find out how he's accessing your devices and get you the evidence you need to stop him."

Ben leaned forward and when he spoke his tone was sharp. "How long will it take?"

"Hard to say," Jake replied. "I'll start with the metadata from the emails he's sent and see if I can trace his IP address. If he's been accessing your devices, there should be a trail."

Dana swallowed hard; a headache threatening in her temple. "What if he's watching us right now? What if he's listening?"

Jake's expression softened slightly. "I can't promise he's not, but we'll find out. In the meantime, be cautious. Change your passwords, update your security software, and don't click on anything suspicious."

The call ended, leaving Dana and Ben sitting in heavy silence. The faint hum of the washing machine in the utility room was the only sound, a stark contrast to the chaos in Dana's mind. She stared at the darkened laptop screen, her chest tight.

Her phone buzzed on the coffee table, and she flinched, her heart racing. She picked it up with trembling hands, her breath catching when she saw the message.

Justin:

"Cute. Hiring a hacker? You're wasting your time. I'm always one step ahead. Enjoy the show."

. . .

A second later, a video appeared. Dana hesitated, her thumb hovering over the play button. Ben reached out. His jaw tight. "Don't," he said. "It's what he wants."

But curiosity and fear got the better of her. She pressed play, her stomach churning as Justin's face filled the screen. He was seated in what appeared to be a lavish office, his expression smug and taunting.

"Hello, Dana," Justin began, his voice smooth and confident. "I hope you've been well. I couldn't help but notice you've been busy. A hacker? Really? You should know better by now. You can't outsmart me. But it's adorable that you're trying."

Dana's grip on the phone tightened as he continued. "Oh, and Ben—I see you're still standing by your wife. Admirable, really. But tell me, how long will that last? How long before you realize she's not worth the trouble?"

Ben's fist slammed onto the coffee table, the sound echoing through the room. "That son of a..."

Dana paused the video, her hands trembling. "He's mocking us," she whispered. "He's always watching, always a step ahead. And he's clever because he doesn't make physical threats and hovers just outside breaking the law. That message could just be construed as a spurned man venting his frustration and exerting his prowess. You know how lawyers twist things to get their client off, and he can afford the best, so we have no chance."

Ben ran a hand over his face, his anger barely contained. "He's scum. I can't get his supercilious face out of my head... I want to smash it into tiny pieces." Ben took a deep breath and once he was in control continued. "I can't bear talking about that fucking waste of space so let's just leave Jake to do his job. Justin's going to slip up. And when he does, we'll nail him."

Dana nodded, but her fear was growing. Justin's reach felt endless, his control absolute. She hesitated before speaking, her voice barely above a whisper. “Ben, I’m scared Justin will find out about... the pregnancy. About the termination.”

Ben’s face hardened, and for a moment, he said nothing. The silence stretched between them, heavy and unbearable.

“I didn’t want to keep it from you,” Dana continued, her voice breaking. “But I’m terrified of what he’ll do if he finds out. I can’t let him use it against us.”

Ben finally looked at her, his eyes filled with a mixture of pain and anger. “I don’t know what you want me to say, Dana. I... I can’t even process this right now.”

She wiped her tears, her heart sinking. “I just need to know we’re in this together. That we can stop him.”

Ben stood, running a hand through his hair and before he turned, said, “I’m trying, Dana. I’m here, aren’t I?”

Dana watched him walk away, her chest aching with a mix of regret and fear. She was more alone than ever, but she couldn’t afford to fall apart. Justin was still out there, watching, waiting. And she had to find a way to fight back—before it was too late.

The hours passed in a blur. Dana remained on the couch, staring blankly at the coffee table as her thoughts raced. She replayed Justin’s taunts in her mind, his smug face burned into her memory. Every time she thought about the video, her stomach twisted with a nauseating mix of fear and rage.

Ben had retreated to the garage, the faint clinking of tools occasionally breaking the oppressive quiet of the house. Dana considered going to him, trying to bridge the widening gap between them, but she couldn’t bring herself to move. She felt paralyzed.

Her phone buzzed again, and she flinched, half-expecting another message from Justin. But it was a notification from Jake. She opened it quickly, her heart pounding.

Jake: I've traced some activity back to his IP. He's been using a remote-access tool to monitor your devices. We've got a lead, but it'll take time to gather enough evidence to take to the authorities. Hang tight.

Dana exhaled shakily, a glimmer of hope breaking through her fear. At least someone was making progress. She forwarded the message to Ben, hoping it would ease some of his frustration.

Moments later, he appeared in the doorway, his expression unreadable. "Jake's making headway," he said. "That's something, at least."

Dana nodded. Her reply spoken softly. "It's a start."

Ben hesitated, his eyes lingering on her before he retreated to the garage leaving her alone. She wanted to believe in Jake, but the fear still lingered, a shadow that refused to lift. Justin's words echoed in her mind, a chilling reminder of how far he was willing to go. For now, all they could do was wait—and hope that they could outsmart him before it was too late.

23

Dana sat stiffly on the plush couch in the therapist's office, her hands folded tightly in her lap. The room was warm and inviting, with muted earth tones and a soft rug that seemed designed to put clients at ease. Bookshelves lined one wall, filled with neatly arranged volumes on psychology, self-help, and trauma recovery. A potted fern sat in the corner, its green leaves vibrant against the soft beige walls. The large window let in a gentle stream of natural light, diffused by gauzy curtains, casting the room in a serene glow.

Dr. Harper sat across from Dana in a high-backed chair upholstered in a calming shade of blue. She was a middle-aged woman with silver-streaked hair pulled back into a neat bun. Her glasses perched low on her nose, giving her an air of intellectual authority, while her warm brown eyes radiated kindness and patience. She wore a simple cardigan over a blouse, her appearance understated but professional, a reassuring presence that immediately put her clients at ease.

"It's a lot," Dr. Harper said gently, her pen poised over a notepad balanced on her lap. "You'd been carrying all of this by yourself."

Dana shuffled in her seat. "I didn't know what else to do. Everything just spiraled so quickly, and I... I made terrible choices. I know that. I should have stopped it before it got this far."

Dr. Harper's eyes remained fixed on Dana, her expression one of quiet understanding. "It's easy to look back and say what you should have done. But at the time, you were vulnerable. Can you tell me what drew you to Justin in the first place?"

Dana hesitated, her gaze dropping to her lap. "I don't know," she murmured. "He made me feel... noticed. I'd been feeling invisible for so long—not at work, at home. Ben and I... we weren't connecting. And then Justin came along, and he... he said all the right things. He made me feel like I mattered."

Dr. Harper nodded, her pen moving across the notepad in measured strokes. "That's not unusual. When someone feels unseen or undervalued, they can be more susceptible to attention from others who make them feel special. It doesn't excuse Justin's behavior, of course. What he's done goes far beyond manipulation."

Dana's chest tightened, and she took a shaky breath. "I feel so stupid. I should have known he was dangerous. I should have..." She trailed off, her voice breaking.

"Dana, be kind to yourself," Dr. Harper said softly. "You're not responsible for Justin's actions. What matters now is how you move forward. How you regain control of your life and your narrative."

Dana looked up. Her eyes glassy with unshed tears. "How do I do that?"

"One step at a time," Dr. Harper said. "You've already taken a significant step by coming here. By acknowledging your fears and your guilt. Now we need to unpack those feelings and find ways to address them."

Dana hesitated, then said, "There's something else. Something I haven't talked about with anyone except Ben."

Dr. Harper's expression remained steady and encouraging. "Take your time."

Dana swallowed hard, her hands twisting in her lap. "I was pregnant. A few weeks ago, I found out. And... I terminated the pregnancy."

She waited for Dr. Harper's reaction, bracing herself for judgment, but none came. The therapist simply tilted her head. Her gaze radiated compassion. "How are you feeling about that decision?"

Dana let out a shaky sigh. "Guilty. Relieved. Both, I guess. I knew I couldn't keep the baby. It wasn't Ben's, and the thought of bringing Justin's child into the world... I couldn't do it. But I can't stop thinking about it. About what kind of person that makes me."

"It makes you a human being who made a difficult choice in an incredibly challenging situation," Dr. Harper said firmly. "You were protecting yourself and your family. That doesn't mean you won't feel conflicted or grieve the decision. Those feelings are valid, and we can work through them together."

Dana nodded, her eyes welling with tears. "I'm also scared. Justin doesn't know about the pregnancy, but if he ever finds out..." She shuddered, unable to finish the sentence.

Dr. Harper leaned forward slightly, her voice steady. "Justin thrives on control and fear. He wants you to feel powerless. But you're not powerless, Dana. You have resources, people who care about you, and steps you can take to protect yourself and your family. Have you talked to the police about his threats?"

"Yes, but they are so slow and have other more important matters to deal with, and they're still looking for Lexy. And we're working with someone privately," Dana said. "A tech expert. He's trying to gather evidence of Justin's cyberstalking. But it feels like Justin is always one step ahead. Like he's untouchable."

"No one is untouchable," Dr. Harper said firmly. "It's important to focus on what you can control. Document everything. Lean on your support system. And remember that you don't have to go through this alone."

Dana wiped her eyes, a small flicker of hope igniting in her chest. "I want to believe that. I'm just so tired of being afraid."

"Fear is natural," Dr. Harper said. "But it doesn't have to define you. You're stronger than you think, Dana. And you've already shown incredible courage by facing this head-on."

As the session ended, Dana felt a faint sense of relief, as though a small weight had been lifted from her shoulders. For the first time in weeks, she felt like she had a glimmer of control. She wasn't alone in this fight. And she was determined to take back her life, one step at a time.

24

Dana pulled into the school parking lot, her heart lifting slightly at the sight of Ethan's small figure standing with a group of other children near the playground. It was one of the few times in her day she could feel a shred of normalcy, seeing her son's carefree smile and hearing his laughter. But as she stepped out of the car and scanned the area, a cold chill ran down her spine. Across the street, leaning casually against a parked car, was Justin. He was watching her.

Dana's breath hitched, and her hand instinctively tightened on her purse strap. She froze, her mind racing. Justin's face was unreadable, apart from a slight smirk playing on his lips. He made no move to approach, but his presence was enough to send her heart into a panicked frenzy. She quickly looked away, trying to act natural as she walked toward Ethan.

"Hi, Mom!" Ethan said brightly, running toward her with his backpack bouncing against his shoulders.

Dana forced a smile, leaning down to hug him. "Hi, sweetheart. How was your day?"

"It was great! We're learning more about space. Did you

know Jupiter has sixty-seven moons?" Ethan's excitement was palpable, his little face lighting up as he chattered.

Dana nodded along, her eyes darting back to the street. Justin was still there, his gaze locked on them. Her stomach churned. She couldn't let Ethan see her fear. "That's amazing, honey. Why don't you hop in the car, and we'll talk more about it on the way home?"

Ethan nodded and climbed into the backseat, oblivious to the tension radiating from his mother. Dana stood for a moment, her hands trembling as she glanced back at Justin. He lifted a hand in a mock wave, his smirk widening.

That was the last straw. On impulse, Dana told Ethan to get out of the car, that she'd remembered she had to speak to the principal about a fundraising event, so with her son in tow she marched back toward the school building, her pulse pounding. She couldn't ignore this anymore. She had to do something. She'd put herself and her shame before Ethan, too weak and selfish to say the words out loud, admit what she'd done and risk the whole school finding out. It was time to grow the fuck up.

The school itself was a charming brick building with large windows framed by white shutters. Brightly colored banners advertising upcoming events hung near the entrance, and the hum of children's voices echoed faintly through the air. Normally, Dana found the environment comforting, a reminder that Ethan was in a safe and nurturing place. But today, the warmth of the school felt far away, overshadowed by the icy grip of Justin's presence.

Inside, the air was cool and filled with the faint hum of conversations and ringing phones. The hallways were lined with art projects—painted handprints, crayon drawings of families, and posters about kindness and inclusion. With Ethan dawdling behind, Dana approached the front desk, her voice strained but firm. "I need to speak to the principal. It's urgent."

The receptionist, a young woman with a friendly smile, looked up, clearly startled by Dana's sudden appearance and tone. "Of course. Let me see if she's available."

Dana waited, her heart hammering in her chest as she told Ethan to take a seat on one of the chairs in the foyer. "Why don't you read while I speak to the principal, this shouldn't take long, honey. Then we can go get something to eat. A special treat." Ethan did as he was told, the promise of food always did the trick.

She glanced back toward the glass doors, half-expecting to see Justin standing there, watching her through the panes. When the receptionist returned and ushered her toward the principal's office, Dana's hands were damp with sweat, her nerves mounting with every step. Turning back to where Ethan sat, she reminded him, "you wait here, okay. No wandering off."

Seeing him nod and then his eyes refocus on his book reassured Dana, who followed the receptionist's lead. Mrs. Carmichael's office was a tidy, well-organized space that reflected the principal's no-nonsense personality. A large desk dominated the room, its surface neatly arranged with stacks of papers, a framed family photo, and a small potted plant. Behind her chair was a bookshelf filled with educational texts and binders, and the walls were adorned with certificates and photos from school events.

Mrs. Carmichael herself was a composed woman in her fifties, her short, graying hair styled neatly. She wore a navy blazer over a patterned blouse, her sharp eyes assessing Dana as she gestured for her to sit. Despite her professional demeanor, there was a warmth to her presence that offered a small measure of reassurance.

"Mrs. Taylor, what can I do for you?" she asked, folding her hands on the desk.

Dana sat down; her hands clasped tightly in her lap. She

hesitated, unsure how to begin. "This isn't easy for me to talk about," she said finally. "But I... I'm worried about my son's safety."

Mrs. Carmichael's expression grew serious. "Go on."

Dana took a deep breath, her voice shaking as she spoke. "There's a man. His name is Justin, and he... he's been stalking me. He's outside right now, watching us. I think he's trying to intimidate me. And I... I'm scared he might try to get to Ethan."

The principal's brow furrowed, and her concern was evident. "Have you contacted the police?"

"Yes, and a lawyer," Dana said, her voice barely above a whisper. "But he's... he's very good at staying just within the boundaries of the law. He's smart, and he knows how to manipulate people. The police are snowed under and I'm not a priority I suppose but I... I need to know that my son is safe here. That Justin won't be able to come near him."

Mrs. Carmichael nodded slowly. "We take our students' safety very seriously, Mrs. Taylor. If this man is a threat, we can work with you to ensure he's not allowed on school grounds. But I'll need more information to understand the situation fully."

Dana hesitated, the words catching in her throat. Finally, she forced herself to speak. "Justin... Justin was someone I was involved with. It was a mistake, a terrible mistake. But when I tried to end things, he became... obsessed. He's been harassing me and my family ever since."

The principal's expression didn't change, but Dana could sense the weight of her words sinking in. "I appreciate your honesty, Mrs. Taylor. This is clearly a very serious matter. I'll speak with our security team immediately, and we'll put measures in place to protect Ethan. Could you provide me with a description of him? A photograph would be very helpful and perhaps the name of the officer dealing with your complaint, just in case we have occasion to need him. But I also encourage you to keep working with the police. This man sounds dangerous."

Dana nodded, tears pricking at her eyes. "Thank you. I'll get those to you as soon as I can. I just... I don't know what else to do. I'm so scared for my son."

Mrs. Carmichael reached across the desk, her voice firm but compassionate. "You're doing the right thing by speaking up. We'll do everything we can to keep Ethan safe."

As Dana left the office, her heart still pounding, she felt a small flicker of relief. It wasn't enough to dispel her fear, but it was something. She and Ethan walked back to the car, her steps quick and purposeful. Justin was gone, but the unease he left behind lingered.

She climbed into the driver's seat and once he was settled, glanced back at Ethan. "Ready to go, sweetheart?" she asked, forcing a smile.

Ethan looked up and grinned. "Yep! Can we go for food now? I want ice cream."

"Of course," Dana said, her voice steady despite the turmoil inside her. As she pulled out of the parking lot, a voice, deep in the recesses of her mind whispered a warning. That Justin's games were far from over. But for now, she focused on the road ahead and the little boy who needed her to stay strong.

25

Dana and Ben entered the police department, the sterile scent of disinfectant and the faint buzz of fluorescent lights adding to the oppressive atmosphere. The front desk, a long counter topped with scratched Plexiglas, was manned by a weary-looking officer in his mid-forties. Behind him, the walls were covered with bulletin boards pinned with flyers and wanted posters. Dana noticed a clock ticking loudly on the wall, each second stretching her nerves tighter.

The waiting area was sparse, with a few hard plastic chairs bolted to the floor and a vending machine humming in the corner. A couple of other people sat quietly, their expressions mirroring the tension Dana felt in her chest. She glanced at Ben, who stood rigid beside her, his jaw clenched, and his hands stuffed into his jacket pockets. The silence between them was heavy, laden with strain.

"We need to speak to the officer who's looking into a stalking matter," Ben said to the officer at the desk, his tone clipped and formal.

The officer raised an eyebrow, pulling out a clipboard. "Alright. Name and nature of the complaint?"

Ben exhaled sharply. "I just told you. It's about harassment. Stalking. This man... he's been threatening my wife and our family. The officer who we spoke to was called Walker, but we've not heard a word for days."

The officer's demeanor shifted slightly, his professional detachment giving way to mild concern. "Alright, let me get someone who can help. Have a seat."

They sat side by side in the waiting area, the space between them feeling like a chasm. Dana fidgeted with the strap of her purse, her mind racing. She could still see Justin's smirk in her mind's eye, the way he had waved at her outside the school as if they were playing some sick game. Her stomach churned, the fear and guilt twisting into a tight knot that she couldn't shake.

After what felt like an eternity, a young officer with a kind face and a neat uniform approached them. His name tag read "Officer Martinez."

"Mr. and Mrs. Taylor?" he asked, his tone polite but direct.

Ben stood, gesturing for Dana to follow as they were led to a small interview room down a narrow hallway. The room was simple, with a metal table and a few mismatched chairs, the walls painted a dull gray. A recorder sat in the center of the table, and Officer Martinez gestured for them to sit.

"Look, I'm going to level with you. Officer Walker is on leave right now and I can't go into details as to why. But I have checked on the system and it appears there's been a lack of shall we say, communication and administration and unfortunately I can't find any record of your complaint. Only that a dispatcher sent him to your address."

Dana thought Ben was going to explode, his face turned ashen, and his hands slammed down onto the table in front of them. "You have got to be joking... so you're telling me that absolutely nothing has been done, while a lunatic is still out there stalking my family. I want to make a formal complaint right now... get me someone senior immediately or I'm calling my lawyer."

Placing a hand on his arm Dana attempted to calm Ben. "Ben, stop. This isn't helping the situation is it? Look, why don't we tell this officer what's been going on and then we can decide whether to make a complaint afterwards but for now, we need to get the ball rolling, again."

Martinez spoke next. "Sir, your wife is correct, and I am really sorry that this has happened but if this matter is as serious as it sounds, I think we should focus on getting a report filed, do you agree?"

Ben harrumphed, then shook Dana's hand free, an action that wounded and embarrassed her in one go.

"Alright," he began, flipping open a notebook. "Why don't you tell me what's been going on?"

Ben spoke first, his voice tight with anger. "There's a man named Justin Birch. He's been harassing Dana for months. He's sent threatening messages, followed her, showed up at places where he knows she'll be. Yesterday, he was outside our son's school."

Martinez's pen moved quickly across the page. "Has he made any direct threats against you or your family?"

Dana hesitated, her voice trembling as she spoke. "He's sent messages implying that he could hurt us. He sent me photos... intimate photos that I didn't know he had. He's used them to threaten my reputation, my job. And yesterday, he... he waved at me. Outside the school. Like he wanted me to know he's watching."

Martinez's expression darkened slightly. "Do you know how he got those photos?"

Dana nodded, her voice barely above a whisper. "He must have had cameras in his apartment. I didn't know. I... I made a mistake. I was involved with him, briefly. But when I ended it, he wouldn't let go. He's been doing this ever since. And there's something else. My best friend Lexy Rivers has disappeared, and I think he has something to do with it."

At this, Martinez paused, his pen still on the notebook. "I think you need to tell me more about Lexy."

The whole story about Lexy's disappearance and her own admission hung in the air, and Dana felt Ben stiffen beside her. She glanced at him, but his gaze was fixed on the table, his expression a mask of quiet fury.

"Alright," Martinez said, his tone careful. "I'm going to have to liaise with my colleagues who are investigating Lexy's case so for now, let's focus on yours. Have you kept any of the messages he's sent? Emails, texts, anything like that?"

Dana nodded again. "Yes. We've been documenting everything and we have a tech expert gathering evidence."

"Good," Martinez said, jotting down more notes. "That will help. Based on what you've described, we'll need to escalate this. I'll file this report and pass it along to the detectives who handle stalking and harassment cases. In the meantime, I suggest you consider getting a restraining order."

Ben's voice was sharp. "We spoke to a lawyer, and she advised we let the police deal with it."

Martinez met his gaze evenly. "That was good advice, but I suspect things have moved on since then. A restraining order is a legal tool, not a shield. But it does give us more leverage if he violates it. And it sends a clear message that you're not afraid to act."

Dana's hands tightened on her purse strap. "What about Ethan? How do I keep him safe?"

Martinez's voice softened slightly. "You've already talked to the school. Made sure they're aware of the situation. If you or school think Justin poses an immediate threat at any time, call us. We'll respond. And if you ever feel unsafe, don't hesitate to get out of the situation and contact us right away."

Dana nodded, her chest tightening with a mix of fear and determination. But then Martinez leaned back in his chair, his expression turning more cautious.

"One thing to keep in mind," he said. "The information you've provided—the messages, the implied threats—it's a good start, but it's not enough to build a solid case. We'll need more concrete evidence to take significant action. Right now, what you're describing could be interpreted as harassment, but it's walking a fine line."

Dana's stomach sank. "What do you mean? He's stalking me. He's threatening me."

Martinez nodded sympathetically. "I understand how it feels, Mrs. Taylor. But without direct threats of harm or physical actions, it's harder to prove criminal intent. A lot of what you're describing could be seen as circumstantial or even dismissed as a domestic issue. We're not saying it's not serious—it absolutely is. But the law requires us to be very precise about how we proceed."

Ben's frustration boiled over. "So, what are we supposed to do? Wait until he hurts her? Hurts our son?"

Martinez raised a hand in a calming gesture. "I understand your frustration, Mr. Taylor. Believe me, I do. That's why documenting everything is so important. If he escalates, every piece of evidence you've gathered will strengthen your case."

Dana's shoulders slumped, the weight of the officer's words pressing down on her. She felt trapped, as though Justin had managed to manipulate not only her life, but the very system meant to protect her.

Martinez slid a card across the table. "Here's my direct line. If anything happens, call me immediately. Give my details to your son's school. We'll do everything we can to help. And I'll make sure this report gets to the right people."

As they left the police department, the tension between Dana and Ben was palpable. He hadn't spoken a word since they'd left the interview room, his silence heavier than any argument. Dana climbed into the passenger seat of their car, her hands trembling as she buckled her seatbelt.

"Ben..." she began, but he cut her off, his voice low and tight.

"Not now, Dana."

She swallowed hard, her heart sinking. The drive home was silent, the distance between them growing with every mile. And yet, beneath her fear and guilt, there was a flicker of hope. They had taken another step, however small, toward standing up to Justin. And for now, that was all she could hold on to.

26

The house was quiet as Dana paced back and forth in the living room. The faint scent of the candles she'd lit in an attempt to create a semblance of peace weren't working.

The living room was warm but cluttered, a space that spoke of a family's life lived within its walls. The couch, slightly worn but still comfortable, was draped with a soft throw blanket. A few framed photos sat on a wooden shelf above the fireplace—smiling moments frozen in time: Ethan's first day of school, a family vacation at the beach, and a candid shot of Ben laughing at something out of frame. A stack of unopened mail rested on the coffee table alongside Ethan's schoolbooks and a lone toy car. The soft beige walls, decorated with Ethan's colorful artwork pinned here and there, made the room feel lived-in, but tonight it felt heavy and unwelcoming.

Ben sat, leaning forward with his elbows on his knees, his face buried in his hands. He'd barely spoken since they returned from the police department, and his silence was worse than anything he could have said. Dana paused her pacing and turned to him, the words spilling out before she could stop them.

"You've barely looked at me since we got home," she said, her voice trembling. "I know you're angry, but we must talk about this. We need to figure out how to move forward."

Ben lifted his head, his eyes hard and unreadable. "Move forward? Dana, do you even hear yourself? You've jeopardized everything. Our life, our family... and now our son is in danger. How am I supposed to just move forward?"

Dana's chest tightened, guilt and frustration warring within her. "I made a mistake, Ben. A terrible mistake. But I'm trying to fix it. I'm trying to protect us."

Ben stood abruptly, his sudden movement making her flinch. "Protect us? You should have thought about protecting us before you let Justin into our lives. Before you let him get this close to Ethan. Do you know what it feels like to see him suffer because of this? He's already lost his kitten, and now we're going to have to explain to him that someone might want to hurt him or his family. What the hell am I supposed to say to him?"

Dana's eyes filled with tears, her voice breaking. "I didn't mean for any of this to happen. I never wanted him to be a part of our lives."

"But he is," Ben snapped, his voice rising. "Because of you. Because you let him in. And now he's watching our son. Do you understand how terrifying that is? How helpless that makes me feel?"

Dana nodded, tears streaming down her face. "I'm scared too, Ben. Every moment of every day, I'm scared. For Ethan, for you, for us. But we can't let Justin win. We must stay united."

Ben let out a bitter laugh, shaking his head. "United? Do you really think we're united right now? I don't even know if I can forgive you, Dana. I don't know if I can ever look at you the same way again."

The words cut deeper than any threat Justin had made. Dana wrapped her arms around herself, as though trying to hold herself together. "I don't know what else to do," she whispered. "I've told you everything. I've admitted my mistakes. I'm trying to make it right."

Ben turned away, running a hand through his hair. "You can't just make this right, Dana. This isn't something you can fix overnight. You've broken something between us, and I don't know if it can be repaired."

Dana sank onto the edge of the armchair, her head in her hands. The silence that followed was heavy, the weight of their shared pain and anger filling the room. For a moment, neither of them spoke, the only sound the faint ticking of the clock on the wall.

Finally, Ben turned back to her, his voice quieter but no less intense. "You need to think about how we're going to keep Ethan safe. How we explain about stranger danger without terrifying him. That's the priority right now. Not us. Not this mess."

Dana's reply was barely audible. "I know. I'll do whatever it takes."

Ben didn't respond. He moved to the kitchen, opening the fridge and pulling out a bottle of water. Dana watched him, her heart aching with the distance between them. She wanted to reach out, to apologize again, to promise that she would find a way to make things right. But she knew it wouldn't be enough. Not yet.

As Ben leaned against the counter, sipping the water and staring out the window into the dark backyard, Dana forced herself to take a deep breath. She couldn't undo what had happened. She couldn't erase the pain she'd caused. But she could fight to protect her family, no matter how broken they felt in this moment.

"We'll figure it out," she said softly, more to herself than to Ben. "We have to."

He didn't turn around, didn't acknowledge her words. The

silence stretched on, and Dana felt the fragile threads of their life unraveling further.

Suddenly, the soft patter of footsteps came from the hallway. Both Dana and Ben turned toward the sound as Ethan appeared, clutching a worn stuffed animal to his chest. His eyes were wide and filled with tears.

"Why were you yelling?" he asked, his voice trembling. "Are you mad at me?"

Dana's heart broke at the sight of him. She knelt, opening her arms as Ethan rushed into them. "No, sweetheart. We're not mad at you. We... we were just talking loudly. I'm sorry if we scared you."

Ethan buried his face in her shoulder, his small frame shaking with quiet sobs. Ben stood frozen for a moment before he sighed deeply and knelt beside them. He rested a hand on Ethan's back, his voice soft. "We're sorry, buddy. We didn't mean to upset you."

Ethan looked up at his father, his tear-streaked face breaking Ben's stoic facade. Ben pulled him into a hug, his own eyes glistening with unshed tears. "You're the most important thing to us," he said quietly. "I promise."

The three of them stayed like that for a while, the weight of their fears and arguments momentarily set aside. In that moment, Dana clung to the fragile hope that they could still find a way to piece their family back together, one bit at a time.

27

The ballroom of the downtown hotel was a vision of elegance, bathed in golden light that reflected off crystal chandeliers hanging high above. Round tables draped in white linen were arranged around a glossy parquet dance floor, each one adorned with tall vases of fresh roses and flickering candles. Guests mingled in the soft hum of polite conversation, their voices blending with the soothing strains of a live string quartet tucked away in one corner.

Dana adjusted her dress—a sleek, dark green gown that hugged her figure—and clutched her glass of champagne, her eyes scanning the room. The gala was a work event, a fundraiser for one of the company's major clients, and the stakes were high. She had convinced Ben to join her, needing him by her side in case Justin turned up while hoping the evening might serve as a brief escape from the tension that had consumed their lives.

Ben stood stiffly beside her, his sharp black suit fitting him perfectly but doing little to soften his strained expression. He'd barely said a word since they arrived, his discomfort palpable. Dana didn't blame him; she'd been walking on eggshells herself, terrified that every polite smile or casual glance might trigger another argument.

"Do you want another drink?" she asked softly, breaking the silence.

Ben shook his head, his eyes scanning the room. "No, I'm fine." His tone was clipped, and Dana's stomach tightened. She forced a smile, trying to project a calm she didn't feel.

They had just settled at their table, surrounded by Dana's colleagues and a few high-profile clients, when the atmosphere shifted. A murmur spread through the room, heads turning toward the entrance. Dana followed their gaze, her heart sinking as she saw him.

Justin.

He was dressed to perfection in a tailored navy suit, his confident stride and easy smile exuding charm. But his presence felt like a knife to Dana's gut. He had no reason to be here, no business attending an event so deeply tied to her professional life. And yet, there he was, gliding into the room as though he belonged.

"Dana," Ben said under his breath, his tone sharp with warning. "What the hell is he doing here?"

"I don't know," she whispered, her voice trembling. "He's not supposed to be here."

As Justin made his way closer, Dana's colleagues began to exchange curious glances. Caroline, leaned toward her with a raised eyebrow. "Who's that? He looks familiar."

Dana didn't answer. She couldn't. Her pulse was racing, and her hands were trembling under the table. She felt Ben stiffen beside her; his jaw clenched tightly.

Justin stopped just short of their table, his eyes locking onto Dana's with a predatory glint. "Dana," he said smoothly, his voice loud enough to draw the attention of those nearby. "It's been too long. You look stunning, as always."

The blood drained from Dana's face. "Justin, what are you doing here?" she asked, her voice barely above a whisper.

He smiled, ignoring her question. "I couldn't resist the chance to see you in your element. You've always been so impressive at these events." He glanced around the table, his gaze lingering on Ben. "And you must be Ben. Dana has told me so much about you."

The tension at the table was excruciating. Ben's hands curled into fists on the tablecloth, his knuckles white. "Get out," he said, his voice low and dangerous. "Now."

Justin's smile didn't falter. "Oh, come on, Ben. No need to be hostile. We're all adults here, aren't we?" He turned back to Dana, his tone light but laced with malice. "You didn't tell them, did you? About us? About all those late nights? The way you..."

"Stop," Dana said sharply, her voice shaking. "You need to leave."

But it was too late. The damage was done. Her colleagues' curious stares had turned to wide-eyed shock, whispers rippling around the table. Caroline's expression was a mix of confusion and disbelief, her eyes darting between Dana and Justin.

"Dana," another colleague, Michael, began hesitantly. "Is everything okay?"

Ben stood abruptly, his chair scraping loudly against the floor. "Come on," he said to Dana, his voice tight with anger and humiliation. "We're leaving."

Dana rose unsteadily, her vision blurring with tears as she avoided the judgmental gazes of her peers. Justin's smirk followed her as she and Ben hurried toward the exit, her heart pounding in her chest.

Outside the ballroom, the cool night air hit her like a slap. Ben was already several steps ahead, his pace brisk and furious. "Ben, wait," she called, but he didn't stop.

Finally, she caught up to him near the parking lot, her heels clicking frantically against the pavement. "I'm sorry," she said, her voice breaking. "I didn't know he would be here. I didn't know he would do this."

Ben turned to her, his face a mask of rage and pain. "You didn't know? Dana, this is what he does. He ruins everything he touches."

"I didn't invite him here," she pleaded, tears streaming down her face. "I never wanted this."

Ben shook his head, his voice heavy with bitterness. "It doesn't matter what you wanted. He's here, and now everyone knows. Your colleagues, your clients... everyone. How do we come back from this?"

Dana had no answer. The weight of Justin's actions, of her own mistakes, pressed down on her like a crushing force. She felt as though she might collapse under it, but she couldn't afford to. Not now. Not with everything at stake.

"We'll figure it out," she said desperately, though she wasn't sure she believed it. "We have to."

Ben didn't respond. He turned and walked to the car, leaving Dana standing alone in the cold, the echoes of Justin's taunts still ringing in her ear.

~

The drive home from the gala was silent, the tension in the car oppressive. Dana sat with her hands clasped tightly, her fingernails digging into her palms as she stared out of the window. Ben gripped the steering wheel, his jaw clenched, and his eyes fixed on the road ahead. Neither of them spoke; there was nothing to say that hadn't already been shouted in the parking lot.

When they arrived home, Ben slammed the car door shut and

stormed into the house without waiting for her. Dana followed, her heels clicking softly on the pavement. As she stepped into the dimly lit foyer, the usual familiar warmth of their home was absent and instead it felt cold and uninviting. Ben disappeared into the kitchen, leaving her standing alone in the hallway.

With a shaky breath, Dana pulled out her phone. Her fingers hovered over the screen for a moment before she made the call she'd been dreading.

"Cambridge Police Department, how can I help you?" a woman's voice answered.

"This is Dana Taylor," Dana said, her voice trembling. "I filed a report about a man named Justin Birch. He's been stalking me and my family. I need an update on the investigation. Is Officer Martinez on duty?"

There was a brief pause. "One moment, ma'am. Let me transfer you to the officer handling your case."

Dana paced the hallway as she waited, her free hand gripping the edge of the staircase banister. She could hear faint noises from the kitchen—the clink of glass, the sound of Ben's heavy footsteps—but she couldn't bring herself to face him. Not yet.

"Mrs. Taylor," a man's voice finally came on the line. "This is Officer Martinez. How can I assist you?"

"Officer, I need to know what's happening with my case," Dana said, her voice firm despite the tremor beneath it. "Justin Birch showed up at a gala tonight. He humiliated me in front of my colleagues and clients. He's escalating, and I'm terrified of what he might do next."

There was a heavy sigh on the other end of the line. "Mrs. Taylor, I understand your concern. Unfortunately, we're still gathering evidence. The messages and photos you've provided are being reviewed, but as I mentioned before, proving criminal intent in stalking cases can be challenging. We're doing everything we can within the limits of the law."

Dana's frustration bubbled over. "Challenging? How much more evidence do you need? He's following me, threatening me, and now he's showing up at public events to humiliate me. What more does he have to do before you take this seriously?"

"Mrs. Taylor, I assure you we are taking this seriously," Martinez said evenly. "But these cases take time. I recommend continuing to document everything and considering additional security measures for your home and family."

Dana closed her eyes, her grip on the banister tightening. "What about my friend? Lexy Rivers. She's been missing for weeks now. Is there any update on her case?"

Martinez hesitated. "I've checked with the team handling that investigation, and as of now, there are no significant updates. Her disappearance remains under active investigation, but we haven't uncovered anything conclusive. I understand how difficult this must be, but these cases also take time."

Dana felt a wave of despair wash over her. "So, you're telling me there's nothing? No progress on Justin, no progress on Lexy? What am I supposed to do in the meantime? Just wait for him to hurt someone?"

Martinez's tone softened. "I know it's frustrating, Mrs. Taylor. I can assure you we are doing everything we can. But I strongly recommend you prioritize your safety and that of your family. Consider speaking to a private security consultant if you feel the immediate threat is escalating."

Dana swallowed the lump in her throat. "Fine. Thank you, Officer Martinez." She hung up before he could respond, her hand trembling as she lowered the phone.

She turned and walked into the kitchen, where Ben stood at the counter with a glass of whiskey in his hand. He didn't look at her as she entered, his focus fixed on the amber liquid swirling in his glass.

"They don't have anything," she said, her voice barely above a whisper. "Nothing on Justin. Nothing on Lexy."

Ben let out a bitter laugh, shaking his head. "Of course they don't. Why would they? People like Justin always get away with this kind of thing until it's too late."

Dana leaned against the doorframe, her exhaustion and despair evident. "What do we do, Ben? I don't know how much more of this I can take."

Ben finally looked up, his eyes hard and unforgiving. "We protect Ethan. That's what we do. Everything else comes second."

His words, while practical, felt like a dagger to Dana's heart. She nodded, unable to muster a response. The divide between them felt wider than ever, and she couldn't see a way to bridge it.

As the house fell into an uneasy silence, Dana retreated to the living room. The weight of the evening pressed down on her, the image of Justin's smug smile burned into her memory. She clutched a throw pillow to her chest, her tears finally spilling over as she sat in the dim light, wondering how much more she could endure before everything fell apart completely.

28

Dana sat in the kitchen the next morning, staring at her untouched cup of coffee. The house was eerily quiet, the silence broken only by the ticking of the clock on the wall. Ben entered the room, his face drawn and his movements deliberate as he placed his mug in the sink. There was an air of finality in his demeanor that made Dana's stomach drop.

"We need to talk," he said, his voice devoid of warmth.

Dana's heart began to race. "Ben, please..."

He held up a hand, silencing her. "This isn't working, Dana. I've tried to make sense of everything, but I can't. You've put us in danger—put Ethan in danger—and I can't just stand by and let it happen again."

Tears welled in Dana's eyes. "I'm doing everything I can to fix this. I called the police again last night. I'm trying to protect us."

"It's not enough," Ben said, his voice firm but laced with pain. "Justin is relentless, and you... you let him into our lives. I can't trust that you won't make another mistake that puts Ethan in harm's way."

Dana rose from her chair, her hands trembling. "Ben don't

do this. Don't tear us apart. We're supposed to face this together."

Ben's jaw tightened. "I can't face this with you. Not anymore. I'm taking Ethan, and we're going to stay with my sister for a while. At least there, I know he'll be safe."

Dana felt like the ground had been ripped out from under her. "You can't just take him," she said, her voice cracking. "He's my son too."

"I'm not saying you can't see him," Ben said, his tone hardening. "But right now, this house isn't safe. Justin knows where we live, and I'm not willing to take any more chances."

Dana shook her head, tears streaming down her face. "Please, Ben. Don't do this. We can figure this out. We can make it work."

Ben's expression softened for a moment, but then the resolve returned to his eyes. "I've already made up my mind. I'm leaving this afternoon. I'll pack some things for Ethan and myself. You need to focus on dealing with Justin, on figuring out how to stop him. Once this is over, we can... we can talk about what happens next."

Dana sank back into her chair, her body trembling as the weight of his words settled over her. She opened her mouth to argue, to plead, but no words came. She watched as Ben left the kitchen, the sound of his footsteps retreating up the stairs.

The rest of the day passed in a haze. Dana heard the faint rustling of bags being packed, the sound of Ethan's voice as Ben gently explained that they were going to visit Aunt Rachel for a while. She stayed in the kitchen, unable to face either of them, her mind consumed by guilt and fear.

When the front door finally closed behind them, the silence that followed was deafening. Dana sat alone at the kitchen table, staring at the empty chairs. She had never felt so utterly alone.

Her phone buzzed on the table, pulling her from her

thoughts. She picked it up with trembling hands, half-expecting another message from Justin. Instead, it was a text from Ben.

"I'll let you know when we're settled. Take care of yourself."

Dana stared at the screen, her vision blurring with tears. She placed the phone down and buried her face in her hands. She had lost her family, her sense of safety, and now, she wasn't sure how much more she could endure.

The long drive to Rachel's house was quiet, the car filled only with the soft hum of the engine and Ethan's occasional questions about their destination. Ben answered him patiently, his voice softer than it had been in weeks, but his eyes stayed focused on the road ahead. He was determined, though every mile they traveled away from Dana felt like a heavy weight pressing on his chest.

Rachel's house came into view just as the sun began to dip below the horizon, casting a golden glow over the sprawling countryside. The two-story farmhouse, painted a cheerful yellow with white shutters, sat nestled among rolling green hills. A tire swing hung from an old oak tree in the front yard, and flowerbeds bursting with color lined the path to the front door.

As Ben pulled into the gravel driveway, the front door swung open, and Rachel stepped onto the porch. She was dressed casually in jeans and a cozy sweater, her fair hair pulled back into a loose ponytail. Her face lit up when she saw them, and she hurried down the steps to greet her brother and nephew.

"There's my favorite little man!" she called, opening her arms wide as Ethan bolted out of the car and ran to her. She scooped him up in a warm hug, laughing as he chattered excitedly about the long drive and the new house. "You've grown so much! I'm going to need a chart just to keep up with you."

Ben walked up behind them, his expression softening as he watched his sister fuss over Ethan. "Thanks for letting us stay, Rachel," he said.

Rachel set Ethan down and placed a hand on Ben's arm. "You don't even have to thank me. You know my door's always open for you two." She glanced at him, her smile fading slightly. "Are you okay?"

Ben hesitated, then lowering his voice said, "I'll be fine. I just need to make sure Ethan's safe."

Rachel didn't press him further, sensing his need for space. Instead, she turned her attention back to Ethan. "Come on, kiddo. Let me show you your room. I set it up just for you."

Ethan's eyes lit up. "Really? What does it look like?"

"You'll just have to come see for yourself," Rachel teased, taking his hand and leading him inside.

Ben followed them, his steps slowing as he took in the familiar comfort of his sister's home. The smell of fresh-baked cookies wafted from the kitchen, and the living room was warm and inviting, with a crackling fire in the stone fireplace and a soft rug spread across the hardwood floor. It was a stark contrast to the tension and fear that had consumed his own house.

Ethan's laughter echoed from upstairs as Rachel showed him his new room, and for the first time in weeks, Ben felt a glimmer of peace. He knew this wasn't a permanent solution, but for now, it was enough. Ethan was safe, and that was all that mattered.

29

Dana sat staring blankly at the muted television. The house was deathly quiet, and every creak of the old wood floors felt magnified in the silence. She hadn't moved much since Ben and Ethan left, her body heavy with exhaustion and despair. The ticking of the clock on the wall marked each passing second, a cruel reminder of how slowly time dragged on in her isolation.

Her phone buzzed on the coffee table, breaking the stillness. The sudden noise startled her, and she grabbed it hesitantly, half-expecting another message from Justin. Instead, it was an email notification from her company's HR department.

Her stomach tensed as she opened the email, her eyes scanning the carefully worded message:

Dear Dana,

Considering recent events at the gala, we believe it would be in the best interest of all parties for you to take a temporary leave of absence. We understand this is a difficult time, and we want to support you in any way we can. Please let us know how we can assist during this transition.

. . .

The words blurred as tears filled her eyes. She read the email again, hoping she'd misunderstood. But the meaning was clear. Her colleagues and clients had seen the spectacle Justin caused, and now she was being sidelined—not out of concern, but because she was a liability.

Dana dropped the phone onto her lap and buried her face in her hands. The humiliation and frustration swirled inside her. Her career had been her sanctuary, the one part of her life where she felt competent and in control. Now, even that was slipping away, thanks to Justin.

After several minutes, she forced herself to sit upright and take a deep breath. She couldn't afford to break down completely. Her mind raced with questions: Would this leave of absence turn into something permanent? How would she explain this to anyone who asked? And most pressing of all—how had Justin's reach extended so deeply into every corner of her life?

Her gaze drifted to the framed photo on the bookshelf—a picture of her, and Ethan taken on a family vacation years ago. They looked so happy, so carefree. She felt like she was looking at a different person, a version of herself that no longer existed. The thought filled her with a hollow ache.

She rose wearily and wandered into the kitchen. The remnants of the morning coffee still sat in the pot, cold and stale. Mechanically, she poured herself a glass of water, her hands trembling slightly as she brought it to her lips. The kitchen, once a lively center of their family life, now felt barren and alien. The absence of Ethan's laughter and Ben's presence was almost unbearable.

As she set the glass down, her phone buzzed again. She

walked back to the living room and picked it up, bracing herself for another blow. It was a message from Caroline.

Hey, Dana. I heard about the leave. I just wanted to say I'm sorry about how everything went down at the gala. I hope you're okay. Let me know if you need anything.

Dana stared at the screen, a bitter smile tugging at her lips. Caroline meant well, but the message only reminded her of the pity and judgment she would face from everyone at work. She typed out a brief reply:

Thanks, Caroline. I appreciate it.

As she put the phone down, a wave of anger surged through her. This wasn't fair. She'd worked too hard to let Justin's manipulations destroy everything she'd built. She couldn't let him win.

Her thoughts were interrupted by movement—was it a shadow or her imagination? Near the bushes by the front window. Dana froze, her heart pounding in her chest. She crept toward the window and peeked through the curtains, her breath catching as she scanned the yard. Nothing seemed out of place, but the unease lingered.

Paranoia. That's what Justin had reduced her to. She double-checked the locks on the front door and every window, her hands shaking as she secured each one. The house felt like a fortress, but not a safe one. Instead, it was a prison, and Justin's shadow loomed over every corner.

Returning to the living room she sat and then pulled a blanket around herself and stared at the darkened screen of the television. The email, the movement outside, the weight of her mistakes—it all pressed down on her, determined and relentless.

As the night deepened, Dana resolved through her tears that she wouldn't let Justin destroy her completely. But as the hours ticked by and the shadows in the room grew longer, she couldn't help but wonder if it was already too late.

30

Dana sat at the dining table, her laptop in front of her and the dim glow of the screen casting a pale light on her face. She'd been staring at the search bar for nearly fifteen minutes, her fingers hovering above the keyboard, hesitant to take the next step.

Finally, she typed in the words: *Justin Birch restraining orders*. Her hands shook as she pressed Enter, the search results filling the screen in a matter of seconds. She scrolled through them, her breath catching as she saw headlines and snippets that hinted at a pattern she hadn't fully understood until now.

Businessman Accused of Harassment by Former Partner Restraining Order Filed Against Entrepreneur Justin Birch Stalking Allegations Rock Prominent CEO's Reputation

Clicking on the first link, Dana began to read. The article described a relationship Justin had several years ago with a woman named Lydia Cole. According to the report, their relationship ended abruptly after Lydia accused Justin of controlling behavior and harassment. She had filed for a restraining order after claiming Justin showed up uninvited at her workplace and sent her threatening messages when she refused to engage with him.

Dana's stomach churned as she clicked on another link. This time, it was an account from a woman named Sarah Jacobs, who had also filed a restraining order against Justin. Her story was unsettlingly similar: a whirlwind romance, followed by manipulation, possessiveness, and, ultimately, stalking when she tried to end things. Sarah had described Justin as "charming and magnetic at first, but deeply unstable underneath."

Dana realized that the public articles barely scratched the surface. She needed more details. Thinking quickly, she opened a private browser window and logged into a background check website she'd used once before when hiring a nanny. She typed in Justin's full name and hit search, her fingers drumming anxiously on the table as the page loaded.

Justin's profile appeared, accompanied by a list of civil and legal cases. Dana scanned the results, her pulse quickening as she spotted multiple filings for restraining orders over the years. Each one was tied to a different woman, and the accompanying summaries painted a grim picture. Harassment. Trespassing. Threats.

She clicked on one of the cases, which led her to court documents that detailed a woman's testimony. Justin had shown up at her apartment unannounced multiple times, once leaving flowers and another time leaving a shattered picture frame on her doorstep. He had sent dozens of messages, alternating between apologies and veiled threats.

Dana jotted down the names of the women she'd uncovered so far: Lydia Cole, Sarah Jacobs, Emily Foster. Each story was disturbingly similar, a testament to Justin's calculated and repetitive behavior. She searched their names next, finding interviews and statements they'd given to local newspapers or blogs. The details were horrifying.

As she dug deeper, Dana stumbled upon a forum thread where people discussed high-profile stalking cases. Justin's name came up more than once, with users speculating about his past relationships and his ability to evade serious consequences. One comment caught her attention:

He's smart, that's for sure. Knows how to charm the right people and keep just enough plausible deniability to avoid legal trouble. But everyone who's crossed paths with him says the same thing—he's broken, and he lashes out when he feels rejected.

Broken. The word stuck with her as she leaned back in her chair, her hands falling to her lap. Justin wasn't just a predator; he was a deeply damaged man, incapable of dealing with rejection or failure. But knowing that didn't make her feel safer. If anything, it made her more afraid. A man like Justin, desperate and spiraling, was capable of anything.

Dana closed her laptop and rubbed her temples, trying to process what she'd just learned. She thought back to their early interactions, how he'd seemed so attentive, so flattering. It had been intoxicating at first, the way he made her feel seen and valued in a way she hadn't felt in years. But now, with the clarity of hindsight, she realized how calculated it all had been. Justin hadn't been interested in her—he'd been interested in control.

Her phone buzzed on the table, pulling her out of her thoughts. She picked it up and saw a message from an unknown number. Her breath hitched as she opened it.

You're digging into things you shouldn't, Dana.

Her hands went cold, and she dropped the phone onto the table as though it had burned her. Justin knew. He always seemed to know. Her heart pounded in her chest as she stood up, pacing the room in a futile attempt to calm herself.

What had she expected? That she could quietly uncover his secrets without him finding out? Justin had spent years perfecting his ability to manipulate and intimidate. He wasn't going to let her expose him without a fight.

But Dana was done being afraid. She thought of Ethan, of Ben, of everything Justin had already taken from her. Taking a deep breath, she picked up her phone and began drafting an email to the detective handling her case. She included links to the articles she'd found, along with a plea for them to act before Justin's behavior escalated further.

When she hit send, a wave of resolve washed over her. She didn't know what the next step would be, but she knew she couldn't sit idly by any longer. Justin's vulnerability wasn't a weakness she could exploit—it was a warning of just how far he might go.

~

Dana sat at her kitchen table. Her notebook open. The pages were blank, but her pen hovered over the paper, poised to write. She took a deep breath, steeling herself. Enough was enough. She had spent weeks reacting to Justin's threats and manipulations, but tonight, she resolved to take the first step toward reclaiming her power.

She titled the first page: ***Justin Birch – Incidents and Evidence.***

Underneath, she began to write in neat, precise lines:

1. **First Contact** – Met Justin at a networking event. He was charming, attentive, and persistent.
2. **Affair** – One stupid night. Ended it due to guilt and realization of his controlling behavior.
3. **First Threat** – Text message: "I don't like being ignored." This was after I cut off contact.

4. **Unwanted Gifts** – Flowers and gift sent to my office. Assistant witnessed delivery. Unprompted and unwelcome.
5. **Murdered Snowball.**
6. **Gala Incident** – Public humiliation. Implicated me in front of colleagues and clients.
7. **Messages** – Numerous texts and emails, including veiled threats.
8. **Stalking** – Sightings outside Ethan's school and soccer game. Interactions with other parents.

Dana paused, the weight of the list sinking in. Seeing it all written out made Justin's behavior feel even more sinister, more calculated. She flipped to a fresh page and jotted down another heading: ***Evidence Collected.***

- Screenshots of text messages.
- Photos of flowers and unwanted gift.
- Emails forwarded to the detective.
- Witnesses: Linda (assistant), Ethan's coach, colleagues at gala.

Her pen slowed as she thought of what she could add next. If she could keep this record meticulous, undeniable, she'd have a stronger case for the police. Maybe they couldn't act yet, but she wouldn't let him slip through their fingers.

A new thought struck her. Dana reached for her phone and opened the voice recorder app. She pressed record, her voice trembling at first but growing steadier as she spoke.

"This is Dana Taylor. It's February 10th, 9:42 PM. I'm documenting the harassment I've experienced from Justin Birch. I've compiled a written log of incidents, but I'll summarize here as well."

She paused, gathering her thoughts before continuing. "Justin Birch began contacting me after I ended our brief relationship. His behavior has escalated over time, including threats, stalking, and attempts to humiliate me publicly. He's inserted himself into my professional and personal life, and I believe he poses a significant threat to my safety and the safety of my family."

Her voice cracked, but she pushed through. "I am keeping a detailed log of his actions and collecting evidence to support my claims. I've reported these incidents to the police, but I'm terrified of what might happen if this continues unchecked. This recording is part of my effort to ensure that, if something happens to me, there's a clear record of what I've experienced."

She pressed stop, her heart pounding as she set the phone down. Hearing her own voice made it all feel real in a way she hadn't expected. But instead of despair, she felt a flicker of determination. Justin wanted her to feel helpless, but she wasn't going to give him that power.

Dana stood and grabbed her coat. She needed to get out of the house, to clear her head. As she locked the door behind her, she resolved to take her notebook and evidence to the police again tomorrow. She'd make them listen.

The night air was crisp, filling her lungs with a sharp chill that felt bracing and alive. For the first time in weeks, Dana felt like she was no longer running. She was preparing for battle.

31

The street outside Dana's house was quiet, the occasional passing car the only sign of life in the otherwise still neighborhood. Parked a few houses down, Justin sat in his car, his fingers drumming idly on the steering wheel. The tinted windows concealed him, though his vantage point gave him a clear view of Dana's front door and the windows on the ground floor. He had been there for hours, his patience unwavering.

Through the long-range lens of his camera, Justin zoomed in on Dana's living room window. The sheer curtains obscured some of the details, but he could see her pacing, her phone in hand. Every so often, she would stop and glance toward the front door, as though expecting someone. Justin's lips curled into a small, satisfied smile. She was rattled. Good.

He adjusted the focus, snapping a series of photos. Dana's expression was tense, her movements agitated. She had no idea he was there, watching her every move. To Justin, the distance made it more thrilling—to observe her in her natural state, vulnerable and unaware.

As the hours wore on, the lights in the house began to flicker off one by one. Justin watched as Dana retreated upstairs, a silhouette moving behind the curtains of what he assumed was her bedroom. He leaned back in his seat, considering his next move. The usual tactics were becoming predictable. He needed to be more creative, more personal.

A few minutes later, Justin stepped out of his car. He moved quietly, his shoes barely making a sound as he approached the house. The trash bins by the side of the garage caught his eye. He hesitated for only a moment before lifting the lid of the nearest bin. The faint odor of discarded food and paper filled the air, but Justin barely noticed. He began to sift through the contents, his gloved hands meticulous as he searched for something—anything—that might give him further insight into Dana's life.

His search was methodical. He pushed aside empty food containers, crumpled receipts, and scraps of paper. Then he saw it: a small, crumpled paper pharmacy bag. Justin's brow furrowed as he examined it, but when he looked inside, a strange sense of satisfaction washing over him. An empty pregnancy test box. Importantly, it was the type that detected early pregnancy. It said so on the front.

Then realization dawned, and his smile widened. The fact the packaging was empty spoke volumes. Had the test been negative she'd have put it back in the box and discarded both. The fact that she'd kept the test meant something, he just knew it.

"Interesting," he murmured to himself, tucking the empty box back into the bin before lowering the lid quietly.

He returned to his car, his mind racing. If his suspicion was correct, then Dana had been keeping secrets far more significant than he'd imagined. His grip on the steering wheel tightened as the possibilities unfolded in his mind. This changed everything.

Justin's phone buzzed on the passenger seat. He picked it up and stared at the screen for a moment before typing out a message.

"Goodnight, Dana. Sweet dreams."

He hit send, watching her darkened house as he waited. Sure enough, moments later, the glow of her phone illuminated the bedroom window. Justin's smile grew. Even if she didn't know what he'd discovered tonight, she would know one thing: she was never truly alone.

Satisfied, Justin started the engine and drove off, the thrill of the night fueling his resolve. He had the upper hand now, and he wasn't going to let her forget it.

But Justin's obsession didn't end there. In the following days, he began to escalate. The thrill of simply watching wasn't enough anymore. He needed more.

He started timing her routines. He knew when she left the house, when she returned, and even when she turned the lights off to sleep. He memorized her movements like a script, every detail feeding his growing fixation. Justin started following her car at a safe distance, noting her stops at the grocery store or gas station. He stayed just far enough to avoid detection but close enough to feel connected to her.

One afternoon, Justin parked near the local coffee shop Dana frequented. Through the large windows, he watched as she ordered her usual drink, her face drawn and distracted. She sat at a corner table, her laptop open, oblivious to the fact that he was outside. Justin didn't approach—he didn't need to. Instead, he took out his camera again, snapping photos of her sitting there, alone. The way she tucked her hair behind her ear, the way her fingers hovered over the keyboard—it all felt intimate, like he was part of her world even though she had no idea.

That night, Justin broke into her backyard. The shadows cloaked his movements as he crept closer to the house. He peered through the windows, his breath fogging the glass as he watched Dana, her notebook in her lap. She was writing something, her expression focused. Justin's fingers itched to know what she was documenting. Was it about him? Did she think she could outsmart him?

He circled the house, taking mental notes of potential entry points. The back door had a simple lock—too easy to break if he needed to. The upstairs windows were often left slightly ajar, likely for ventilation. Justin filed this information away, his mind already forming plans for how he could get closer without her knowing.

As he returned to his car that night, Justin felt a sense of satisfaction. Dana might think by making notes she would outwit him, but Justin was always one step ahead. His obsession had grown beyond control, but to him, it wasn't madness—it was destiny. She belonged to him, whether she knew it or not.

~

The night air at Rachel's countryside home was crisp, carrying the faint scent of freshly cut wood from a nearby stack beside the porch. Inside the warm, cozy living room, Ben sat slumped in an armchair, a glass of whiskey in his hand. The fire crackled in the stone hearth, its glow casting flickering shadows on the rustic walls adorned with family photos and Rachel's collection of handwoven baskets. Ethan was asleep upstairs, nestled in the room Rachel had lovingly prepared for him, complete with soft flannel sheets and a small shelf of children's books.

Rachel walked into the room, a steaming mug of tea in her

hands. She handed it to Ben, who gave her a small nod of thanks. She sat down in the armchair across from him, her expression tender but tinged with concern. For a long moment, neither of them spoke, the sound of the fire filling the silence.

Finally, Rachel broke the quiet. “You’ve been sitting there for an hour. You’re not one to sulk, Ben. What’s on your mind?”

Ben sighed, swirling the whiskey in his glass. “Everything, Rachel. I don’t even know where to start.”

“Start with Dana,” Rachel said softly. “Do you think you’ll ever forgive her?”

Ben stiffened, his jaw tightening. He stared into the glass, searching for answers that wouldn’t come. “I don’t know. I want to say yes, for Ethan’s sake, but it’s not that simple. She didn’t just betray me... she jeopardized our family. Our son.”

Rachel leaned forward. When she spoke, her tone was gentle. “I can’t imagine how hard this is for you, but you’ve always been the steady one. The rock. Maybe Dana needs that now more than ever.”

Ben’s laugh was bitter. “She needs a rock. Rachel, she had one. She had me. And she chose someone else. Someone dangerous.” He shook his head, his voice breaking. “I can’t stop thinking about what Justin has done to her... to us. And the worst part? She opened the door and invited him into our lives.”

Rachel’s eyes softened with sympathy. “People make mistakes, Ben. Big ones, yes. But I’ve known Dana for a long time, and I know she loves you. She loves Ethan. I think she’s scared and lost, and she’s trying to fix it the only way she knows how.”

Ben’s shoulders slumped, and he ran a hand through his hair. “I keep asking myself how we got here. How did everything fall apart so fast? I know that we’d been gradually drifting. Focusing so much on work that we took our eyes off what was important, not making time for one another and barely having enough left in the tank for our son. So, I accept I made mistakes too but why didn't she speak out, tell me how she was feeling? And now, when I look at Ethan, I see how much he misses his mom. And part of me misses her too. But then I remember what she did, and I..." His voice trailed off, and he shook his head. "I just don't know if I can forgive her, Rachel. Not completely."

Rachel reached out and placed a hand on his knee, her touch grounding. "Maybe you don't have to figure it all out right now. Take it one day at a time. But don't close the door completely. Sometimes love needs time to heal."

Ben looked up at her, his eyes filled with a mixture of pain and gratitude. "I just don't want Ethan to grow up thinking this is normal. That this is what a family is supposed to look like."

"Ethan's stronger than you think," Rachel said with a small smile. "And he has you. That counts for a lot. Whatever happens, you'll make it through this. You always do."

Ben sighed, leaning back. "I hope you're right."

Rachel hesitated, then said, "What if it were the other way around? If you had made the mistake? Do you think Dana would forgive you?"

The question hit Ben like a punch to the gut. He frowned, considering it. "I don't know," he admitted. "But I'd like to think she'd at least try. She's always been... kinder than I deserve, in some ways." He shook his head. "But this isn't about me. It's about protecting Ethan. I can't... I can't put him at risk because of her mistakes."

"She's doing everything she can to fix it," Rachel countered gently. "You said yourself that she's been working with the police, documenting everything. She's trying, Ben. Isn't that worth something?"

Ben's hand tightened around the glass. "It's worth something, yeah. But I don't know if it's enough. Not yet."

Rachel tilted her head, her expression thoughtful. "Then

maybe you don't need to decide right now. Give yourself time. Give her time. But don't let anger make the decision for you."

Ben stared at the fire, the flames dancing in the hearth. "It's not just anger, Rachel. It's... fear. I'm scared of what Justin might do next. I'm scared of what happens if I let my guard down and he comes after Ethan again. I don't know how to live like this."

Rachel got up and moved to where he sat, squishing into the space beside him before wrapping an arm around his shoulders, pulling him into a comforting embrace. "You don't have to figure it all out tonight, Ben. But I know one thing: you're a good father. And whatever happens, you'll do what's right for Ethan. That's what matters."

Ben rested his head in his hands, his voice barely above a whisper. "I just want my family back. But I just don't know if it's even possible anymore."

They sat together in silence, the crackling fire filling the room. Outside, the stars sparkled in the clear night sky, and the house felt safe and warm—a bubble of peace in the chaos of their lives. But even as Ben sat there, surrounded by his sister's unwavering support, a small part of him couldn't stop wondering if Dana was okay, if she was safe. The thought gnawed at him, refusing to let him rest.

32

The morning was cold and misty, the kind of day where the world felt muted, wrapped in a pale gray haze that softened the outlines of the towering trees. The woodland was dense, the skeletal branches of winter-stripped oaks and birches interwoven like a cathedral ceiling overhead. Frost clung to the undergrowth, glinting faintly as the weak sunlight struggled to penetrate the mist. The ground was damp, covered in a carpet of decaying leaves and patches of stubborn moss.

A lone jogger moved along the narrow dirt trail. Her breath visible in the frigid air. She was in her mid-thirties, clad in black leggings and a bright red windbreaker, her movements rhythmic and precise. Her running shoes crunched softly against the gravel-strewn path. Her earbuds pumped out an upbeat track, blocking out the natural world around her—the distant call of a crow, the rustle of unseen creatures in the underbrush.

The woodland was her sanctuary. She jogged this trail every weekend, a ritual that helped her clear her mind and reconnect with herself. Today, however, the woods felt different. The mist was thicker than usual, and a strange stillness hung in the air, as though the forest was holding its breath. She glanced around, slowing her pace, a faint prickle of unease crawling up her spine.

It was then that she noticed something off the path. At first, it seemed like nothing more than a bundle of discarded clothing, dark and crumpled among the leaves. She frowned, pulling out her earbuds and stopping in her tracks. The forest seemed to grow quieter still as she stepped cautiously closer, her pulse quickening.

As she approached, the shape became clearer, and dread pooled in her stomach. It wasn't clothing. It was a body.

The woman lay sprawled on her side, her hair tangled and matted with dirt. Her skin was unnaturally pale, almost waxen in the dim light, and her lifeless eyes stared blankly into the canopy above. A thin trickle of dried blood ran from her nose, staining her cheek. Her clothes were torn and disheveled, and her hands, curled into loose fists, were smeared with mud.

The jogger's breath hitched, and she stumbled back a step, her hand flying to her mouth. She fought the urge to scream, her body trembling as she fumbled for her phone. Her fingers were numb with cold making it difficult to unlock the screen. Finally, she managed to dial 911, her voice shaking as she gave the dispatcher her location.

"There's a body," she stammered. "In the woods, off the trail by Silver Creek. A woman. She's... she's dead."

The dispatcher's calm and measured voice instructed her to stay on the line, to remain at the scene but not to touch anything. The jogger nodded, even though no one could see her, and cast another glance at the body. She noticed more details now: the way the woman's fingers were bent unnaturally, the faint bruising around her neck, and the torn edge of her sleeve that revealed a deep scratch along her forearm. The scene was disturbingly quiet, the only sounds her own ragged breathing and the faint rustle of leaves in the breeze.

She backed away, her gaze darting around the forest as paranoia crept in. Was someone still out here? Had they seen her? The thought sent a fresh wave of terror coursing through her, and she gripped her phone tightly, the dispatcher's voice a fragile lifeline.

The mist seemed heavier now, the trees looming like silent sentinels. The jogger hugged her arms around herself, her body trembling not just from the cold but from the overwhelming shock of what she'd stumbled upon. She felt the weight of the moment pressing down on her, the realization that someone's life had ended here, in this quiet, unassuming woodland. And whoever had done it... might still be nearby.

In the distance, the faint wail of approaching sirens broke the silence, and the jogger exhaled a shaky breath. Help was coming, but the image of the woman's lifeless face was seared into her mind. She knew she would never run this trail again without seeing her, without remembering the cold, empty eyes staring up at the unfeeling sky.

~

Dana sat on the couch, her legs curled under her and a threadbare blanket draped loosely over her shoulders. The coffee table in front of her was a mess of discarded takeaway containers, crumpled napkins, and empty wine bottles. The faint smell of soy sauce and stale grease lingered in the air, mingling with the scent of lavender from a candle that had burned out hours ago. The dim light from the television cast flickering shadows on the walls, the room otherwise shrouded in a heavy, oppressive silence.

She stared blankly at the screen, barely registering the sitcom rerun playing in front of her. The canned laughter jarred against the numbness that had taken up residence in her chest, but she didn't bother to change the channel. She hadn't laughed in days, hadn't really felt anything except an all-consuming exhaustion that seemed to settle in her very bones.

The sitcom faded to black, replaced by the opening notes of the evening news. Dana's eyes flickered to the screen; her interest piqued for only a moment. The anchor's polished voice filled the room, introducing the night's top stories, and then the image shifted to a live shot of a reporter standing outside a wooded area. Yellow police tape fluttered in the background, and the flashing lights of squad cars lit up the edges of the scene.

"Breaking news tonight from Woodland Ridge Park," the reporter said, her breath visible in the chilly night air. "Authorities have confirmed that the body of an unidentified woman was discovered earlier today by a local jogger. Police are currently treating the area as a potential crime scene and have not released any further details."

Dana's brow furrowed slightly, her gaze lingering on the screen. The camera panned over the scene, zooming in on a cluster of investigators huddled near the tree line. The sight should have stirred something in her—curiosity, concern, unease—but she felt nothing. Just another piece of bad news in a world filled with it.

The reporter continued, "We'll bring you updates as more information becomes available, but for now, authorities are asking anyone with information to come forward."

Dana reached for the remote, her movements sluggish, and changed the channel. The screen flipped to an old movie, the black-and-white image of a dramatic confrontation playing out in silence. She settled back, pulling the blanket tighter around her shoulders. The news was someone else's problem, someone else's tragedy. She had enough of her own to deal with.

Her eyes drifted to the coffee table, to the chaos of takeaway cartons and empty bottles that had become the new normal in her life. For a moment, a flicker of shame passed through her, but it was gone as quickly as it came. She couldn't summon the energy to clean up, couldn't summon the energy to care.

Outside, the wind rattled the windows, a lonely sound that seemed to echo the hollow feeling in her chest. The movie continued to play, its grainy images casting flickering light across her face. Dana stayed like that for hours, unmoving, lost in the haze of her own apathy.

33

A few days had passed since her decent into slovenliness and after giving herself a stern talking to, Dana had pulled herself and the house together and then decided to take matters into her own hands. She sat at the small café table, her hands wrapped around a steaming cup of coffee. The place was busy, the murmur of conversation blending with the clinking of cups and the occasional hiss of the espresso machine. Sunlight streamed in and

the air smelled of freshly brewed coffee and pastries, with the faint hum of a nearby blender adding to the lively atmosphere. She'd chosen this place deliberately—a crowded, public space where Justin couldn't easily intimidate her. Yet, despite the safety in numbers, her stomach fluttered with unease.

She glanced at the door for the third time in as many minutes, her heart skipping a beat when she finally saw Justin enter. He was impeccably dressed, his dark coat buttoned neatly, and his sharp eyes scanned the room with a confidence that made her skin crawl. When his gaze landed on her, a slow, knowing smile spread across his face. He walked over with deliberate strides, pulling out the chair across from her and sitting down without a word.

Her heart was racing but her face work a mask. She forced herself to appear composed. The buzz of chatter and the clinking of cups around them helped attain this, gave the scene a false sense of normalcy. Justin leaned back in the chair, his sharp gaze pinned on her, an unnerving smile curling at the corner of his lips. She slipped her hand into her coat pocket, brushing against her phone, the recording app running silently. She needed him to trip up, to say something that could end this nightmare and was relieved when he opened the conversation.

"Dana," he said smoothly. "You look tense." His eyes then roamed her body. "This isn't a date, is it? You didn't dress up for me."

She forced herself to meet his gaze, refusing to let him see her fear. "I wanted to talk. Clear the air."

Justin chuckled softly, shaking his head. "Clear the air? That's rich, coming from you. I've wanted to meet for a while so we could have a friendly chat, but you turned everything into a drama. So, why the U-turn? What is it you really want, Dana? I'm a busy man so let's skip the false pleasantries."

Ignoring the sarcasm in his voice, keeping hers light, almost casual, Dana began. "I've been thinking a lot about everything that's happened. About how... complicated things have gotten."

Justin tilted his head, amused. "Complicated is an understatement, don't you think? You cheated on your husband with me then told him all about it, can't get much more complicated than that."

Dana forced a small laugh. "You're right. And no matter how many times I told you it was a mistake and I didn't want to see you again, you didn't take my rejection well. But I can't help wondering why? Surely one night didn't mean that much to you that you'd go to all the trouble of punishing me."

Justin responded by inclining his head and giving her a quizzical look. Like he was having trouble understanding. Irritated but unfazed, Dana ploughed on.

"I know it's you, Justin. What you did to my son's kitten, the way you've insidiously infiltrated my work and home life and I find it... very sad. That you have so little in *your* life that you feel the need to wreck mine. I mean, don't you have work to do or other women you can stalk? I'm sure you're not short of female attention, or do they all tire of you eventually or even after one date?"

He raised an eyebrow, his smirk widening. "I really have no idea what you mean by wrecking your life an if sending flowers and gifts to a woman I admire is a crime and being hurt when she throws that back in my face, then yes I'm guilty as charged. You make what happened between us that night and afterwards sound so nefarious oh, and for the record you're correct. Where female attention is concerned I'm definitely not going short in that department. Why, are you a teeny bit jealous?"

Dana ignored his taunt and focused on facts. "Well," she pressed, leaning forward slightly, her tone softening, "for the record, someone's been watching me. At my house, at Ethan's school. It's unsettling. You wouldn't know anything about that, would you?"

Justin's expression didn't falter. He simply stared. His eyes gleaming with something unreadable. "Watching you?" he repeated, his tone feigning innocence. "Dana, if I wanted to see you, I'd just ask you to meet me for coffee. Like today. We could even have cake but," his eyes roamed her body once more, "maybe you're watching what you eat. Looks like you've gained a few pounds to me."

At this her face flushed which made her feel ridiculous, that his comment bothered her and frustrated too, at how easily he deflected. Still she refused to take the bait and forged on. "But the things that have been happening... the vandalism, the photos, the threats," she continued, her voice trembling slightly now, more from a wave of irritation than fear. "Why would anyone do this?"

Justin leaned in, his face mere inches from hers. "Why indeed?" he said softly. His voice was calm, almost soothing, but the menace in his words was unmistakable. "Perhaps you have a lot of enemies, Dana. Maybe you've underestimated how much damage you've caused. I'm sure your colleagues and family are rather upset with you right now."

Her pulse thundered in her ears as she resisted the urge to snap at him. Refute his lies and scream in his face that he was a liar. A freak, a pervert. But that would be stupid because she realised now that he was far too clever to fall into her trap, too practiced at turning things around. She felt the weight of her phone in her pocket, the recording app catching nothing incriminating, and she fought the despair rising in her chest.

Their tense standoff was interrupted by the arrival of a waitress, a young woman with a polite smile and a notepad in hand. "Can I take your order?"

"Coffee, black" Dana said quickly, her voice betraying the tension she tried to hide.

The waitress jotted it down and turned to Justin.

His smile returned, wider this time, but with a wicked edge. "I'll have the same," he said, before turning his attention back to Dana. His voice dropped to a near whisper, his words slicing through the air. "Should you really be drinking coffee in your condition?"

Dana froze, her breath catching in her throat. Her mind raced as his question lingered between them, a silent declaration that he knew about her pregnancy.

The waitress left, oblivious to the bomb Justin had just dropped. Dana stared at him, her hands gripping the edge of the table to steady herself. Justin reclined in his chair, looking completely at ease, his gaze locked on her like a predator savoring the game.

Dana knew she had to fight back, pour water on his assumption no matter how he'd come to it. But she couldn't even contemplate the ramifications of that right now because the mere idea of him having access to her medical records freaked her out, terrified her in fact.

"What condition? What the hell are you talking about? I'm not sick and stop trying to change the subject. I can drink whatever I want." Dana shook her head, feigning exasperation at his remark.

Again Justin smirked. "If you say so."

Dana leant forward slightly, narrowing her eyes, the finger of her left hand pointing in the direction of his smug face. He wasn't falling for her plan so the only alternative was to be direct. "I mean it, Justin. If you don't leave me and my family alone I'll go back to the police and keep going back until they do something" she said, her voice firm despite the tremor in her hands. "I've been keeping a record of everything. Every message, every time you've shown up where you don't belong. Our lawyer is ready to act and all we need to do is say the word. You think you're untouchable, but you're not."

At this, Justin tutted then stood, taking his time, adjusting his coat with practiced ease, adding a sigh and a disappointed look for dramatic effect. "You know, I've had quite enough of your ramblings for one day, Dana and it's a shame because I was so looking forward to our date. Anyway, do enjoy your coffee, if you think it's wise, that is," he said with a smirk. "Oh, and Dana. You can switch your phone off now.'

While Dana stared, her mouth agape, Justin winked and walked away, leaving her trembling with a mix of fear and fury. She watched him disappear into the crowd outside, her mind racing. He hadn't fallen for the trap, but she'd seen something in his eyes when she mentioned the police—something unguarded, if only for a moment. She clung to the hope that it might be enough even as his comment about her 'condition' echoed in her ears.

The café's warmth suddenly felt stifling, the cheerful clinking of cups and chatter grating against her raw nerves. Dana took a deep breath, steadying herself. She wasn't giving up. Not now, not ever. Justin might think he had the upper hand, but one way or another, this was going to end.

~

Dana cursed under her breath as she navigated through the city streets, ignoring the constant buzz of her phone, alerting her to messages and voicemails that she had no intention of opening. The late afternoon sun was beginning to dip below the horizon, casting a pale orange glow over the urban sprawl. The faint chatter of the radio host in the background her only companion. She barely registered the soothing tones of a pop song that had given way to a news bulletin.

Her meeting with Justin had left her confused and deflated, her carefully laid plans crumbling in the face of his unshakable confidence. She had hoped to catch him off guard, to lure him into saying something incriminating, recording their conversation on her phone but instead, she was left feeling more vulnerable than ever. His words echoed in her mind, taunting her: "In your condition." She clenched her teeth, anger and despair swirling together in a toxic brew. How did he know? Who had told him? Had he been following her? Had he paid someone at the clinic to divulge her details? One thing she did know for sure, was that she'd made the right decision, terminating the pregnancy.

"This is breaking news," the voice on the radio announced, cutting through her thoughts. Dana's focus sharpened slightly as she glanced at the dashboard, her foot easing off the accelerator.

"Authorities have identified the body discovered in Woodland Ridge Park earlier this week. The victim has been named as Lexy Rivers, a local private investigator. Police have yet to release details surrounding her death, but sources say it is being treated as suspicious."

Dana's heart stopped. Her breath hitched, and she gripped the steering wheel so tightly her fingers ached. *Lexy?* She replayed the name in her head, certain she had misheard. But the reporter continued, her calm voice clashing with the storm building inside Dana.

"Ms. Rivers was well-known for her work in uncovering fraud and corporate misconduct. Friends and colleagues describe her as tenacious and fearless. We will provide more updates as the investigation unfolds."

The blood drained from Dana's face. Her mind raced. Was that why her phone had been buzzing? The police trying to inform her about Lexy. Then images of her dear friend flashed through her head: her bold laugh, her sharp wit, the determination in her eyes. Lexy had been helping her, digging into Justin's past, and now... now she was gone. The realization hit her like a physical blow.

"No," Dana whispered, shaking her head as if denying it could make it untrue. Tears blurred her vision, and she blinked rapidly, trying to clear them. Her chest tightened, and her breaths came in short, panicked gasps.

The world outside the car seemed to tilt. She barely registered the red light ahead or the horn blaring as she drifted into the next lane. Her foot faltered on the brake; her shaking hands unable to correct the steering in time. A sharp screech of tires sliced through the air, followed by the sickening crunch of metal on metal.

The impact jolted her forward, her seatbelt locking across her chest. The car spun slightly before coming to an abrupt halt, the hood crumpled against a streetlight. The sudden silence that followed was deafening, broken only by the faint hiss of steam rising from the engine and the distant shouts of bystanders.

Dana sat frozen, her hands still clutching the wheel, her mind reeling. Pain bloomed in her shoulder where the seatbelt had dug in, but she barely noticed. All she could think about was Lexy. Her friend, her ally, taken from her in the most brutal way imaginable.

A knock on the driver's side window startled her, and she turned her head sluggishly to see a concerned face peering in. She fumbled with the door handle, her movements uncoordinated, and managed to push the door open.

"Ma'am are you okay?" the man asked, his voice urgent but kind. "Do you need an ambulance?"

Dana opened her mouth to respond, but no words came out. Her throat felt tight, her chest constricted. She shook her head, tears streaming down her face as she tried to steady her breathing.

"You're in shock," the man said, crouching beside her. "Just stay here, okay? Help is on the way."

She nodded numbly, her thoughts a chaotic swirl of grief, fear, and guilt. The news about Lexy, the crash, Justin's threats—it all felt like too much to bear. As she sat there, trembling and broken, one thought rose above the rest: Justin had to be stopped. Whatever it took, she couldn't let him destroy anyone else.

The sound of approaching sirens grew louder, their wail piercing through the fog in her mind. Dana took a shuddering breath, steeling herself. She wasn't sure how, but she knew she had to find a way to fight back. For Lexy. For Ethan. For herself.

34

The sterile scent of antiseptic filled the air, mingling with the soft hum of machines in the corner of the hospital room. Dana lay propped up on the stiff hospital bed, her left wrist encased in a thick plaster cast and resting awkwardly on a stack of pillows. A thin tube ran from her arm to an IV drip, and the faint ache in her ribs reminded her of the force of the crash. The fluorescent lights overhead buzzed faintly, casting a pale glow over the beige walls and linoleum floor.

She stared out the window, watching the rain streak against the glass. Her mind was a whirl of thoughts, but they all returned to one constant: Lexy. The news of her death had been a blow she hadn't yet fully processed, and every time she closed her eyes, her friend's face flashed before her. The grief felt debilitating, and her helplessness only added to the weight.

The sound of the door opening pulled her from her thoughts. She turned her head to see Ben stepping into the room, his expression a mix of concern and weariness. His coat was damp from the rain, and he carried a takeaway coffee cup in one hand. He hesitated in the doorway for a moment before stepping closer to her bedside.

"Hey," he said softly, setting the cup down on the small table beside her bed. "How are you feeling?"

Dana managed a small, strained smile. "I've been better. The doctors say it's just a broken wrist and some bruised ribs. I'll live."

Ben nodded, his gaze drifting to her cast. He pulled up the chair beside the bed and sat down. For a moment, neither of them spoke, the silence stretching between them like a fragile thread.

Finally, Dana broke it. "Lexy's dead, Ben. The body they found in the woods... it was her." Her voice cracked, and she looked away, blinking back tears. "I know Justin is behind it. I... I'm sure of it."

Ben's jaw tightened, his hands gripping the edge of the chair. "I was afraid of that," he said quietly. "Dana, I... I'm so sorry. I know how much she meant to you."

Dana shook her head, frustration and grief boiling over. "She was helping me, Ben. She was trying to find something, anything, to stop him. And now she's gone. He's taken her away, and I couldn't do anything to stop it."

Ben reached out, placing a hand gently over hers. "This isn't your fault," he said firmly. "Justin is the one to blame, not you."

She looked at him, her eyes brimming with tears. "I'm so scared, Ben. What if he comes after Ethan? Or you? I can't lose anyone else."

Ben's grip on her hand tightened. "I left Ethan with Rachel. He's safe there. I... I needed to come and see you. To make sure you were okay."

Dana's lips trembled, and she nodded, the weight of his words bringing a small measure of relief. "Thank you," she whispered. "For being here."

Ben leaned forward. His voice low but resolute. "I'm not leaving, Dana. Not this time. Whatever happens, we'll face it together. Justin doesn't get to win. He doesn't get to take everything from us."

Her heart ached at his words, a bittersweet mixture of hope and guilt swelling within her. She reached up with her uninjured hand, brushing a tear from her cheek. "Do you think we can fix this? Us?"

Ben hesitated, his gaze searching hers. "I don't know," he admitted. "But I want to try. For Ethan. For us. We've been through too much to give up now."

A tear slipped down Dana's cheek, and she squeezed his hand. "I'm sorry for everything, Ben. I... I never meant for any of this to happen."

"I know," he said softly. "We'll figure it out. One step at a time."

The rain outside softened to a gentle drizzle, the rhythmic patter against the window a soothing backdrop to their moment of connection. For the first time in weeks, Dana felt a flicker of hope. It was fragile and faint, but it was there. She wasn't alone in this fight, and maybe, just maybe, they could find a way back to each other.

As Dana drifted off to sleep, she felt comfort knowing Ben was by her bedside.

~

Dana stirred awake to the sound of murmured voices and the soft creak of the hospital door opening. She blinked against the dim light of the room, her mind sluggish from the pain medication coursing through her system. The faint glow of the wall-mounted monitor cast a pale light on her cast and the thin hospital sheet pulled over her legs.

"Mrs. Taylor?" A firm, unfamiliar voice broke through her haze. She turned her head to see two police officers standing at the foot of her bed, their faces serious and their uniforms crisp. The taller officer, a man with salt-and-pepper hair, stepped closer, while the other—a younger woman with sharp eyes and a no-nonsense demeanor—remained by the door.

Ben, who had been dozing in the chair beside her bed, snapped awake at the sound of the officer's voice. He sat upright, his eyes narrowing as he took in the unexpected visitors.

"Is everything okay?" Ben asked, his voice rough with sleep but laced with protectiveness. "Why are you here?"

The older officer cleared his throat. "I'm Detective Marshall, and this is Detective Hayes. We need to ask Mrs. Taylor a few questions regarding an ongoing investigation."

Dana's heart began to race, a sick sense of foreboding settling over her. "Investigation?" she echoed, her voice barely above a whisper. "This is about the crash, isn't it? I told the doctors it was an accident."

"This isn't about the crash," Detective Hayes interjected, her tone sharp and deliberate. "This is about Lexy Rivers."

The mention of Lexy's name was like a slap to Dana's already fragile state. She sat up straighter, wincing as pain shot through her ribs. "Lexy?" she repeated. "What about her?"

Detective Marshall's expression hardened. "Mrs. Taylor, during the course of our investigation into Ms. Rivers' death, forensic evidence was collected from her... personal effects. DNA analysis revealed a match to you."

Dana froze, the words not fully registering at first. "What?" she managed, her voice trembling. "That... that's impossible. How? How the hell have you obtained my DNA?"

The detective replied, unfazed by Dana's question. "Your details are stored on a familial database which we accessed. I'm presuming that at some point in the past you've signed up to a heritage search, lots of people do."

Dana gasped, remembering the hereditary site and her

desire to trace her Irish ancestors, more for fun and out of curiosity than anything else. She had no idea her DNA could be accessed by the police or anyone but herself.

At this juncture Ben stood, his body tense and his eyes blazing with anger. "What the fuck are you accusing her of? She had nothing to do with Lexy's death."

"We're not making any accusations at this time," Detective Hayes said carefully, though her sharp gaze remained fixed on Dana. "But the presence of your DNA in Ms. Rivers' clothing—specifically, her undergarments—raises questions that need answering."

Dana's stomach turned, a wave of nausea rising in her throat. "I don't understand," she stammered. "I haven't seen Lexy in weeks. I... I don't know how my DNA could be there. Look, I've just been in an accident, my head if foggy and I can hardly think straight or remember the crash let alone months ago."

Ben stepped closer to the bed, his hand gripping the railing tightly. "My wife is right. You're putting her under pressure when she's been through enough and anyway, this must be a mistake," he said firmly. "Someone's trying to frame her. You need to investigate Justin Birch. He's the one who's been threatening her. Messing with our lives. He's dangerous."

Detective Marshall's eyes narrowed slightly. "Justin Birch's name has come up during our investigation, but that doesn't explain the presence of Mrs. Taylor's DNA."

Dana shook her head vehemently, tears welling in her eyes. "I didn't hurt her. I didn't... I wouldn't. She was my friend."

"We're not here to draw conclusions," Detective Hayes said, her voice softer now but still unyielding. "We're here to gather information. If there's an explanation for the DNA, we need to hear it."

Dana looked at Ben, her chest tightening as she saw the

worry and doubt flickering in his eyes. "You have to believe me," she whispered, her voice cracking. "This isn't what it looks like."

Ben reached for her hand, gripping it tightly. "I believe you," he said, though his voice was strained. Turning back to the detectives, he added, "If you want answers, look at Justin. He's the one orchestrating this."

Detective Marshall exchanged a glance with Hayes before nodding curtly. "We'll be following every lead," he said. "In the meantime, Mrs. Taylor, we ask that you stay available for further questioning."

Dana nodded numbly, the weight of their words pressing down on her like a physical burden. As the detectives left the room, the sound of the door clicking shut felt final, like the closing of a trap.

Ben sat down heavily in the chair beside her bed, his hand still clutching hers. "We'll figure this out," he said, his voice low but steady. "No matter what it takes, we'll prove the truth."

Dana nodded, but her mind was racing. If Justin was behind this—and she was certain he was—then he was more dangerous than she'd ever imagined. And now, he had managed to turn even the authorities against her. The fight to stop him was no longer just about survival. It was about clearing her name and protecting everything she held dear.

35

The ride home from the hospital was quiet, the tension in the car so thick it felt like a physical presence. Dana stared out the window, her wrist throbbing in its cast, her thoughts racing. Ben's gaze was fixed on the road ahead. He hadn't said much since they left the hospital, and his silence weighed on her like a stone.

When they pulled into the driveway, Dana hesitated before opening her door. The house loomed in front of them, its familiar shape now tinged with an ominous air. She felt a pang of unease as she stepped out of the car, the cool evening air biting at her skin. Ben grabbed her bag from the back seat and walked ahead, unlocking the door without waiting for her.

The moment they stepped inside, Dana froze. Something felt off. The air was different, heavy and stale, as if the house had been holding its breath. She glanced around the living room, her eyes scanning the familiar space. It looked the same as always—at first.

But then she noticed the small details. The pile of mail on the table had been shuffled through, the top envelope slightly crumpled. A blanket that usually draped over the back of the couch was now folded neatly on the armrest. Her favorite mug, the one she always left on the kitchen counter, was in the sink, a faint ring of coffee staining the bottom.

"Ben," she said, her voice tight. "Someone's been here."

Ben turned to look at her, his brow furrowing. "What are you talking about?"

"My things have been moved," she said, stepping cautiously into the living room. "The blanket, the mug... This isn't how I left it. The house was immaculate the last time I was here. I spent ages cleaning, and I never use that mug it's ugly. Always the one's with the daisy pattern."

Ben's frown deepened as he set her bag down by the stairs. "Maybe you're just imagining things. It's been a stressful few days."

"I'm not imagining it," Dana insisted, her heart pounding. She moved to the hallway and opened the closet. Her coat, which she distinctly remembered hanging neatly, was now crumpled on the floor. Her stomach spasmed as the unease morphed into a cold certainty. "He's been here. Justin's been in the house."

Ben sighed heavily, running a hand through his hair. "Dana, we don't know that. It could have been anyone. Maybe it's nothing."

She turned to face him, her eyes blazing. "Nothing? You think this is nothing? He's been stalking me for months, Ben. He killed Lexy, and now he's trying to make me look like a suspect. Do you really think he'd stop short of breaking into our home?"

Ben's expression hardened, his jaw tightening. "I don't know what to think anymore, Dana. I'm trying to make sense of all this, but every time I turn around, there's another twist, another thing you didn't tell me."

Her chest tightened at his words, and she took a step back. "You think I'm lying?"

"I think..." He trailed off, shaking his head. "I think I don't know who to trust right now. Your DNA was found on Lexy's body, Dana. Do you have any idea how that looks?"

Tears welled in her eyes, but she refused to let them fall. "You think I'm capable of hurting her? Lexy was my friend. She was trying to help me."

Ben looked away, his silence cutting deeper than any words could have. He walked past her and into the kitchen, leaving her standing alone in the hallway. The sound of him opening a cabinet and slamming it shut echoed through the house.

Dana stood there for a long moment, her breathing shallow. She felt the walls closing in, the house that had once been her sanctuary now feeling like a trap. Every creak of the floorboards, every shadow seemed to carry Justin's presence. She turned and locked the front door, double-checking the bolt before moving to the windows to ensure they were secure.

As she walked through the house, her unease grew. In the bedroom, she noticed her jewelry box slightly ajar, a pair of earrings missing from their usual spot. In the bathroom, a hand towel was damp, though she hadn't used it since before the crash. The evidence was everywhere, small but undeniable. Justin had been here, and he wanted her to know it.

When she returned to the living room, Ben was sitting in front of the television, his face buried in his hands. She stood in the doorway, her voice soft but firm. "I need you to believe me, Ben. I need you to be on my side."

He looked up at her, his eyes tired and filled with conflict. "I want to, Dana. I really do."

Her heart broke at his words, but she refused to let the fear and doubt consume her. "Then help me prove it. Help me show them that Justin is the one behind all of this. I can't do it alone."

Ben stared at her for a long moment, then nodded slowly.

"Okay. We'll figure it out. But you need to be honest with me about everything. No more secrets."

Dana nodded, a flicker of hope igniting within her. "No more secrets."

The tension in the room eased slightly, but the shadow of Justin's presence lingered.

~

The knock on the door was sharp and commanding, reverberating through the house. Dana froze, her hands trembling as she clutched the edge of the kitchen counter. Ben looked up, his face tightening as he rose to answer it. The tension in the air was palpable, and Dana's stomach turned over with a mix of dread and defiance.

When Ben opened the door, two uniformed officers stood on the porch, their expressions neutral but firm. Behind them, Detective Marshall and Detective Hayes lingered, their presence a stark reminder of the gravity of the situation.

"Mr. Taylor? Mrs. Taylor?" Detective Hayes stepped forward. "We'd like to ask you some more questions, if you don't mind."

Ben opened the door wider, gesturing for them to come in. "Do we have a choice?" he muttered under his breath, but loud enough for them to hear.

Detective Hayes didn't react, stepping into the living room with her partner in tow. Dana forced herself to move from the kitchen to join them, her casted wrist resting awkwardly at her side. She nodded. "Please, sit."

"We'll stand, thank you," Detective Marshall replied curtly. He pulled a notepad from his pocket, flipping it open. "Mrs. Taylor, we'd like to discuss the evidence you provided and revisit some of the circumstances surrounding Lexy Rivers' death."

Dana's heart sank. She had been hoping this visit would

mean progress—an acknowledgment of Justin's involvement—but the detectives' rigid posture and unyielding gazes told her otherwise.

"Of course," she said, trying to steady her voice. "I've compiled everything I have on Justin Birch. His threats, the stalking, his connections to Lexy... It's all here." She gestured to a folder on the coffee table, neatly labeled and bulging with printed emails, screenshots, and notes.

Detective Hayes glanced at the folder but didn't reach for it. Instead, she looked directly at Dana. "We'll review that, but first, we need to address some inconsistencies."

"Inconsistencies?" Dana's voice wavered.

"Your DNA was found on Ms. Rivers' body," Detective Marshall said bluntly. "I'll ask again. Can you explain how it got there?"

Dana swallowed hard. Her mouth dry. "I... I don't know. I told you. I haven't seen Lexy in weeks. The last time we met, we shook hands, hugged maybe, but that's it."

"When was this last meeting?" Detective Hayes pressed.

"About five weeks ago," Dana replied. "We met at a café to discuss Justin. She was helping me gather information on him."

Detective Marshall scribbled something in his notebook. "Do you have anyone who can confirm your whereabouts during the likely time of death? Specifically, last Tuesday evening?"

Dana's mind raced. Tuesday. She had been home, alone, trying to piece together her next steps. "I was here," she said carefully. "Alone. Ben was with Ethan at Rachel's house."

Ben's face darkened, but he remained silent, his jaw clenched.

"No one can corroborate that?" Detective Hayes's tone was probing.

Dana shook her head. "No. But Justin... he's the one you

should be looking at! He has a history of violence, of stalking. Lexy was digging into his past, and now she's dead. Don't you see the connection?"

"We're aware of Mr. Birch's background," Detective Marshall said evenly. "But right now, we're focused on the evidence at hand. Your DNA, Mrs. Taylor, puts you at the center of this investigation."

Dana's chest tightened. "I'm being framed," she said desperately. "Justin's done this before. He's manipulative, he's calculated. You have to believe me."

Detective Hayes's sharp gaze bore into Dana. "Framed or not, Mrs. Taylor, the evidence doesn't lie. Your DNA was found in an intimate location on Ms. Rivers' body. Can you explain that?"

Dana's stomach turned. Intimate location? The words hit her like a physical blow. "No," she stammered, her voice cracking. "That doesn't make sense. Someone must have planted it."

Detective Marshall's pen scratched across the notepad. "Do you have any items of personal clothing or toiletries missing? Anything Justin could have used to obtain your DNA?"

Dana's mind raced back to the unsettling discoveries at home: the moved blanket, the crumpled coat, the missing earrings. Her throat tightened. "I... I think so. Some of my things have been... tampered with. He's been in my house. I'm sure of it."

Detective Hayes exchanged a glance with Marshall, her expression skeptical. "Do you have proof of that? Security footage? Witnesses?"

"No," Dana admitted, her voice shaking. "But you must believe me. He's doing this to punish me, to make me look guilty."

"Or" Detective Marshall said, his tone measured but pointed, "you're trying to shift blame onto Justin Birch to cover up your own involvement."

Dana's eyes widened, her chest heaving. "How can you say that? I loved Lexy. She was my friend."

"People have killed for less," Hayes said coldly. "Until we have more evidence, every possibility remains on the table."

Ben finally spoke, his voice low but firm. "This is ridiculous. You're wasting time harassing my wife while Justin Birch walks free. Why aren't you investigating him?"

Detective Marshall closed his notebook with a snap. "Thank you for your time, Mr. Taylor. Mrs. Taylor, we'll be in touch."

As the detectives turned and left, Dana collapsed onto the couch, her entire body trembling. Ben stood silently for a moment before sitting down beside her, his face etched with worry and frustration.

"He's framing me," Dana whispered, tears streaming down her face. "And they're falling for it."

Ben put a hand on her shoulder, his grip firm but his words not entirely reassuring. "I think you need to be prepared, Dana. This isn't going away anytime soon."

As the door clicked shut behind the detectives, Dana felt a chilling certainty settle over her. She was running out of time to prove her innocence.

36

The evening air was unusually still, the kind of quiet that seemed to amplify every small noise. Dana sat in the living room, the glow of the television washing over her as the latest news played in the background. She wasn't really watching it, her mind too clouded with fear and exhaustion to focus. Ben was in the kitchen, clanging dishes and muttering under his breath—a poor attempt at masking his frustration. They'd hardly spoken since the police visit earlier that day, the weight of their unspoken tension thickening the air between them.

A sudden noise outside startled Dana. It was faint at first, a metallic clinking that seemed to come from the driveway. She stiffened, her pulse quickening. "Ben?" she called, her voice trembling.

Ben appeared in the doorway, wiping his hands on a dish towel. "What is it?"

"Did you hear that?" she asked, her eyes darting toward the window. "I think... I think someone's outside."

Ben frowned, his expression shifting from irritation to concern. He grabbed a flashlight from the utility drawer and headed to the front door. "Stay here," he said firmly, slipping on his shoes and stepping out into the night.

Dana's heart raced as she watched him through the window. The flashlight beam cut through the darkness, sweeping across the driveway and the front lawn. Ben stopped abruptly, his posture stiffening. "Dana," he called, his voice tight. "You need to see this."

She hesitated for a moment before grabbing her sweater and stepping outside. The cold air hit her like a slap, but it did little to numb the sinking feeling in her chest. She joined Ben in the driveway, her breath catching when she saw the state of his car. The windshield had been shattered, spiderweb cracks radiating across the glass. Deep gouges were carved into the paint, stretching from the hood to the trunk, as though someone had taken a key or a sharp object and methodically scratched every surface. The side mirrors dangled uselessly, and the tires were completely slashed, the car sitting lopsided on its rims.

"Oh my God," Dana whispered, her hand flying to her mouth. "He did this. Justin did this."

Ben's face darkened; his knuckles white as he gripped the flashlight. "We don't know that" he said, though his tone lacked conviction.

"Who else would it be?" Dana snapped, her voice rising. "This is what he does, Ben. He's trying to scare us, to make us feel powerless."

As Ben moved closer to inspect the damage, he opened the driver's door. A foul smell immediately wafted out, causing him to recoil. "What the hell?" he muttered, shining the flashlight inside. The seats were soaked, dark stains spreading across the upholstery. Dana stepped closer, her stomach turning as the acrid stench hit her.

"Is that... urine?" she asked, horrified. The smell was

unmistakable, sharp and invasive, permeating the air around them.

Ben's jaw tightened, his face a mask of anger and disgust. "He's escalating," he said through gritted teeth. "This isn't just vandalism. This is personal."

Before Dana could respond, a deafening screech filled the air, making them jump. The house alarm had gone off, blaring in every room. The sound was shrill and relentless, echoing through the neighborhood like a siren. Dana clutched her ears, her heart pounding. "What now?" she shouted over the noise.

Ben ran back toward the house, his flashlight beam bouncing wildly. Dana followed, her ears ringing from the alarm. Inside, the lights flickered erratically, casting disorienting shadows across the walls. The security panel by the front door was flashing red, the word "TAMPERED" displayed on the screen.

"The system's malfunctioning," Ben said, his voice barely audible over the screaming alarm. He pressed a series of buttons on the keypad, but nothing happened. "It's completely fried."

Dana's hands trembled as she watched him work. "He's been here," she said, her voice cracking. "He's been watching us, Ben. He's inside our heads."

Ben slammed his fist against the wall in frustration. "We need to call the police. Now."

Dana nodded, though a part of her felt defeated. The police hadn't believed her before. Why would this time be any different? Still, she followed Ben into the kitchen, where he grabbed his phone and dialed the non-emergency number. The shrill alarm continued to wail, making it nearly impossible to hear the dispatcher on the other end of the line.

When Ben hung up, he turned to Dana, his expression grim. "They'll send someone over, but it could take a while."

Dana's whole body slumped, her head in her hands. The

noise of the alarm felt like a physical assault, amplifying her sense of helplessness. Ben sat beside her, his presence a small comfort despite the growing chasm between them. "We'll get through this," he said quietly, though his voice lacked its usual steadiness.

Dana looked up at him, her eyes filled with a mixture of fear and determination. "I don't know how much more I can take, Ben. He's not just trying to scare us. He's trying to destroy us."

Ben hesitated, then placed a hand on her knee. "Then we fight back. We'll get the security system fixed, and we'll make the police listen. He won't win, Dana."

She nodded, though the doubt lingered. As Ben got up to check the windows and doors again, she stared at the wreckage of his car through the window. Justin's message was clear: he wasn't done. And deep down, Dana feared the worst was yet to come.

37

The countryside air was crisp, carrying the faint scent of pollen and freshly mown grass. Rachel's charming stone cottage was nestled on a quiet lane, surrounded by rolling fields that stretched as far as the eye could see. The garden behind the house was spacious and well-kept, a mix of vibrant flowerbeds and lush green lawn bordered by a low wooden fence. A weathered picnic table sat beneath the shade of a towering oak tree.

Ethan's laughter rang out across the yard as he chased Rachel's golden retriever, Max, who bounded playfully ahead of him with a stick in his mouth. The boy's cheeks were flushed with excitement, his dark curls bouncing as he ran. Rachel stood nearby, her hands on her hips, smiling warmly as she watched her nephew. She wore a simple floral sundress and a pair of muddy boots, a practical choice for keeping up with an energetic boy and an equally rambunctious dog.

"Come on, Ethan! Don't let him win!" Rachel called, her voice teasing.

Ethan doubled his efforts, sprinting after Max and finally grabbing hold of the stick. The dog barked happily, wagging his tail as he tugged back, turning it into a game of strength. Ethan giggled, his grip firm but his small frame no match for Max's exuberance.

"Max, you're cheating!" Ethan exclaimed, laughing so hard he nearly fell over. Rachel walked over and gently pried the stick from the dog's mouth, holding it high above her head.

"There, now it's fair," she said with a grin, handing the stick back to Ethan. "But you'd better throw it before he jumps for it again."

Ethan obediently hurled the stick across the garden, and Max took off like a shot, his golden fur gleaming in the afternoon sunlight. The boy clapped his hands in delight and turned to Rachel. "Did you see that? He's so fast!"

"I did," Rachel replied, ruffling Ethan's hair affectionately. "You're pretty fast yourself. I think Max has met his match."

Ethan beamed up at her, his eyes shining with happiness. "I love it here, Aunt Rachel. It's so much fun. Max is the best dog ever."

Rachel's heart swelled at his words. "I'm glad you're having fun, sweetheart. It's nice to have you here. The house feels a lot livelier with you around."

They wandered back toward the picnic table, where Rachel had set out a pitcher of lemonade and a plate of cookies. The sun filtered through the branches of the oak tree, casting dappled shadows on the table. Ethan climbed onto the bench, pouring himself a glass of lemonade with a careful precision that made Rachel smile.

"Your mom and dad must be missing you," she said gently, taking a seat beside him. "But I'm glad I get to spend some time with you."

Ethan's expression grew a little more serious, and he looked down at his glass. "Mom and Dad have been fighting a lot," he admitted softly. "That's why I'm here, isn't it?"

Rachel's chest tightened. She reached out and placed a comforting hand on his shoulder. "Sometimes grown-ups have things they need to work out," she said carefully. "But that doesn't mean they don't love you. They just want to make sure you're safe and happy while they figure things out."

Ethan nodded slowly, his young mind processing her words. After a moment, he looked up at her with a small smile. "I feel safe here. And I'm happy."

Rachel smiled back, her throat tightening with emotion. "That's all that matters, sweetheart. And while you're here, we'll have as much fun as we can, okay?"

"Okay," Ethan said, his smile widening. He took a big bite of a cookie and glanced toward Max, who had returned with the stick and was lying in the grass, chewing contentedly.

The peaceful scene felt like a world away from the turmoil that had brought Ethan to her doorstep. Rachel silently vowed to protect her nephew from the shadows that loomed over his family, if only for a little while longer.

~

But as the sun began to dip lower in the sky, casting long shadows across the garden, a figure stood hidden behind the dense line of trees that bordered Rachel's property. Justin watched the scene unfold from a distance; his piercing eyes locked on Ethan. His expression was a mix of curiosity and cold determination. A camera hung from his neck, and he lifted it to snap several photos of the boy as he played with Max, his laughter carrying faintly on the breeze.

Justin's lips curled into a sinister smile as he lowered the camera. He adjusted the strap on his shoulder and muttered under his breath, "Soon, little one. Very soon."

~

Rachel and Ethan remained oblivious to his presence, their laughter and conversation filling the garden. Max barked happily, chasing the stick Ethan threw again and again, but the dog's ears twitched slightly as if sensing something amiss. He paused, his head tilting toward the trees, a low growl rumbling in his throat. Rachel glanced at him, her brow furrowing slightly.

"What's wrong, Max?" she asked, her gaze following the dog's fixed stare. She saw nothing but the gently swaying trees and the fading light of the evening. "It's probably just a squirrel," she said with a laugh, patting the dog's head.

Justin stepped back deeper into the shadows. His presence undetected. The game he was playing was far from over, and he was ready to take his next move.

38

The two detectives stood in the shadow of the towering oak that bordered Rachel Sterling's back garden. The winter sun offered no warmth, casting long, cold shadows over the crime scene. Yellow tape fluttered in the wind, cordoning off the meticulously maintained garden that now served as the site of something gruesome and unnatural. Rachel's body had been discovered sprawled near the edge of her ornamental pond, her lifeless form disturbingly at odds with the tranquility of the setting.

Detective Inspector Harriet Blake crouched by the edge of the garden path, her gloved hand brushing against a tuft of grass. She examined the ground, noting the faint, uneven footprints that had already been photographed and marked.

"They dragged her," she muttered, half to herself. The thought made her stomach churn.

Detective Sergeant Tom Fielding stood behind her, a gash to her head, arms crossed tightly over his chest as if trying to ward off the chill. His eyes, sharp and dark, roamed the garden, darting between the evidence markers and the gnarled branches above.

"This isn't random," he said finally, his voice low and steady.

"Someone wanted her dead. Subdued her with a blow to the head then strangled her." She gestured vaguely toward the pond, the bruises visible on Rachel's neck.

Blake straightened up and removed her gloves, rubbing her temples. "It's personal," she agreed. "But there's no sign of a break-in, no defensive wounds on her hands." She trailed off, glancing back at the pond, its surface frozen over, the cracks in the ice mirroring the fracture lines in her own thoughts.

Fielding responded grimly. "Could be a lover. A friend. Someone she trusted."

"Or someone she feared," Blake countered, folding her arms tightly against her chest. She glanced toward the house, its windows dark and empty, the door still swinging slightly from the bustle of the forensic team moving in and out.

"Fielding picked up the narrative. "From what the attending officers got out of the kid who was in a state then they arrived, he's staying here because there's a bad man who has been mean to his mom. His dad left him here with his aunt Rachel. He was in the house with the dog," he checked his notes, "Max, and from the kitchen window saw the man hurting his aunt, so he took the dog and hid in the downstairs closet. That's all they got out of him. It was a neighbor that found Rachel," again he referred to his notes, "Mrs. Ida Green, who called with some muffins for Ethan. She rang 911 immediately then found Ethan and the dog in their hiding place."

Blake whistled out a breath. "Looks like this could be some kind of grudge killing then. We need to speak to the parents as a matter of urgency. I take it they are on their way."

Fielding replied. "Heading here as we speak. Hopefully they'll shed some light on who this bad guy is and maybe get some more out of the kid. It takes a particular kind of mind to do this. Someone patient. Methodical. Not just a crime of passion. I think this was planned."

Blake nodded, her eyes narrowing as she processed his words. "You're right. They took their time.

Fielding murmured again, almost to himself. "Did he know her nephew was inside? The sick fuck. And lord only knows what would've happened if the dog had gone to her rescue. Who would be brazen enough to walk into someone's garden and attack like this in broad daylight?"

Blake's voice was steady but cold when she replied. "Someone who thinks they're untouchable. Someone who thinks they're clever enough to get away with it." She turned to him, her eyes hard. "But they're wrong."

"Or someone who doesn't care if they get caught." Fielding countered.

Blake glanced back at the house, the garden, the pond, and the faint footprints that told a fragmented story. They would piece it together. She would make sure of it. Whoever had done this—whatever kind of person they were—they wouldn't stay at liberty for long.

~

Ethan sat in the corner of the living room, curled up on the oversized armchair. His small frame seemed even smaller, tucked into itself like he was trying to disappear. His eyes stared blankly at the floor, unblinking, while his hands gripped the fabric of his jeans so tightly his knuckles were white. The boy hadn't uttered a single word since he'd been brought home by the police.

Dana knelt in front of him, her broken wrist awkwardly held against her chest as she tried to meet his vacant gaze. "Ethan, sweetheart," she said gently, her voice trembling. "It's Mommy. Can you look at me? Please?"

But Ethan didn't respond. His breathing was shallow, his

chest rising and falling in quick, uneven bursts. Dana reached out, but he flinched, shrinking further into the chair. The sight broke her heart into pieces.

Ben stood nearby; his arms crossed tightly over his chest. His face was pale, his expression torn between grief and rage. He looked at the two officers standing in the doorway, their notepads in hand and their faces grim.

"This isn't helping," Ben said sharply, his voice thick with frustration. "He's traumatized. He just watched his aunt get murdered. What do you expect him to do?"

Detective Marshall cleared his throat. "We understand this is difficult, Mr. Taylor, but any description he can give us might help us identify the suspect. Time is critical in cases like this."

Dana turned to the officers; her tear-streaked face filled with desperation. "He's a child," she pleaded. "Can't you see he's in shock? He can't talk right now."

Detective Hayes stepped forward. Her voice softer but no less insistent. "Mrs. Taylor, we're not asking him to relive everything. Just a few questions about what the man looked like. Did he have a beard? Was he tall or short?"

At that moment, Ethan let out a small whimper. His eyes darted toward the officers, and then he quickly looked away. His hands trembled, and his breathing became more erratic. Dana reached for him again, but before she could comfort him, he suddenly wet himself, the dark stain spreading across his jeans.

Dana gasped, her hands flying to her mouth. Ben moved quickly, kneeling beside the chair and wrapping an arm around his son. "It's okay," he said softly, his voice shaking. "You're safe now, Ethan. You're safe."

Ethan buried his face in his father's chest, his small body trembling uncontrollably. Dana's tears fell freely as she watched the scene, her helplessness almost unbearable.

"That's enough," Ben said, his voice cold and hard as he

looked up at the officers. "He's done for tonight. No more questions."

The officers hesitated, but eventually, Detective Marshall nodded. "We'll step outside. If he remembers anything, please let us know immediately."

As the officers exited the house, Ben scooped Ethan up, carrying him toward the bathroom to clean him up. Dana followed, her hands trembling as she tried to help, but Ethan wouldn't let go of Ben. He clung to his father as though his life depended on it. His sobs muffled against Ben's chest.

When they finally settled Ethan into his bed, his face was pale, and his eyes remained wide open, staring at the ceiling. Dana sat on the edge of the bed, stroking his hair gently, but he didn't react. Ben stood at the door, his hands gripping the frame as though he needed it to steady himself.

"We have to do something," Dana said quietly, her voice barely above a whisper. "Justin... this is Justin's doing. He's not going to stop until... until he takes everything from us."

Ben's face darkened, his jaw tightening. "We're going to make them listen," he said firmly. "Tomorrow, we go to the station. We demand they bring Justin in. If they don't, I swear to God I'll drag him in myself."

Dana nodded, her tears falling silently as she looked back at Ethan. The weight of the night's events pressed heavily on her chest, but beneath the despair was a burning determination. They had to protect their son. They had to end this nightmare.

Later that evening, the house was cloaked in a heavy silence. Ethan had finally fallen asleep, though his quiet whimpers still echoed in Dana's mind. Ben sat on the edge of the couch, staring blankly at the coffee table. His face was pale, his eyes rimmed red from tears he hadn't tried to hide.

"I can't believe she's gone," Ben said finally, his voice raw and hollow. "Rachel... she didn't deserve this. She didn't..." His voice broke, and he buried his face in his hands.

Dana sat beside him, her own grief and guilt threatening to suffocate her. She placed a trembling hand on his shoulder, but he didn't move. "I'm so sorry, Ben," she whispered. "I never wanted any of this to happen. This is my fault. If it weren't for Justin..."

Ben's head snapped up, his eyes blazing with anger and anguish. "You think saying sorry will fix this?" he demanded. "My sister is dead. Dead, Dana. And Ethan... he saw it. He saw her die because that lunatic is obsessed with you. How am I supposed to forgive that? How am I supposed to live with this?"

Dana flinched at his words, her throat tightening. She knew he was right. She knew the guilt was hers to bear. But before she could respond, a sudden thought struck her, chilling her to the core.

"Ben," she said softly, her voice shaking. "There's something else you need to know."

He frowned, his expression hardening further. "What now?"

Dana stood and moved to the utility room, where a bouquet of white lilies lay on the counter. She had placed them there earlier, hoping to ignore their presence until she had the courage to tell Ben. She picked up the small card that had come with the flowers and held it out to him, her hand trembling.

Ben took the card, his brow furrowing as he read it. His face darkened, his hands clenching around the small piece of paper. The words were scrawled in a sharp, jagged hand:

If you erase my child. I will erase yours.

. . .

Ben's head shot up, his eyes wide with fury and horror. "Is this some kind of sick joke?" he demanded, his voice rising. "When did this get here?"

"It was delivered earlier while you were in the shower," Dana admitted, her voice barely above a whisper. "I didn't know how to tell you. I... I was scared."

Ben threw the card onto the counter as if it had burned him. "Scared?" he repeated, his voice shaking with anger. "You should have called the police the second this arrived. He's threatening Ethan now, Dana. Our son. This isn't just about you anymore."

"I know that!" Dana shot back, her own voice trembling with emotion. "Don't you think I know that? I've been trying to protect you and Ethan, but he's everywhere, Ben. He knows everything. I don't know what to do."

Ben paced the room, his fists clenching and unclenching. "We're calling the police again," he said firmly. "If they don't take this seriously, I swear I'll handle Justin myself. He doesn't get to threaten my family and walk away."

Dana sank into a chair, her head in her hands. "He's unhinged, Ben. I... I don't know if the police can stop him in time."

Ben stopped pacing and looked at her, his expression softening just slightly. He knelt in front of her, his hands gripping her knees. "Then we make them listen," he said quietly but firmly. "We do whatever it takes to protect Ethan. He's all that matters now. You hear me?"

Dana nodded, tears streaming down her face. "I hear you," she whispered.

But deep down, she couldn't shake the feeling that Justin was always one step ahead. And with Rachel gone and Ethan now in his sights, she feared they were running out of time.

39

The following morning was unnaturally quiet. Dana shuffled down the stairs, her body still heavy with exhaustion from the night before. Ben was already in the kitchen, his back to her as he stared into a mug of coffee. The house felt hollow, each step she took echoing unnaturally.

She reached the front door, intending to check the mail, but stopped short when she noticed something lying on the doormat. A single folded leaflet sat there, stark against the neutral tones of the hallway. Frowning, she bent down and picked it up, her stomach flipping at the sight of the bold black text on the cover:

"Who Is Dana Taylor Really?"

Her hands shook as she opened it. The contents made her blood run cold. Photographs of her—intimate, invasive, and deeply humiliating—were plastered across the pages. Images of her with Justin, moments she hadn't even realized had been captured, filled the leaflet. Her breath hitched, and she felt a wave of nausea rise as she recognized the bedroom from Justin's penthouse. The captions beneath the photos were cruel and damning: "**A Mother and a Mistress,**" and "**The Real Reason Behind the Drama.**"

Dana staggered backward, her knees nearly giving out. "Ben!" she called out, her voice barely above a whisper.

He appeared in the doorway, his brows furrowed in concern. "What is it?"

Wordlessly, she handed him the leaflet. His eyes scanned the pages, his face darkening with every passing second. "What the hell is this?" he growled, gripping the leaflet tightly.

Before Dana could answer, a gust of wind blew through the slight crack in the door, scattering more leaflets that had been piled on the porch. Dana stepped outside, her heart sinking as she took in the scene. The leaflets weren't just on her doorstep—they were everywhere. They littered the street, caught in bushes and gutters, some stapled to trees and telephone poles. A few fluttered down the road, carried by the breeze like grotesque confetti.

Neighbors were already outside, their faces a mixture of curiosity and disdain as they picked up the leaflets. Dana's chest tightened as she saw Mrs. Henderson from across the street holding one, her lips pursed in disapproval.

"This can't be happening," Dana whispered, her voice cracking.

Ben stepped out beside her; his jaw clenched as he scanned the street, his tone grim. "This is his way of humiliating you. Of humiliating us."

Dana turned to him, her eyes wide and filled with tears. "What do we do? Ben, what do we do?"

He looked at her, his face hard but resolute. "Whatever it takes to put a stop to this."

Dana nodded, though her legs felt like jelly beneath her. She looked down the street again, watching as more leaflets fluttered by, their glossy images flashing like a cruel reminder of her mistake. The humiliation was overwhelming, but beneath it all was a growing fire of anger.

"He thinks he can ruin me," she muttered, more to herself than to Ben. "He thinks he can destroy everything I have."

Ben placed a hand on her shoulder, grounding her. "He won't. We won't let him."

But as Dana looked back at the leaflets scattered like debris, she admitted to herself that Justin had already won this round. And she wasn't sure how many more she had left in her.

This time, presented with the leaflets and the unavoidable fact that the photos showing inside Justin's apartment could be used as evidence against him, the detectives had taken Dana's claim a lot more seriously. With luck, the urine samples taken from Ben's car would also be linked to Justin and the case made stronger.

They'd also assured Ben and Dana that all leads were being followed to find Rachel's killer, including speaking to Justin but it seemed like he'd gone off grid and for the time being, was untraceable. The detectives hinted that rather than make a rookie error leaving DNA in Ben's car, Justin's behavior was becoming dangerously erratic, a sentence that struck fear into Dana's heart.

Left alone with the detective's solemn words, Dana and Ben sat at the kitchen table, the stack of leaflets between them like a silent accusation. Ben's face was drawn, his lips pressed into a thin line as he flipped through the pages again. Dana couldn't bring herself to look. Her stomach heaved with nausea and shame.

"These are disgusting," Ben said finally, his voice low but laced with anger. "How could you not know that piece of shit was taking these photos?"

"I didn't know," Dana whispered, her head in her hands. "I swear, Ben. I had no idea. He must have had cameras set up in his apartment. I never saw them."

Ben slammed the stack down on the table, making her flinch. "This is sick. How many people have seen these, Dana? How many?"

Dana's voice cracked as she tried to answer. "I don't know. But Ben... there's more. Something I just realized."

He looked at her, his eyes narrowing. "What?"

Dana's throat tightened, and she struggled to get the words out. "The... the DNA they found on Lexy. I think I know how it got there."

Ben's eyes widened, his expression shifting from anger to horror. "What are you talking about?"

"I left something at Justin's apartment," Dana admitted, her voice barely audible. "A pair of... panties and stockings. I was in such a panic to leave and get home. He must have kept them. He must have used them to frame me."

The color drained from Ben's face. He pushed back from the table, standing abruptly and pacing the room. "You're telling me that the reason your DNA is on Lexy's body is because of your... your underwear?"

Dana nodded, tears streaming down her face. "I didn't think about it until now. My head has been all over the place. It's the only explanation. He's been planning this, Ben. He's been planning everything."

Ben turned away from her, his hands on his hips as he stared out the window. "This just keeps getting worse," he muttered. "Every time I think it can't get worse, it does. That freak has gone missing, and we both know that with his money and contacts, it's highly likely he's paid someone to help him disappear and now, you suddenly remember a vital piece of the puzzle."

"Ben, please," Dana said, standing and reaching for him. "I'm so sorry. I'll ring the detectives straight away and tell them."

He turned back to her, his face hard. "You must. Because if you don't, I will. I don't care how embarrassed you are telling them your seedy tale. This has gone too far, Dana. I can't do this anymore."

Dana's breath hitched. "What do you mean?"

"I mean I'm taking Ethan to stay with my parents," Ben said firmly. "They're devastated about Rachel, and they need us. And Ethan needs to be somewhere safe. Away from this. Away from you."

Dana felt like the air had been knocked out of her. "Ben, no. Please don't do this again. I need you. I need both of you."

"You need to fix this," Ben said, his voice breaking. "But I can't let Ethan get caught in the middle anymore. Not after what happened to Rachel. Not now Justin is off grid."

He turned and left the room, leaving Dana alone with the stack of leaflets and the crushing weight of her mistakes.

40

The sound of Ben's heavy footsteps on the stairs echoed through the house, each one a reminder to Dana of the widening chasm between them. Her eyes flicked to the window, where she could see the outline of the police cruiser parked outside, the faint glow of its headlights cutting through the early evening gloom. A police escort, waiting to take her husband and son to safety—away from her.

Dana's heart clenched painfully as she heard the faint murmur of Ben's voice as he spoke to Ethan. She imagined the little boy's confused face, his wide eyes filled with questions he was too afraid to ask. The thought was almost unbearable.

Unable to sit still any longer, Dana rose and climbed the stairs, her steps tentative. She paused at the doorway to Ethan's room, where Ben was kneeling in front of their son, zipping up a small blue suitcase. Ethan clutched his favorite stuffed animal, a worn-out bunny, to his chest, his lower lip trembling as he looked between his parents.

"I don't want to go," Ethan whispered, his voice breaking.

Ben placed a hand on Ethan's shoulder. "I know, buddy," he

said gently. "But it's just for a little while. Grandma and Grandpa are excited to see you. They'll take good care of you."

Dana stepped into the room, her throat tightening. "Ben, please," she said, her voice trembling. "Don't do this. Don't take him away from me."

Ben stood, turning to face her. His expression was hard, his eyes filled with a mixture of pain and determination. "He needs to be somewhere safe, Dana. After everything that's happened... after Rachel... I can't risk him getting hurt."

"You think I don't want him to be safe?" she asked, her voice rising. "I'm his mother, Ben. I love him more than anything. Please don't take him away from me. Don't take both of you away."

Ben sighed heavily, running a hand through his hair. "This isn't about punishing you, Dana. It's about protecting him. And right now, I'm not sure he's safe here."

Tears streamed down Dana's face as she stepped closer, her hands trembling. "Ben don't leave me. Please."

Ben's jaw tightened as he looked at her, his eyes glistening with unshed tears. "You should have done that already," he said quietly. "You should have gone to the police the moment Justin started threatening you. But you didn't, and now Rachel is dead. And Ethan... he's scared of his own shadow. I've got to do what's best for him, Dana. Even if it hurts."

Dana shook her head, her voice breaking. "Ben, please..."

Before she could say more, Ethan let out a small sob. "Mommy," he whispered, reaching for her. Dana knelt, wrapping her arms around him as he buried his face in her shoulder.

"It's okay, sweetheart," she said softly, stroking his hair. "It's going to be okay."

Ben's voice was firm but gentle. "Dana, the officers are waiting. We need to go."

She looked up at him, her tears blurring her vision. "I... I can't say goodbye. Not like this."

Ben's expression softened for a moment, but he quickly steeled himself. "It's not goodbye. It's just for now."

Ethan clung to Dana, his small body trembling. "I don't want to go," he whispered again.

Dana kissed the top of his head, her tears falling into his hair. "I know, baby. I know. But you'll be safe, and that's the most important thing."

After a long moment, Ben gently pulled Ethan away. The boy's cries pierced Dana's heart as she watched them leave the room, the small suitcase trailing behind. She followed them to the front door, where the two officers stood waiting. Ethan looked back at her, his tear-streaked face breaking what little resolve she had left.

As the door closed behind them, Dana collapsed onto the floor, sobbing uncontrollably. The house felt emptier than ever, and the silence that followed was deafening.

The silence stretched long after Ben and Ethan were gone, broken only by the occasional sound of traffic outside. Dana sat, her body frozen, eyes staring at the front door as though willing it to open and bring them back. Instead, the creak of the floorboards startled her, and she turned to see Officer Martinez, the younger of the two officers, standing awkwardly by the doorway. As a precaution, Dana had been given a police guard.

"Mrs. Taylor," Martinez said gently, breaking the stillness. "I'll be here throughout the night. If you need anything, just let me know."

Dana nodded numbly, her voice barely above a whisper. "Thank you."

Martinez hesitated, then moved to stand by the window, his posture straight but his expression unreadable. Dana watched him for a moment before her mind drifted to Justin. The thought of him sent a chill down her spine, and she swallowed hard.

"Have you found him yet?" she asked suddenly, her voice breaking the quiet.

Martinez turned to face her, his brow furrowing slightly. "Not yet," he admitted. "But we're doing everything we can. There's a team dedicated to tracking him down. He won't stay hidden for long."

Dana's fingers dug into the fabric of the chair. "He's not hiding, he's waiting," she said softly, more to herself than to Martinez. "He's been here. Watching. Since the night we..." Her voice trailed off, and she shook her head. "He's always close by."

Martinez's expression grew more serious. "If you suspect he's nearby, that's something we need to know. Any detail, no matter how small, could help us find him."

An idea began to form in Dana's mind, a spark of clarity cutting through the fog of fear and grief. She straightened slightly, her gaze sharpening. "If he's close, maybe there's some way I can draw him out," she murmured.

Martinez's eyes narrowed. "Mrs. Taylor, that sounds dangerous. What are you thinking?"

Dana didn't answer right away, her thoughts racing. If she could anticipate Justin's next move, maybe, just maybe, she could turn the tables.

"I need to think," she said finally, her voice steadying. "But if we're going to stop him, we have to be smarter than he is."

Martinez watched her carefully, his jaw tightening. "Whatever you're planning, make sure you tell us first. I don't want you putting yourself in more danger."

Dana nodded, though she wasn't sure she entirely meant it.

The spark of determination inside her was growing, pushing back against the fear. For the first time in weeks, she felt like she had a shred of control. And she was going to use it.

41

Ben's mind wandered as he drove along the familiar winding roads leading to his parents' home. His thoughts drifted to the life he'd once imagined for himself, long before the chaos of recent months.

He had grown up in a quiet New England town, nestled among rolling hills and thick forests. The cozy home where he and his sister Rachel were raised had always felt sturdy, immovable—much like their family. His father, Robert, was a high school history teacher, the type who commanded respect with his booming voice and genuine passion for the Revolutionary War. His mother, Margaret, was a nurse, sharp-eyed and no-nonsense, who ran the household like a well-oiled machine. She loved her family fiercely but expected the best from everyone, especially her children.

Rachel and Ben couldn't have been more different. Where Rachel was the outspoken dreamer, always pushing boundaries, Ben was the dependable one. He was the kid who helped his dad mow the lawn without being asked, who brought home good grades without needing much encouragement. Rachel would roll her eyes at his predictability, calling him "Dad's little soldier," but she loved him for it, even if she rarely admitted it.

Ben had always wanted stability in life, perhaps because Rachel's chaos had so often tipped the balance at home. After high school, he chose a practical path, earning a degree in finance and landing a job at a mid-sized firm in Boston. He had a knack for numbers and problem-solving, rising quickly through the ranks thanks to his work ethic and steady demeanor. It wasn't glamorous work, but it gave him the sense of control and security he'd always craved.

Meeting Dana had been the curveball he never expected. He still remembered the first time he saw her. Her laughter cutting through the chatter like a bright summer breeze. She was radiant, with her intelligent eyes and infectious smile, and she had a way of making everyone around her feel like they were the most important person in the world. For someone like Ben, who lived by rules and routine, Dana was a revelation. She brought color to his ordered world, and he had fallen for her faster than he cared to admit.

They married a few years later, building what Ben had thought was a solid, dependable life together. They moved to a charming suburban home, had Ethan, and balanced their careers with family time as best they could. It wasn't perfect—no marriage was—but it had felt unshakable.

Now, as the weight of Rachel's death and Dana's betrayal hung over him, Ben wasn't so sure of anything. His parents were devastated, and Ethan had been pulled into a nightmare that no child should ever have to endure. Then he thought about Justin. A predator like him didn't just destroy lives—he shattered every illusion of safety and normalcy.

Ben's career had taught him how to think strategically, how to weigh risks and manage crises. But nothing in his years of experience had prepared him for this. As he neared his parents' home, he resolved to do whatever it took to protect his son and to rebuild what little was left of their family—if it was even possible.

He glanced at Ethan sat in the backseat, clutching his stuffed bunny tightly, his eyes fixed on the passing scenery but not really seeing it. The police cruiser following them at a steady distance was a constant reminder of the precariousness of their situation.

When they finally turned onto the gravel driveway of his childhood home, Ben felt a momentary pang of nostalgia. The house was a modest, two-story structure with a wraparound porch, its white paint slightly weathered but still charming. Large oak trees framed the yard. Warm light spilled from the windows, creating a welcoming glow that contrasted with the darkness looming over their lives.

As Ben parked the car and turned off the engine, Ethan stirred slightly. "Are we safe here, Daddy?" he asked, his voice small and uncertain.

Ben turned in his seat, his face softening as he looked at his son. "Yes, buddy. You're safe here. Grandma and Grandpa will take good care of you."

Ethan nodded, though his grip on the bunny didn't loosen. Ben stepped out of the car, opened the back door, and helped Ethan out. As they approached the house, the front door opened, and his mother, Margaret, stepped out, her face lined with worry and grief. She was a petite woman with silver-streaked hair pulled back into a bun, her blue eyes filled with a mixture of concern and sadness. Behind her was Ben's father, Robert, a tall, broad-shouldered man who suddenly appeared somewhat diminished, cowed by loss.

"Oh, Ben," Margaret said, pulling him into a brief hug before kneeling to Ethan's level. "Hello, my sweet boy. We've been waiting for you."

Ethan hesitated for a moment before stepping into her arms. She held him tightly, stroking his hair as she whispered comforting words. Robert placed a hand on Ben's shoulder, squeezing it firmly.

"Rachel..." Robert started. His voice gruff. "We can't believe she's gone."

Ben's jaw stiffened, and he nodded. "I know, Dad. I can't either."

Margaret stood, holding Ethan's hand. "Come inside. Let's get you both settled."

The house smelled of fresh-baked cookies and lavender, scents that should have been comforting but felt hollow in the wake of Rachel's absence. The living room was cozy, with overstuffed armchairs and a brick fireplace adorned with family photos. One of the photos was of Rachel, her bright smile a painful reminder of what they had lost. Margaret led Ethan to where a pile of toys and a cozy blanket had been laid out.

"Look, sweetheart," she said with a gentle smile. "We have all your favorites here. You can pick whatever you like."

Before Ethan responded, a uniformed police officer entered the room, his presence drawing everyone's attention. He was a tall man in his early forties, with a calm demeanor and a badge that read "Officer Callahan."

Ignoring the officer, Ethan climbed onto the couch, clutching his bunny as he eyed the toys warily. Margaret stood beside him, her presence calming, while Robert motioned for the adults to follow him into the kitchen.

Once inside, with the door closed slightly so Ethan couldn't overhear, Callahan addressed Ben's parents. "Mr. and Mrs. Taylor, I'm Officer Callahan, and I'll be stationed here for the time being. My job is to ensure everyone's safety until Justin Birch is apprehended."

Margaret's brow furrowed, and she exchanged a glance with

Robert. "Who is this Justin Birch?" she asked, her voice trembling slightly. "Why is he doing this to our family?"

Ben sighed heavily, running a hand through his hair as he leaned against the kitchen counter. "Justin is... he's someone Dana got involved with. It was a mistake, and she tried to end it, but he... he's obsessive. Dangerous. He's been stalking her, threatening her... and now he's targeting all of us."

Margaret's hand flew to her mouth, her eyes widening. "You mean to tell me Rachel... Rachel died because of this man?"

"We don't know for sure," Ben said quickly, though the anguish in his voice betrayed his words. "But it's likely. He's capable of anything."

Robert's face darkened, and he clenched his fists at his sides. "Why hasn't he been caught yet?" he demanded, his voice rising.

Callahan stepped forward; his tone measured. "I understand your frustration, sir. We're doing everything we can to locate Justin Birch. He's been careful, but we're tracking him, and we've increased patrols in this area. Your family's safety is our top priority."

Margaret's shoulders sagged, and she shook her head. "This is... it's unthinkable. Rachel... she didn't deserve this. None of us do."

Ben reached out, placing a reassuring hand on her arm. "We'll get through this, Mom. I promise."

Margaret's eyes filled with tears as she looked at her son. "How do we move on from this, Ben? How does a family heal from losing someone like Rachel? And now... now Ethan is caught in the middle of all this? It's too much."

Robert's face was grim as he added, "This Justin Birch needs to be stopped. If the police can't do it, what's to stop him from coming after someone else?"

Callahan interjected again, his voice calm but firm. "We're taking every precaution. Justin Birch is a priority for us. Your family has a dedicated team assigned to this case, and we're doing everything possible to prevent further harm."

When they returned to the living room, Ethan was curled up, his bunny tucked under his chin as he stared at a cartoon playing on the TV. Margaret sat beside him, her hand resting lightly on his back, while Robert stood behind them, his presence reassuring.

Ben knelt beside his son, brushing a stray curl from his forehead. "Hey, buddy. I need to run an errand, but I'll be back soon, okay? You listen to Grandma and Grandpa. They'll take good care of you."

Ethan's eyes flicked to Ben, a small frown on his face. "You're coming back, right?"

Ben's throat tightened, but he nodded. "Of course, buddy. I'll be back before you know it."

Ethan seemed to accept this, though his grip on the bunny didn't loosen. Ben stood, exchanging a glance with his parents who looked confused at his sudden departure but didn't ask questions, before stepping toward the door. As he walked out into the cool evening air, the police cruiser's lights flickered on, and he glanced back at the warm glow of the house.

Turning away, Ben took out his phone and scrolled until he found the name he was looking for. It only took seconds to type his message, and for one to ping back. Within moments Ben was in his car and heading into town, and for the first time in days felt a sliver of hope that he might have found a way to keep his son safe.

~

The bar was dimly lit, its wooden paneling and scuffed floors a throwback to another era. Ben pushed open the door and stepped inside, the murmur of low conversations and the clink of glasses meeting his ears. He scanned the room until his eyes landed on the familiar figure seated at a corner booth. Dressed in a leather jacket and nursing a half-empty pint of beer, the man looked up, his face breaking into a crooked grin.

"Well, well, Ben Taylor," he said, standing to greet him. "Haven't seen that face in years."

"Derek," Ben replied, managing a faint smile as he shook his old friend's hand. "It's been a while."

Derek Malone had aged, but not in the way most men did. His lean frame and sharp features were still intact, though the lines around his eyes hinted at a life lived hard. He gestured for Ben to sit, sliding a fresh drink across the table toward him.

"Figured you could use this," Derek said. "Judging by the look on your face, I'm guessing this isn't just a casual reunion."

Ben sat heavily, his shoulders sagging. "You're not wrong," he admitted, taking a sip of the whiskey. The burn in his throat was welcome—it was something to feel besides the endless churn of guilt and anger.

Derek leaned back, watching him. "You've got that look," he said after a moment. "Like you're carrying the weight of the world. So, tell me, what's going on?"

Ben hesitated, his fingers tightening around the glass. "It's my family," he said finally. "We're in trouble. Big trouble."

Derek's expression grew serious. "What kind of trouble?"

Ben exhaled slowly, his eyes meeting Derek's. "There's this guy, Justin Birch. He's... he's been stalking my wife. Threatening her. It started as... an affair, but she tried to end it, and he didn't take it well. Now he's targeting everyone—me, my son, even my sister. She... she's dead, Derek. Because of him."

Derek's jaw tightened, and he sat up straighter. "Jesus, Ben. That's heavy."

"It gets worse," Ben continued. "The police can't catch him. He's smart, rich, always one step ahead. He could be over the border by now or parked right outside. And I... I don't know what to do anymore."

Derek leaned forward, resting his elbows on the table. "And you came to me," he said, his voice low. "You know the kind of help I offer isn't exactly above board. My job title is security and protection but a lot of the time the boundaries are blurred. I've made a career out of fixing other people's problems at the same time as staying on the right side of the law, just. My methods aren't exactly subtle, just so you know."

Ben nodded. "I know. And I wouldn't ask if I wasn't desperate. I wish I'd come to you sooner, but I thought I could handle this or at least the law would, but now I'm not sure and this guy... he's ruining my life. He killed my sister. I can't just sit back and let him win. Even if you find him and scare the crap out of him, that will give me some satisfaction at least."

Derek studied him for a long moment, his gaze calculating. "You've changed, you know that?" he said finally. "Back in school, you were the guy who always played by the rules. The golden boy. Now you're asking me for help to... what? Take this guy out?"

"I need him gone," Ben said firmly. "Whatever it takes. I'm not asking you to do anything... extreme. Just... find him. Make him stop."

Derek's eyes narrowed. "Finding him is one thing. Making him stop is another. Guys like this don't back down easy, Ben but I'll do my best to persuade him. You sure you're ready for what might come next?"

Ben's grip on the glass tightened. "I'll do whatever I have to. For my family."

Derek nodded slowly, a grim smile tugging at his lips. "Alright. I'll see what I can do. But Ben, once we go down this road, there's no turning back."

"I understand," Ben said, his voice steady. "Thank you."

Derek leaned back, finishing his drink in one swig. "You're lucky I've still got a soft spot for old friends," he said. "But you owe me, Taylor. Big time."

Ben managed a faint smile. "I'll take care of it. Just... help me end this."

Derek's grin widened slightly, a glint of nostalgia in his eyes. "You know, I was thinking about the old days when I saw your name pop up in my messages," he said. "Remember when we got caught sneaking into the gym after hours? You wanted to practice for that big basketball game, and I just wanted to mess around with the sound system."

Ben chuckled despite himself. "Yeah, and Coach Daniels threatened to bench me for the rest of the season. You talked him out of it somehow."

"Talked? More like bribed him with tickets to that concert my uncle scored us," Derek said with a smirk. "Man, those were good times. Simpler times."

Ben's smile faded slightly. "Yeah. Simpler times. Before life got so... complicated."

Derek nodded, his expression sobering. "You were always the strait-laced one, Ben. Honor roll, team captain, all that. And me? I was the guy everyone warned their kids about."

"You weren't all bad," Ben said. "You had my back more times than I can count."

"And here we are again," Derek said, raising his glass. "Different stakes, same loyalty. I'll do what I can, Ben. For old times' sake."

Ben clinked his glass against Derek's, a small measure of relief washing over him. For the first time in weeks, he felt like he wasn't completely alone in this fight.

42

Justin sat in his car across the street from the bar, his eyes trained on the entrance. The darkened windshield shielded him from view, but he remained still and vigilant, his fingers drumming idly on the steering wheel. He had been tailing Ben since he left the house, curious about where he would go. When Ben finally emerged, Justin leaned forward slightly, a smirk playing on his lips.

Ben walked to his car with purpose, his expression tense, and climbed in. Justin waited a moment before starting his own engine, easing out of the parking spot to follow at a safe distance. The streets were quiet, their stillness amplifying the low hum of Justin's car as he kept a steady distance behind Ben. The tension in Justin's chest grew as he considered what Ben might be up to. A late-night meeting? A desperate attempt to find help?

It didn't matter. Justin was always a step ahead.

The drive took them away from the dim glow of the town's nightlife and into quieter, residential streets. Ben turned onto a gravel driveway then slowed, allowing his car to idle just before the property's entrance. Through the darkness, Justin could make out the warm glow of the house nestled behind tall oak trees. A porch light illuminated the front steps, and a police cruiser was parked prominently near the front of the house.

The sight of the police car made Justin's stomach twist with irritation. The presence of law enforcement complicated his plans.

His eyes scanned the property, noting the small details: the weathered white paint of the house, the wraparound porch, the faint shadows of movement inside. It looked like a family home —cozy, inviting, safe. Justin sneered at the thought.

In his mind, he imagined Ben's family sitting inside, thinking they were protected. The thought only fueled his rage. He resented Ben's attempts to outsmart him, to hide behind the law. And Ethan... the boy was an extension of everything Justin hated about Ben: a happy, intact family that Justin was determined to shatter.

"You can't hide forever," Justin muttered to himself. His grip on the wheel tightened, his nails digging into his palm. The image of Ethan's face flashed in his mind, and a dark smile spread across his lips. The thought of his innocence only deepened Justin's resolve.

Pulling his car into reverse, he backed up slowly to avoid drawing attention. His hands flexed on the wheel, and he leaned back in his seat, his mind racing. Ben had been careful, but Justin was patient. He always found a way. For now, he'd retreat, but not for long.

As he drove away, Justin's mind buzzed with possibilities. The police presence was a setback, but it wasn't insurmountable. He'd bide his time, watch and wait. Ben and his precious family wouldn't know what hit them.

"Soon," Justin whispered to himself, his voice low and menacing. "Very soon."

Dana sat alone as the quiet of the house pressed down on her, but her mind was far from still. She replayed every detail of Ben's departure: the hurried way he packed, the set determination on his face, and the soft click of the door as he left with Ethan. Something about the whole situation gnawed at her, a rising dread she couldn't shake.

The police officer stationed at the house stood by the window; his gaze trained on the quiet street outside. He had introduced himself earlier as Officer Reynolds, a tall man with a steady presence that was supposed to reassure her. But Dana felt anything but reassured.

She rose suddenly, pacing the living room. "Something's wrong," she said aloud, her voice trembling. "I... I can feel it."

Reynolds turned to her, his expression calm but wary. "Mrs. Taylor, what you are experiencing is probably paranoia after everything that's happened but we do have this situation under control. The department has officers assigned to your husband and son's location. They'll be safe."

"No, you don't understand," Dana snapped, her voice rising. "Justin's not like other people. He's... he's calculated. He'll find them. He must already know where they are."

Reynolds's brow furrowed. "What makes you say that?"

Dana stopped pacing, turning to face him fully. "Because he's always one step ahead. He's been watching me for months, maybe longer. Do you think he wouldn't have followed Ben?" Her voice cracked with desperation. "He knows where they are. I know it."

The officer hesitated, his training telling him to maintain composure. "Even if that's true, Mrs. Taylor, there's a police presence at their location. Justin can't get near them without being spotted."

Dana shook her head violently. "You don't get it! He'll find a way. He always does. I can't just sit here while they're out there."

"Mrs. Taylor," Reynolds began, but Dana cut him off.

"Take me to them," she demanded, stepping closer. "Please. If I'm there, I'll know. I'll see if something's wrong."

"That's not how this works," Reynolds replied, his tone firm but not unkind. "Your presence could complicate things. You're safer here."

"I don't care about being safe!" Dana's voice broke, tears spilling down her cheeks. "My son is out there. My husband is out there. If something happens to them because I stayed here..." She trailed off, choking on her words.

Reynolds hesitated, clearly torn. His radio crackled softly at his side, a constant reminder of the chaos unfolding beyond this quiet house. "Let me make a call," he said finally, stepping aside and reaching for his radio.

Dana watched him, her heart pounding as he relayed a brief message to dispatch. The minutes stretched unbearably, every second heightening her fear. Finally, he turned back to her, his expression grave.

"Alright," he said. "I'll take you to them. But you stay in the car until I say otherwise. Understood?"

Dana nodded quickly, grabbing her coat and purse. "Thank you," she whispered, her voice raw.

Reynolds led her to the unmarked police car parked outside. The cool night air bit at her skin as she climbed into the passenger seat, her hands trembling. As they pulled away from the curb, her mind raced with scenarios, each more terrifying than the last.

The drive was tense and silent, the weight of her dread filling the car. She glanced at Reynolds, who kept his eyes on the road, his jaw set in determination. The radio on his dashboard crackled intermittently, voices cutting in and out with updates she couldn't quite make out.

When they finally approached the quiet street where Ben's parents lived, Dana's stomach twisted. The police cruiser parked nearby was a reassuring sight, but it did little to calm her nerves.

Reynolds pulled to a stop a short distance away, his sharp eyes scanning the area. "Stay here," he instructed, opening his door. "I'll check in with the officers on duty."

But Dana couldn't sit still. Her hand gripped the door handle, her instincts screaming that Justin was close. She looked toward the darkened edges of the street, her breath catching as shadows seemed to shift and move. She didn't know where he was, but she could feel him. Justin was here.

43

Dana's heart sank as she stepped into the warm glow of the house. The living room, usually a sanctuary of comfort and familial warmth, now felt alien. Margaret and Robert stood near the fireplace, their faces etched with grief and anger. The air was heavy with the weight of unspoken words, and Dana braced herself for the storm she knew was coming.

"You have some nerve showing up here," Margaret said, her voice trembling with barely contained fury. She crossed her arms tightly over her chest, her piercing blue eyes locking onto Dana. "After everything you've done."

Dana's breath caught in her throat. "I… I came because I was worried about Ben and Ethan. I just wanted to make sure they were safe."

"Safe?" Robert interjected, his deep voice shaking the room. "Our daughter is dead, Dana. Dead. And for what? Because of your selfishness? Because you couldn't keep your damn life together?"

Tears welled in Dana's eyes as she shook her head. "I never meant for any of this to happen. I—"

"You didn't mean for it?" Margaret's voice rose, sharp as a

knife. "You had an affair! You brought that man into our family's life. He's destroyed everything, Dana. And Rachel paid the price. My daughter paid the price for your mistakes, your lust. You disgust me."

Dana's knees felt weak, and she gripped the edge of the armchair to steady herself. "I... I'm so sorry. I never wanted anyone to get hurt. I'm doing everything I can to make it right."

"Make it right?" Robert barked out a bitter laugh. "You think you can undo this? Rachel is gone. Ethan will never see his aunt again because of that... that monster you let into your life, whose bed you crawled into."

Dana's tears spilled over as she tried to speak. "I... I've been working with the police. I—"

"Save it," Margaret snapped, her voice cutting through Dana's stammering. "You're not a victim here, Dana. You're the reason this family is in ruins."

Ben appeared in the doorway, his face pale and drawn. His eyes flicked between his parents and Dana, taking in the scene. "What's going on?" he asked, his voice weary.

"What's going on?" Margaret turned to her son. Her voice thick with emotion. "We're telling Dana the truth. That she's not welcome here. That she's the reason our daughter is gone. And that she needs to leave."

"Mom, that's enough," Ben said firmly, though his voice wavered. "Dana's trying to help."

"Help?" Robert's voice boomed. "She's done enough damage, Ben. And now you're letting her drag Ethan into this mess? He's just a boy! He doesn't deserve this."

Dana stepped forward, her voice trembling. "I love Ethan. I'd never let anything happen to him."

"You already have," Margaret said coldly. "And don't you dare pretend otherwise."

From the hallway, a small voice broke the tension like a shard of glass. "Mom?"

All eyes turned to see Ethan standing at the threshold, his face pale and his eyes wide with confusion. His stuffed bunny dangled limply from his hand, and his bottom lip quivered. "What are they talking about? What's going on?"

Dana's heart shattered. She dropped to her knees, reaching out to him. "Ethan, sweetheart, it's okay. Everything's fine."

"No, it's not," Ethan said, his voice rising. "They said you... you did something bad. They said it's your fault Aunt Rachel..." His voice broke, and tears spilled down his cheeks. "Is it true?"

Dana's hands trembled as she tried to hold his gaze. "Ethan, listen to me. I love you more than anything. I would never, ever hurt you or anyone in this family. You have to believe me."

Margaret stepped forward. Her voice sharp. "He deserves to know the truth, Dana. You brought that man into our lives. You're the reason his aunt is gone."

"Stop it!" Ben shouted, his voice cracking with emotion. He turned to his parents, his face red with anger. "This isn't helping. Do you see what you're doing to him?"

But the damage was done. Ethan stared at his mother, his tears falling freely. "You lied to me," he whispered, his voice full of betrayal. "You said everything would be okay, but it's not. It's not okay!"

He turned and ran down the hallway, his small footsteps echoing in the heavy silence. Dana rose unsteadily, her entire body trembling. "I... I didn't want him to find out like this," she said, her voice barely audible.

"What did you expect?" Margaret said bitterly. "The truth always comes out, Dana. And now you've broken your son's heart, too."

Ben looked torn. "I'll talk to him," he said finally, his voice thick. He walked out of the room, leaving Dana standing alone under the weight of his parents' withering glares.

Justin sat in his car, parked under the shadow of a towering oak tree, the dim streetlight casting long shadows across the street. His fingers occasionally tapping a rhythm on the dash that betrayed his anticipation. The house before him was a glowing beacon of warmth and familiarity, emanating an idyllic glow that Justin found almost laughable.

His lips curled into a sly grin as he adjusted the binoculars he held to his eyes. Through the front window, he could see a man pacing near the fireplace, his hands gesturing animatedly as he spoke. A woman sat on the couch, her shoulders stiff and her face a mask of tightly controlled fury. Justin couldn't hear their words, but he could sense the tension even from this distance.

It had taken him little effort to find this place. Ben was predictable, always running to the safety of his family. Justin had followed him to the bar with ease, his car a silent shadow. The presence of the police cruiser parked in the driveway was still a minor annoyance, but Justin knew better than to act recklessly. He was patient. He could wait.

And then, the unexpected happened. The front door opened, and there she was.

Dana.

Justin's heart quickened as he lowered the binoculars, leaning forward slightly. She stood on the porch, her arms wrapped around herself as if shielding herself from the crisp night air. Her face was pale, her movements tense. Even from a distance, Justin could see the exhaustion etched into her features.

"Well, well," Justin murmured to himself, a slow smile spreading across his face. "What do we have here?"

The timing couldn't have been better. Dana, Ben, Ethan, and the parents—all under one roof. It was almost poetic. Justin's fingers stilled as his mind raced with possibilities. He could feel the rush of adrenaline coursing through him, the thrill of control, of having the upper hand.

He adjusted the binoculars again, focusing on Dana as she stepped off the porch and onto the gravel driveway. She paused, glancing around as though sensing something was off. Justin chuckled softly. "So paranoid, Dana. Maybe you should be."

The shadows cloaked his car in near-total darkness, making him invisible to her searching gaze. He watched as she hesitated, then turned back toward the house, retreating inside. The door closed behind her, and Justin let out a long breath, his grin widening.

"All the pieces on the board," he whispered, his voice barely audible over the hum of the engine. "And now, the game begins."

For now, he would wait. Justin thrived on challenges. He had always been meticulous, calculating. Tonight was no different. He leaned back in his seat, the binoculars resting in his lap as his eyes remained fixed on the house.

"Enjoy your family reunion, Dana," Justin muttered, his tone laced with menace. "Because it won't last."

44

The atmosphere inside the house was excruciating. Dana's hands were clasped tightly in her lap, while Margaret's icy glare bore into her from across the room. The air felt heavy, almost unbreathable, as though the weight of their collective grief and anger had settled into every corner of the house. Margaret's disapproval radiated like heat, making Dana feel small and exposed.

Robert stood near the window, his posture rigid, staring out at the dark driveway as though expecting Justin to emerge from the shadows at any moment. His face was a grim mask, and the tension in his jaw betrayed his own inner turmoil. Ben paced the length of the room, his steps heavy and uneven. The animosity radiating from Margaret and Robert was palpable, an invisible force pushing them further apart with every passing second.

"We should call the police again," Margaret said sharply, breaking the silence. Her voice was brittle, each word laced with anger. "They need to do more. They're not taking this seriously enough."

"The police are already patrolling," Ben said, his voice strained. "They've told us to stay here and keep an eye out for anything suspicious. Calling them again won't change anything."

Margaret's lips pressed into a thin line, but she said nothing further. Instead, her eyes flicked to Dana, her disapproval palpable. "And what about her?" she asked, gesturing toward Dana with a nod of her head. "How do we know Justin won't show up just because she's here?"

"Because it doesn't matter to Justin where I am," Dana said quietly, her voice trembling. "He's already watching all of us. It doesn't matter if I'm here or somewhere else—he'll find a way and pick his victim, whoever that may be."

Robert turned from the window, his expression grim. "She's right," he said, his deep voice carrying a weight of reluctant acceptance. "If Justin wants to come after her, or any of us, he will. The police said the best thing we can do is stick together. Safety in numbers."

Margaret's eyes widened in disbelief. "So, what? We're supposed to let her stay here and put us all in more danger?"

Robert's gaze didn't waver. "Yes," he said firmly. "Because if she leaves, she'll be alone, and Justin will go after her. If she's here, we have the police watching the house. And" he hesitated, his tone darkening, "maybe it's better this way."

Ben stopped pacing and turned to his father, confusion and suspicion in his eyes. "What are you talking about?"

Robert sighed, running a hand over his face. "Think about it," he said. "If Justin knows Dana's here, he might make a move. And if he does, the police will be ready for him. We could use this as a way to trap him."

The room fell silent as the weight of Robert's suggestion sank in. Dana's stomach clenched at the thought of being used as bait, but she couldn't deny the logic in his words. She'd thought the same thing earlier and had been desperately trying to think of a way to lure Justin. It was a fact that Justin's obsession with her had been the catalyst for everything. If staying here meant finally ending his reign of terror, she would endure it.

"No," Ben said abruptly, shaking his head. "That's too dangerous. We're not using her as some kind of trap. It's not right."

"And what's the alternative?" Robert shot back, his voice rising. "We sit here and wait for Justin to strike again? You think he'll stop at Rachel? At terrorizing Dana? He'll come for Ethan next, Ben. Do you really want to take that risk?"

The mention of Ethan's name made Ben's face pale. He glanced toward the hallway where his son was sleeping, his shoulders slumping as the fight drained out of him. "I don't like it," he muttered. "But maybe you're right."

Margaret let out a sharp huff, crossing her arms tightly over her chest. "I still don't like it. But if she's staying, she needs to stay out of the way. And she'd better not do anything to put Ethan in danger."

Dana swallowed hard, nodding. "I won't," she said softly.

The air in the room felt heavier, pressing down on everyone present. The faint creak of the house settling and the distant hum of the police radio outside only added to the oppressive atmosphere. Ben rubbed his temples, the weight of the situation pressing heavily on him. "Fine," he said finally, his voice hollow. "She stays. But we're not using her as bait unless it's necessary. And the second things get too dangerous, she's out of here. Understood?"

Robert nodded, and even Margaret offered a begrudging nod of agreement. Yet the tension in her body did not ease, her shoulders remaining stiff, her gaze sharp and unforgiving.

Dana sat back down on the armchair, her heart heavy with the knowledge that she was at the center of this chaos. She glanced toward the window, her eyes searching the darkness outside. Somewhere out there, Justin was watching, waiting.

The hands of the clock had moved slowly, marking the two hours and fifteen minutes that had passed since Ben said Dana could stay. The faint murmur of voices from the kitchen added another layer of disquiet. The family's fragmented interactions —Margaret's curt words, Robert's grim observations, Ben's defeated silence—painted a picture of a family on the brink. Every glance, every word carried an edge, as though one wrong move might make the fragile peace shatter entirely.

In his bedroom, Ethan stirred in his sleep, his muffled voice calling faintly for his father. Ben's eyes darted toward the sound. His anguish clear. For a heartbeat everyone froze, their collective breaths held, as though Justin himself might suddenly step through the door.

And then the lights went out.

The house was plunged into an oppressive darkness. A collective gasp rippled through the room as shadows swallowed the faint warmth of the space. Dana's heart thundered in her chest as her breath caught in her throat.

"What happened?" Margaret's tremulous voice cut through the silence.

"The power's out," Robert said grimly, his voice steady but low. He moved toward the window, peering out into the blackness. "The streetlights are still on. It's just us."

Dana's blood ran cold. "It's Justin," she whispered, her voice trembling. "He's here."

"Stay calm," Ben said firmly, though his own fear was evident in the tightness of his voice. "Everyone stays here. I'll check the fuse box."

"No," Robert interjected. "We need to stick together. If Justin cut the power, he's trying to scare us. We can't give him the chance to separate us."

Margaret's breath hitched audibly. "What if he's already inside?" she asked, her voice barely above a whisper.

Dana began to tremble. Her eyes darted toward the windows, imagining Justin's shadow lurking just beyond the glass.

45

Justin crouched in the cellar, the damp, musty air filling his lungs as he listened intently to the muffled voices above. He'd climbed in through a small hatch that would also provide his escape route. The faint glow of a flashlight illuminated his face, casting eerie shadows that danced along the cracked walls. He allowed himself a quiet smile as he adjusted the bundle of wires he'd pulled from the electrical panel, cutting power to the house. The chaos above had been immediate, the panicked reactions he'd heard giving him a grim sense of satisfaction.

They had no idea he was here.

Above him, the voices rose in tense urgency. Justin tilted his head, his ears trained on the sound of Margaret's question, followed by Robert's low, measured reply. They were scared. Good. Fear made people sloppy. Fear made people predictable.

He leaned back against the wall, the chill of the concrete seeping through his clothes, and allowed himself a moment to savor the situation. This wasn't just about Dana anymore. This was about control. About showing them all that he could reach them anywhere, anytime. They thought they were safe behind locked doors and police patrols. Fools.

From above, he caught the distinct sound of Ben's voice. Justin's smile faltered, replaced by a scowl. Ben Taylor. The golden boy. The perfect husband. The man who thought he could outmaneuver him. Justin's fingers twitched as he imagined wrapping them around Ben's throat, squeezing until the life drained from his eyes.

A thud from above snapped Justin back to the present. He froze, every muscle in his body going taut as he strained to identify the source of the noise. It was faint, like a chair being pushed back, followed by hurried footsteps. He grinned. They were moving around in the dark, scrambling to maintain their false sense of control.

His grin widened as he imagined their faces: pale, tense, their eyes darting toward every shadow. He pictured Dana's trembling hands and Margaret's barely concealed panic. He had them exactly where he wanted them.

Upstairs, Ben fumbled in the darkness, his hand finally closing around his mobile phone. The screen's faint glow was like a beacon in the oppressive blackness as he called the officer stationed outside. No answer. Panic mounting, he quickly typed out a message.

Power's out. We think Justin is here. Send backup immediately.

He hesitated for only a second before composing a second message, this one to Derek, words he couldn't say out loud:

. . .

I need you. Bring a gun. It's Justin. I think he's here and taken out the lights.

He hit send and slipped the phone into his pocket, his heart hammering in his chest. He turned to his father. "I messaged the police and someone else who can help. But we need to stay together until they get here."

Robert's large frame hovered in the dim light. "Good. Now we wait. And we don't let our guard down."

Dana's voice trembled as she spoke. "What if he's already inside? What if he's... watching us?"

Margaret let out a sharp breath, her composure slipping. "He's not inside. He can't be. The doors were locked."

But even as she said it, doubt flickered in Dana's heart. Justin was unpredictable, clever. If anyone could bypass their security, it was him.

In the cellar, Justin shifted slightly, positioning himself to move if necessary. He'd planned this perfectly, but improvisation was always part of the thrill. For now, he would wait. Let them stew in their fear. Let them imagine him in every shadow. The power was out, the house was silent, and their nerves were fraying with every passing second.

Dana eyes darted around the room. She could feel her heartbeat in her throat, each pulse a reminder of how close Justin might be. What were the police doing? Patrolling the garden she hoped.

Margaret's breath came in shallow gasps. Dana knew her mother-in-law had always prided herself on her composure, but the oppressive silence and the knowledge that Justin could be lurking nearby had stripped her of her usual poise.

"This is his game," Dana muttered under her breath, her voice cracking. "He wants us to be scared."

"It's working," Margaret replied, her voice barely audible.

Robert moved toward the window, peering out into the blackness hoping to see the beam of a police flashlight cut through the darkness outside, but the shroud of black that met his eyes did nothing to reassure him.

Ben's hands were shaking as he gripped his phone, the faint glow casting eerie shadows across his face. He hated this—the feeling of helplessness, the constant dread that Justin could be anywhere. Then he smelt it. Smoke.

"Can you smell that? It's smoke." Ben could hear the fear in his own voice, a sound reflected when Robert replied.

"Christ, it is. It must be coming from the cellar. We need to leave, right now."

Ben's mind raced with thoughts of Ethan, sleeping upstairs and completely unaware of the danger that surrounded them. "We need to get Ethan," he said abruptly, breaking the tense silence.

Robert placed a hand on his son's shoulder. "We'll go together," he said. "No one goes anywhere alone."

But Ben's eyes were wide with urgency as he stopped his father. "No," I'll get him them you and Mom need to leave with Ethan, you too Dana. I'll stay here and hold him off, distract him while you get out."

Margaret's breath hitched audibly. "Ben, are you insane? We can't just leave you here!"

"And I'm staying with you, it's me he wants, and we'll face him together, I mean it Ben, I'm going nowhere till that man is stopped." Dana's voice had a steel edge to it.

"Mom," Ben said firmly, his eyes locking with hers. "Ethan's safety is the only thing that matters right now. Justin's focused on me and Dana. He'll come for us first. Please, just get Ethan out of here."

Robert agreed, understanding the gravity of the situation. "She's right, they both are" he said, gripping Margaret's arm. "We don't have time to argue. Let's go."

Margaret hesitated, her face a mask of fear and uncertainty, but she finally nodded, her resolve hardening. Together, they moved quickly but quietly toward the stairs and watched as Ben disappeared into the darkness to retrieve Ethan. Seconds later he returned carrying a sleepy boy clutching his toy rabbit, who he then passed into Robert's arms.

"Dad, what's going on? What's that smell?"

"Nothing to worry about buddy, but I need you to go with Grandpa while Mom and I check it out, okay. We'll be out soon."

Within seconds, the three of them were by the door as Ben gave instructions. "Go straight to the squad car and if the officer isn't there, go across the street to the neighbors and ask them to call 911. You know what to say, Dad, now go. Hurry."

Before Dana could even kiss Ethan goodbye, Margaret had flung open the door and as a cool blast of air rushed into the house, the smell of smoke seemed to intensify. In a heartbeat they were gone.

Ben turned back to Dana who was sobbing quietly, his face pale but determined.

"If Justin's here," he whispered, "we're not letting him win. Not this time."

~

Having set Ethan down onto the path, Robert checked behind them to ensure no one was watching while Margaret whispered softly to her grandson, urging him to move quietly. The darkness pressed in on them, every small noise amplified by the tension in the air. The wind stirred the trees, casting long, flickering shadows that seemed to dance with malevolent intent. Margaret's heart pounded in her chest, her grip on Ethan's hand tightening as though holding him closer might shield him from the horrors lurking in the night.

Now, the cold air wrapped around them like a shroud, and the faint metallic tang of fear seemed to linger with every breath.

"Stick close," Robert whispered, his voice low and firm. He scanned the gravel yard, his eyes narrowing at every shadow that stretched across the lawn. The porch light of the house was out, and the darkness felt almost impenetrable. In the distance, the police cruiser sat parked near the edge of the property, its presence meant to be a reassuring reminder of their safety. But something about the stillness of the car made Robert uneasy.

Margaret tugged Ethan closer to her, her grip on his hand so tight that his fingers squirmed. "It's alright, sweetheart," she murmured, her voice trembling. "We're just going to the officer. He'll keep us safe."

The trio moved quickly but cautiously; their footsteps muffled by the grass. As they neared the car, Robert's unease grew. The cruiser's engine was off, and the beam of the flashlight that had been sweeping the property earlier was gone. The closer they got, the more Margaret's breathing quickened.

"Why is it so quiet?" she whispered, her voice trembling.

Robert didn't answer. Instead, he approached the car slowly, his hand raised in a hesitant wave. "Officer?" he called softly. "It's Robert Taylor. We need your help."

There was no response. The car remained still; its windows darkened. Robert's heart froze as he reached the driver's side and peered inside. His breath caught in his throat.

The officer was slumped against the steering wheel, his face pale and lifeless. A dark stain spread across his uniform, the unmistakable mark of violence. The harsh glare of the moonlight streaming through the windshield illuminated the blood, stark and horrifying against the otherwise still figure.

Margaret froze in place, her hand flying to her mouth as a strangled gasp escaped her lips. Her knees felt weak, and she swayed slightly, the world spinning around her as she stared at the lifeless body. The shadows of the night seemed to press closer, as though they were conspiring to consume her entirely.

"Oh my God," she whispered, her voice breaking. She pulled Ethan back instinctively, shielding his face with her trembling hand. Her pulse thundered in her ears, and tears blurred her vision as her mind raced with fear. "Robert, what do we do?"

Robert sucked in a breath as he stared at the gruesome scene, his mind racing. The oppressive darkness around them felt heavier now, as though it carried Justin's presence, his malice. "We need to get out of here," he said, his voice low and urgent. "Now."

"The neighbors, they can call for help." Margaret's voice was rising in panic.

Ethan whimpered, his small voice breaking through the tension. "I'm scared," he said, his face buried in Margaret's side.

Before Robert could respond, the sound of an approaching engine broke the silence. Headlights cut through the darkness, and Margaret froze, her arms tightening protectively around Ethan. The vehicle rumbled closer, its lights bouncing as it turned onto the uneven driveway. Robert stepped in front of his family, his fists clenched, ready to defend them if necessary.

The truck came to a stop a few feet away, and the driver's door swung open. Derek stepped out; his tall frame silhouetted against the headlights. He was holding a shotgun, the barrel resting casually over his shoulder, but his eyes were sharp and alert.

"What the hell is going on here?" Derek asked, his voice gruff but steady. His gaze swept over the frightened group before landing on the police car. He frowned deeply, his grip on the shotgun tightening.

"Derek," Robert said, relief and tension mingling in his tone. "The officer... he's dead. Justin must be nearby."

Derek's expression darkened as he stepped closer, his boots crunching against the gravel. "Alright," he said. "We're not sticking around here. Get in the truck. Now. I'll take you to the station then come back."

Margaret hesitated, her eyes darting between Robert and the dark expanse of the yard. "What about Ben? And Dana? We can't just leave them."

Derek's jaw tightened. "I'll go back for them. But first, I'm getting you and the boy out of here. Justin's not taking another life tonight."

Margaret nodded reluctantly, her hand never leaving Ethan's shoulder. Together, they hurried to the truck, their fear palpable but their determination stronger. Derek kept his eyes on the shadows, his shotgun ready, as they climbed inside. As the truck's doors slammed shut, Derek turned back toward the house, his face grim and resolute.

"Stay low," he muttered. "Just in case."

46

The oppressive silence in the house felt as though it had taken on a physical weight, pressing down on every surface and corner. Ben held his breath, straining his ears for any indication of Justin's movements. Dana stood behind him, clutching a heavy lamp she had found in the darkness, her knuckles white with tension.

A sudden noise broke the stillness—a deliberate scrape of a boot against the floor, impossibly close. Ben's head snapped toward the sound, and his heart began to pound in his chest. "Justin," he called out, his voice steady despite the fear tightening his throat. "You don't have to do this."

The response came from the shadows, low and mocking. "Oh, but I do, Ben. You took something from me. Now it's my turn."

Dana's breath hitched audibly, and she stepped closer to Ben. The darkness seemed alive, shifting and morphing as if Justin himself was a part of it. Then, with a sudden rush, Justin emerged from the shadows, his face a mask of cold fury. In his hand, a glint of metal—a knife.

Ben barely had time to react as Justin lunged. He grabbed a

chair and swung it in Justin's direction, forcing him to step back. The knife slashed through the air, narrowly missing Ben's arm. Dana screamed, dropping the lamp, and the crash of shattered ceramic echoed through the room.

"You ruined everything!" Justin hissed, his voice dripping with venom. He lunged again, this time aiming for Ben's midsection. Ben twisted away, his hand lashing out to grab Justin's wrist. The two men grappled, their shadows twisting grotesquely on the walls in the faint moonlight filtering through the windows.

Dana stumbled backward, her mind racing. She had to do something, but her body felt frozen in fear. Her eyes darted around the room until they landed on a heavy candlestick on the mantel. Summoning every ounce of courage, she grabbed it and rushed toward the fray.

Ben grunted as Justin's knee connected with his ribs, knocking the wind out of him. Justin used the momentary advantage to shove Ben against the wall, the knife inching closer to his throat. "You think you can protect her?" Justin sneered. "You can't even protect yourself."

"Get away from him!" Dana's voice rang out, trembling but determined. She swung the candlestick with all her strength, striking Justin on the shoulder. He cried out in pain, stumbling backward and loosening his grip on the knife. Ben seized the opportunity to shove Justin away, sending him sprawling onto the floor.

Justin rolled to his feet with animalistic speed, his eyes wild and blazing with hatred. "You think this changes anything?" he snarled. "You're mine, Dana. You've always been mine."

"Stay back," Ben warned, stepping in front of Dana. His voice was firm, but his breathing was labored, and his body ached from the struggle.

Before Justin could respond, he lunged again, this time

knocking Dana off her feet. She fell backward, her head hitting the edge of the coffee table with a sickening thud. Her body went limp, and she crumpled to the floor, unconscious.

"Dana!" Ben shouted, his voice breaking. Rage flared in his chest as he turned back to Justin, his fists clenched. Justin's grin widened; his satisfaction evident as he twirled the knife in his hand.

"She'll be fine," Justin said, his tone mocking. "You, on the other hand..."

Ben didn't wait for Justin to finish. He charged at him, tackling him to the ground. The knife skittered across the floor as the two men wrestled violently. Justin's fists pounded into Ben's sides, each blow sending jolts of pain through his body. Ben retaliated with a savage punch to Justin's jaw, the impact splitting his knuckles.

The fight devolved into a brutal struggle, each man fueled by desperation and hatred. Justin managed to claw his way to the knife, his fingers curling around the hilt. He slashed wildly, the blade grazing Ben's arm and drawing blood. Ben gritted his teeth against the pain, grabbing Justin's wrist and slamming it against the floor until the knife clattered free again.

With a surge of strength, Ben pinned Justin beneath him, his hands wrapped tightly around Justin's throat. "You'll never hurt my family again," he growled, his voice raw with fury.

Justin's face turned red as he struggled against Ben's grip, his hands clawing at Ben's arms. But just as it seemed Ben had the upper hand, Justin kneed him in the stomach, forcing him to release his hold. Justin scrambled to his feet, gasping for air, and stumbled toward the shadows once more.

The sound of distant sirens pierced the tense silence, growing louder with each passing second. Justin's head tilted slightly, his smile fading as he realized his time was running out.

"This isn't over," he said, backing toward the shadows. "Not by a long shot."

Before Ben could react, Justin turned and disappeared into the darkness, leaving behind only the faint echo of his footsteps. Ben sagged against the wall, his chest heaving as the adrenaline began to subside. He crawled to Dana's side, gently cradling her head. Her breathing was steady, but she remained unconscious.

The sirens grew closer, and the red and blue lights of the approaching police cars flickered through the windows. Ben brushed a strand of hair from Dana's face, his hands trembling. "It's going to be okay," he said, though his voice wavered with uncertainty.

For the first time in what felt like hours, the house was silent again.

~

Derek's truck skidded to a stop in the driveway, the headlights casting long shadows against the house. The sound of the engine died abruptly, leaving an eerie silence that seemed to stretch into eternity. He stepped out, his shotgun gripped firmly in one hand and a heavy-duty flashlight in the other. The beam of light cut through the thick darkness, sweeping over the porch, the windows, and the surrounding yard.

The house loomed before him, its once-inviting exterior now an ominous void. Every instinct Derek had told him this was wrong—the lack of light, the oppressive quiet, the gnawing sense that something malevolent lurked within. He took a deep breath, bracing himself, and approached the front door.

The door was locked. Without hesitation, Derek raised his boot and kicked it in. The wood splintered with a loud crack, the sound reverberating through the empty rooms. He stepped inside, the flashlight beam illuminating the chaos left in the wake of a struggle. Shattered glass glinted on the floor, and furniture lay overturned, casting jagged shadows against the walls.

"Ben? Dana?" Derek called out. His voice low but commanding. The house answered him with silence.

He moved cautiously, his boots crunching over broken ceramic as he swept the beam of his flashlight from side to side. The living room was a wreck, but there were no signs of movement. He advanced deeper into the house, his grip tightening on the shotgun.

Each creak of the floorboards beneath his feet felt amplified, echoing in the stillness. Derek's jaw tightened as he moved toward the kitchen. The beam of his flashlight landed on a spilled drink pooling across the floor, the liquid shimmering darkly in the light. He crouched to inspect it, his pulse quickening when he realized it was blood.

"Damn it," he muttered under his breath. Standing, he adjusted his grip on the shotgun and pushed forward.

The hallway stretched ahead of him like a tunnel, the flashlight's beam revealing doorways that yawned open like empty mouths. Derek's muscles were taut, his every sense on high alert. He moved methodically, room by room, his light sweeping corners and shadows, searching for any sign of life.

In the dining room, chairs were toppled and scattered, the table pushed against the wall as if someone had tried to use it as a barricade. The faint scent of something metallic lingered in the air, mingling with the earthy smell of overturned soil from a broken potted plant.

"Ben?" he called again, his voice softer this time, wary of alerting anyone who shouldn't hear him.

As he stepped into the study, he heard a faint noise from upstairs. It was a muffled thump, followed by what sounded like footsteps. Derek's blood ran cold, but his movements remained deliberate as he climbed the stairs, the wooden steps groaning beneath his weight.

The upstairs hallway was darker than the rest of the house, the flashlight barely cutting through the oppressive blackness. Derek stopped at the first door and nudged it open with the barrel of his shotgun. Inside, the room was empty, but the bedclothes were in disarray, as if someone had left in a hurry.

He continued down the hall, his breath shallow and controlled. The sound of footsteps came again, this time more distinct, and Derek's grip on his weapon tightened. He swung the flashlight beam toward the source of the noise—a door at the end of the hall, slightly ajar. A shadow flickered across the crack in the door, and Derek froze.

"Come out now," he barked, his voice cutting through the silence like a blade. "Slow and easy. No sudden moves."

The door creaked open slightly, but no one emerged. Derek stepped closer, his shotgun raised and ready. He kicked the door open fully, the crash echoing down the hall.

The room was empty, but the window was wide open, the curtains fluttering in the cold night breeze. Derek cursed under his breath, stepping closer to the window and peering out. The yard below was empty, but the faint sound of distant sirens reached his ears.

"Where the hell are you?" he muttered, turning back toward the hallway. He moved quickly now, checking each remaining room with precision. The house felt alive with tension, every shadow a potential threat, every creak a possible attack.

Finally, Derek descended the stairs again, his heart hammering in his chest. He paused in the living room, his flashlight beam landing on a figure sprawled on the floor. His breath caught as he recognized Dana, unconscious but breathing. He knelt beside her, quickly checking for injuries.

"Hang on," he said softly, his voice gentler now. "You're gonna be okay."

Blood trickled from a gash on her forehead, and her face was pale, but her pulse was steady. Derek's flashlight swept the room as he stood, his eyes narrowing when he realized Ben and Justin were nowhere to be seen. His pulse increased as he noticed the knife lying nearby, bloodied and abandoned.

A low, muffled sound caught his attention. He froze, his head snapping toward the direction of the noise. It was faint, but unmistakable. It was coming from below.

The basement.

Derek's jaw tightened as he moved toward the door leading to the cellar. His flashlight beam wavered slightly as he reached for the handle, his grip on the shotgun tightening. The sound grew clearer: a scuffle, followed by a pained grunt. His heart pounded as he braced himself and slowly opened the door. The stairs descended into pitch-blackness, the air growing colder and heavier with each step he took.

"Ben?" Derek called out; his voice steady but strained. There was no response, only the faint echo of movement below.

He stepped onto the first stair, the creak of the wood piercing the silence. His flashlight illuminated the narrow staircase, the beam cutting through the dense darkness like a knife. As he descended, the sounds grew louder: labored breathing, the scrape of something heavy against the concrete floor.

Derek's pulse thundered in his ears as he reached the bottom step. His flashlight swept the room, landing on a chaotic scene of overturned shelves and scattered tools. Then he saw them—two figures locked in a violent struggle. Justin was on top of Ben, his hands around Ben's throat, his face twisted with rage.

"Get off him!" Derek roared, raising the shotgun. Justin's head snapped toward him; his eyes gleaming with malice even in the dim light. But Derek wasn't waiting for an invitation. He moved forward, ready to end the fight once and for all.

47

The basement was a dark, claustrophobic space, the dim light of Derek's flashlight slicing through the heavy shadows. Ben struggled beneath Justin, his breath coming in ragged gasps as Justin's hands closed tighter around his throat. His vision blurred, but he refused to stop fighting, his fists weakly pounding against Justin's sides.

Derek's voice rang out again, sharp and commanding. "Get off him!"

Justin's head snapped toward Derek. His eyes gleaming with feral hatred. For a moment, his grip on Ben loosened, just enough for Ben to twist beneath him and shove him off. Justin stumbled backward, crashing into a shelf that sent tools and boxes clattering to the floor. Ben rolled to his side, coughing and gasping for air, his chest heaving.

Derek advanced, his shotgun trained on Justin. "This ends now," he growled. "Don't move, or I swear to God I'll blow you away."

Justin's lips curled into a twisted smile. "You're too late," he said, his voice laced with mockery. His hand darted into his pocket, and before Derek could react, Justin pulled out a small revolver.

"Gun!" Derek shouted, his finger tightening on the trigger. But Justin was faster. He raised the revolver and fired.

The crack of the shot echoed deafeningly in the enclosed space. Derek staggered, his flashlight tumbling from his grasp as his hand flew to his chest. Blood seeped between his fingers, dark and viscous. He fell to his knees, his shotgun slipping from his grip and clattering to the ground.

"No!" Ben's hoarse cry filled the air as he scrambled toward Derek, his own pain forgotten in the face of the horrific scene unfolding before him.

Justin stood over Derek; his revolver still raised. His expression was cold, detached, as though the act of taking a life meant nothing to him. Derek's eyes met Ben's, a mix of determination and regret flashing in them. He opened his mouth to speak, but no words came. With a shuddering breath, he collapsed onto the cold concrete floor, the light in his eyes fading.

"Derek!" Ben's voice cracked with anguish as he reached his friend's lifeless body. His hands hovered uselessly over Derek's chest, the warm blood pooling beneath him a stark reminder of the irreversibility of what had just happened.

Justin's voice cut through the air like a blade. "Touching, really," he said, his tone dripping with disdain. "But this is just the beginning, Ben. You should've stayed out of my way."

Ben's head snapped up; his grief replaced by a surge of raw fury. He pushed himself to his feet, his body trembling with adrenaline. Justin took a step back, his revolver trained on Ben, but there was no fear in Ben's eyes—only rage.

"You're not getting out of here," Ben growled, his voice low and menacing. "Not this time."

Justin smirked, the madness in his eyes shining brighter than ever. "We'll see about that."

As Justin raised the revolver, his finger tightening on the trigger, neither man noticed the soft creak of the stairs behind them. Dana, her face pale and streaked with dried blood, had managed to regain consciousness and was now slowly descending the staircase. Her steps were careful, her breath shallow, as she took in the horrifying scene below: Derek's lifeless body, Ben's battered form, and Justin's cruel smile as he prepared to fire.

Dana's eyes fell on the shotgun lying near Derek's outstretched hand. She moved silently, her trembling fingers curling around the weapon's stock. It was heavier than she expected, but the weight was nothing compared to the determination that gripped her. She raised the shotgun, her heart pounding so loudly she feared Justin might hear it.

Justin spoke again, his voice mocking. "Any last words, Ben?"

Ben's eyes darted to the staircase, catching the faint movement behind Justin. Hope flickered in his gaze as he saw Dana, the shotgun raised and steady despite the tremor in her hands.

"Yeah," Ben said, his voice steady despite the chaos. "You're not as smart as you think."

Justin's brow furrowed in confusion, but before he could turn, Dana pulled the trigger. The shotgun roared, the recoil slamming into her shoulder and sending her stumbling back. Justin's body jerked violently as the blast hit him square in the back. The revolver fell from his hand, clattering to the floor as he crumpled forward.

48

The cemetery was quiet, the air thick with the lingering scent of damp earth and freshly cut grass. Dana walked slowly, the crunch of gravel beneath her feet the only sound as she made her way to Lexy's gravestone. The sky above was a muted gray, the sun hidden behind heavy clouds, casting the world in a somber light. A light breeze tugged at the edges of Dana's coat, but she barely noticed. Her thoughts were elsewhere.

The graveyard stretched out before her, rows of headstones rising from the damp soil like sentinels. Patches of moss clung to the older stones; their inscriptions faded with time. A cluster of tall oak trees stood nearby, their skeletal branches swaying gently in the wind, casting long, shifting shadows on the ground. The air was cool, almost cold, with a faint hint of rain lingering in the breeze. A low, gray mist curled around the bases of the stones, giving the scene an ethereal quality.

She stopped in front of the headstone, its polished surface glistening faintly from a recent rain. The inscription carved into the stone was simple yet poignant:

. . .

Alexis "Lexy" Morgan
Beloved Daughter, Sister and Friend
1987 – 2024

Dana's throat tightened as she stared at the words. She knelt slowly, placing a small bouquet of wildflowers at the base of the stone. The vibrant colors of the blooms stood in stark contrast to the cold, dark granite. Droplets of water clung to the petals, shimmering like tiny diamonds in the dim light.

"Hey, Lexy," she said softly, her voice trembling. "I've been... I've been thinking about you. A lot."

Her fingers brushed against the damp stone, tracing the letters of her friend's name. Tears welled in her eyes as memories of Lexy's laughter and fiery spirit surfaced, moments of their friendship that now felt like they belonged to another life. The coldness of the stone seemed to seep into her fingertips, a stark reminder of the finality of death.

"I'm sorry," Dana whispered, her voice breaking. "I'm so sorry for everything. For letting you down. For dragging you into this mess."

She paused, swallowing hard as the weight of her guilt pressed down on her. "I didn't mean for any of this to happen. I didn't think... I didn't think my mistakes would cost you your life. But they did. And I will have to live with that."

The wind picked up slightly, rustling the leaves of a nearby tree. Dana's shoulders shook as silent tears streamed down her face. She wiped them away with trembling hands, but they kept coming, as though years of pain and regret were pouring out all at once.

"You were the best of us," she continued. "You didn't deserve any of this. If I could trade places with you, I would. In a heartbeat."

Dana's gaze shifted to the flowers she had brought, their petals glistening with tiny drops of rain. "I hope you're at peace now. I hope you know how much you meant to me. To everyone. I… I'll never stop missing you."

The air around her felt heavier now, as though the weight of her confession had settled into the very ground beneath her. She stayed there for a while, kneeling in silence, letting the stillness of the cemetery envelop her. The clouds above churned, their gray depths threatening to spill rain, but the drops held back, as if the sky itself was mourning with her.

Finally, with a shaky breath, she pushed herself to her feet. She brushed the dirt from her knees and placed her hand gently on the gravestone one last time.

"Goodbye, Lexy," she said softly. Her voice grew firmer as she added, "I'm going to make the most of my life now. No more wasting time. No more taking things for granted. I'll do better. For you."

As Dana turned to leave, her eyes fell on the narrow path leading back to the cemetery gates. With each step she reflected. On her mistakes and regrets but most of all the lives lost or damaged by her actions. Justin was gone and while she could never mourn for him, he was still someone's son, despite his crimes. Lexy and Rachel were gone forever. Officer Reynolds survived but his injuries were life changing and even after months of therapy it was touch and go whether he'd be able to return to uniform. Derek had taken what he called a lucky shot and lived to fight, or protect his clients, another day for which she was eternally grateful. Had he and Officer Reynolds died, she knew for a fact Ben would never look her in the eye again.

In the distance, the man at the forefront of her mind stood next to his car, his arms crossed as he watched her. Ben's face was solemn, his expression unreadable. In the backseat, Ethan's small silhouette was visible through the window, his head resting against the glass as he looked out at the sky.

Dana's heart ached as she walked toward them, her steps slow and deliberate. The chill in the air seemed to seep into her bones, but she ignored it, her focus on the figures waiting for her. When she reached the car, Ben opened the passenger door for her without a word. She climbed in, her movements heavy with exhaustion. Ben got in behind the wheel, and for a moment, the three of them sat in silence, the weight of everything they'd endured hanging in the air.

As the car pulled away from the cemetery, Dana glanced back at Lexy's grave, the flowers she'd left now just a blur against the gray backdrop. The mist had thickened, curling around the gravestones like a protective shroud. She turned forward again, her resolve hardening. The road ahead would not be easy, with or without Ben, but for the first time in what felt like forever, she felt the faint stirrings of hope.

THE END

Printed in Great Britain
by Amazon

61660251R00160